Red-Tailed
Odyssey

OTHER BOOKS BY JOHN IRBY

Red-Tailed Rescue

Red-Tailed Odyssey

John E. Irby

WiDō Publishing
Salt Lake City

WiDō Publishing
Salt Lake City, Utah
www.widopublishing.com

Cover Design by Steven Novak
Book Design by Marny K. Parkin

ISBN: 978-1-937178-95-6
Printed in the United States of America

FOR ALL TEACHERS EVERYWHERE

To bring force to bear upon an indomitable diamond requires a second diamond to cleave an edge to catch the light.

Likewise, to shape a precious child, the teacher must become childlike, playful, and yet remain strong. Two children together, gathering the light.

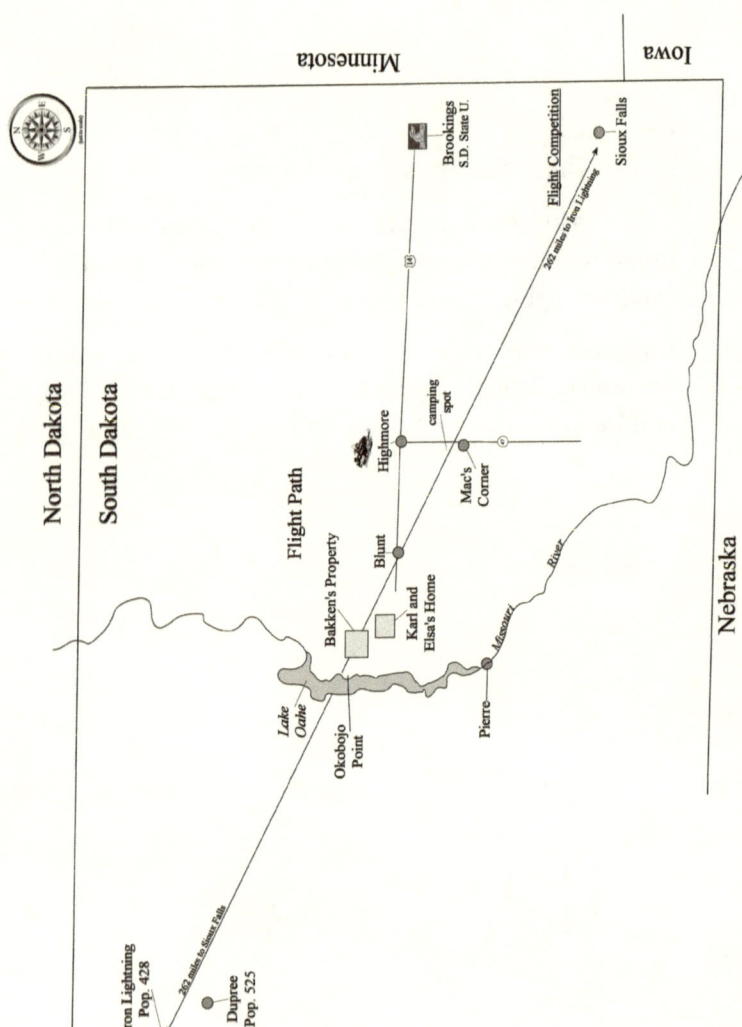

Figure One: Flight Route

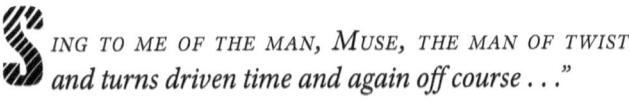"S*ING TO ME OF THE MAN, MUSE, THE MAN OF TWISTS and turns driven time and again off course . . ."*

The Odyssey
Homer

Chapter One

To fly, one must first still the beating of a timid heart and conquer the deepest, oldest fear of falling . . .

EARLY SUNDAY MORNING THE TEMPERATURE plummeted. The wind pushed back. Thick cloud cover forced them low. Twenty-eight chilled red-tail hawks representing Prairie Winds School of Flight flew northwest in a true line toward Dupree. On Friday and Saturday they had performed at the annual South Dakota *October Fly* aerial competition in Sioux Falls, placing second in the junior class. Thirty-eight schools had entered, including powerhouse Ride The Air Academy from Rapid City, and perennial champion, Sky High, out of Belle Fourche. True to form, Belle Fourche took home the gold medal for the third straight year.

A mile back, Ms. Chawla Ride did her best to keep her students in sight. On Thursday, the day before the competition began, Ms. Ride had severely sprained her left wing driving off a murder of ill-tempered crows attempting to harass the class as they approached Sioux Falls. On Friday and Saturday during the competition she iced and rested her injured wing as much as possible. By Sunday morning, the injury still caused great pain whenever she opened her wing. As they flew home toward Dupree, the wing, weak and painful, prevented her from leading her students from her customary position at the point of the phalanx.

After breakfast Sunday morning as they prepared for the flight, she pulled Rowdy aside.

"I cannot lead," she said. "You will fly the point. The weather reports are most worrisome, but I'm hopeful we'll arrive home before the worst of it hits. Fly as high as visibility allows just below the cloud cover," she instructed. "Navigate at four hundred-fifty feet, laser-straight and level. Keep the pace at a steady twenty-two and make certain no one falls behind. Chloe woke up with a sore throat and a bit of a fever. If she cannot keep up, allow her to fall back and I will escort her home. Everyone else is fit for the flight. Understood?"

"Of course, Ms. Ride," Rowdy replied. "I'll make certain Chloe is attended to." Rowdy's demeanor, always calm and earnest, made him perfect for a leadership role and he readily accepted the heavy responsibility she placed on his young wings.

"Another concern, Rowdy," she cautioned. "If the temperature falls below freezing or the clouds continue to thicken and obscure your visibility, be prepared to lead the others to ground. If the smallest shred of doubt for safety enters your mind, descend at a steep angle immediately. We cannot fly safely below three hundred feet. Much danger lurks there."

She paused and sought his eyes, where courage and trust are stored in all red-tails. "If you are forced to land, keep everyone together until I arrive. We'll seek shelter together." Ms. Ride scanned her student's face for any signs of uncertainty. His eyes mirrored the confidence born of proper training and youthful strength. Seeing nothing of weakness, her only concern was he might be too cocky and become reckless.

He smiled at his teacher. "We'll be safe, Ms. Ride. "I'll see to it. You may be sure."

She raised her voice slightly. "Class," she called. The single word brought immediate silence to the excited assembly of flyers. She waited patiently for them to turn and face her. For emphasis she fluttered her wings, shook the gold bangles she favored, causing a pleasant tinkling sound.

A moment later, satisfied with their attention, she announced, "Rowdy will fly point for us today, and carry this home for us." She pulled a small black satin bag from her wing holster. From it she removed a silver medal dangling from a shimmering silver chain: the second-place award the class had earned in the flight competition.

She held it up for all to see, glittering brilliantly in the early morning light. Then she placed it around the young flyer's neck and an exuberant cheer erupted from the class.

When it was quiet again she said, "The chain has twenty-nine pure silver links, one for each of you, and one for me. Each link represents your dedication of effort and skill to our school, our community, and to each other. The links also symbolize not only our precious individuality, but our strength in unity."

Another rousing cheer went up. "One last photo op," she said. The class eagerly pressed together around Rowdy and she raised her cell phone high overhead to snap a grinning flockie.

Cell phones are relatively new to the red-tail community, but just as they've become essential to human society, so too they've become widely used by hawks. Many red-tails carry tiny, lightweight but almost indestructible cells called Tammers; the phones were developed specifically for hawks at a plant near the Tammerkoski Rapids on the Nokiavirta River in southwestern Finland. Needless to say, the Tammers are popular with school age red-tails in South Dakota and across the globe.

Young red-tails are trained to fly at six hundred-fifty feet, the optimum surveillance and attack altitude for hunting, but today's weather conditions prevented flying that high. Besides, there would be no hunting today. They would have to fly over two hundred miles with only the water and food already in their bellies.

In clear weather young hawks can fly, depending on their physical capabilities, between thirty-five and forty miles per hour and have a safe range of nearly three hundred miles. Like a sleek cheetah racing in pursuit of a desperate gazelle across the African savanna, higher bursts of flight speed can only be sustained by red-tails for short intervals, usually during an attack or the rare need for escape from a predator.

Ms. Ride gathered them in a tight circle around her. Raising her wing for silence, she waited. When the excited whispering ceased, she said, "I've never been so proud. You all flew with distinguished courage and precision in the competition." Her gold eyes gleamed as she sought each student's face, one by one. "You have proven yourselves to be among the very best student flyers in the entire state, and I suspect—no, I predict—next year as seniors, you will sweep the competition, and we will fly home with a gold medal around our point's neck." She paused and flashed a mischievous smile. "Next year, ladies and jelly beans, I say—we will own Belle Fourche. What say you?"

The class erupted as one, sang out their class motto: *Beware the Prairie's arrow, fast and true. Belle Fourche, boo hoo.*

"It's settled then," Ms. Ride replied. "As you know, my wing is still out-of-whack and I can't fly point." She waited until the giggles caused by her slangy choice of words had ceased. "Rowdy will lead us home. He's been instructed to fly at twenty-two and as close to the ceiling as vision allows. As usual, Emma and Owen will start in row two. The rest of you will follow in your normal ranks. It's a straight line two hundred sixty-two miles to Dupree. Assuming the weather doesn't worsen and force us down, we face almost twelve hours of continuous flight."

When no qualms were forthcoming she continued, "I know we stopped for lunch at Mac's Corner on the way down, and I remember I promised you three-meat pizza if we finished in the top three, but unfortunately today's weather forbids any delay on our part. We dare not get caught short after dark. Your parents will be most anxious if we arrive after sunset. The wind and cold will test us severely. Our journey will take us to our physical and mental limits. We must draw strength from each other and not rest until the school is in sight. Your parents will greet you there, and you can sleep all day tomorrow."

The students cheered.

"I've already ordered the pizzas for Friday's celebration party."

More cheers broke out.

She stretched her right wing above them and they leaned in, like spokes on a feathery bicycle wheel, each straining to touch a wingtip to her wing in agreement. They stood in silence for a full minute, gathering strength from her and each other, joined in body and spirit, a class of twenty-eight becoming a determined and powerful single engine of flight.

Ms. Ride gazed upward at the threatening sky. A few steely bits of wind-driven ice, not yet fully formed snowflakes, a weak flurry, pelted her eyes. A sudden chill came upon her and she shuddered. Her beak barely moved as they, in unison, vocalized the ancient Red-tail Prayer of Safe Travel: "Deikerrt-Deimerrt-Deisoorrt." *God grant speed. God grant courage. God grant vision.*

Ms. Ride consulted her Breitling wing watch. It showed exactly zero six thirty. The temperature at ground level, the default setting for most modern refrigerators, was thirty-six degrees. "Air," she commanded. "Be gone, you twits. Fly true. I love you all."

Without hesitation or complaint, they launched themselves. There was an almost silent whirr of furious wings, ruffled feathers catching the woven wind, but nothing more.

Rowdy, the class's silver medal dangling from his neck, climbed quickly to four hundred and fifty feet, leveled off and waited for the others to form the arrowhead behind him. A heartbeat later, Owen, wearing his trademark Maui Jim Kapalua goggles and leather flying helmet; and Emma, a pink ribbon tied smartly round her neck, snugged in mere inches aft of Rowdy's red-stained tail feathers, and within thirty seconds the formation was complete. Four of the class's more acrobatic flyers, Oliver, Lily, Brady, and Gabe formed the protective trailing edge. If predators attacked from the rear, they would be the first to defend.

Gripping her cell with her wing tip by its cleverly designed hawk handle, Chawla Ride tapped the *power off* button on her cell phone with her beak and snugged it into its custom-made leather wing holster next to her chest. Enduring a burst of sharp pain, her beak clamped tight as a blacksmith's fist, she opened her wings, caught air for the first time in three days, and hurried after.

From the ground, looking upward, they appeared as a tiny, red-tinted version of the American military's lethal Northrup Grumman B-2 Spirit, more commonly known as the Stealth Bomber. They slid through the gloomy air in near invisible silence in the regulation red-tail Point of the Arrow formation:

Rowdy
Owen Emma
Noah Quinn Sven
Riley Sadie Cork Carter Ben
Casey Ian Chloe Parker Daisy Sophie
Caroline Olivia Mandy Logan Eli Jack Isabella
Oliver Lily Brady Gabe

Unknown to her, Ms. Ride's sluggish rise into the somber sky was marked by a solitary spy obscured in a nearby towering maple tree, resplendent in its autumnal, lipsticked leaves. As she fought the pain in her injured wing, she overlooked the shadowy stalker. A moment later, as she leveled off a hundred yards behind her brood, the black-feathered sentry cawed with soft satisfaction and flapped off to share information with those who patiently waited—and plotted.

Chapter Two

. . . and in her youth she was lovely, vigorous of mind and body. So too, she wove lofty dreams of the future.

KATE FLANNERY SLID HER CHAIR BACK FROM THE long desk, yawned, and stretched her arms overhead. She'd been reading and entering notes in her MacBook for almost two hours without a break. The library would close in another hour and her dorm, Binnewies Hall, was a quick five-minute walk away. She had eaten lunch hours earlier with her roommate, Amy Mitchell, and her stomach grumbled. Kate glanced around the cavernous room. Two female students were huddled a few tables behind her and across the room, a young man with a wild jumble of blond hair rested his head on his backpack, sound asleep. A jumble of piled books surrounded him. At the far end of the room, a sloth of a student librarian collected research materials from empty tables.

Shouldering her backpack, Kate headed for the exit. September had been an exciting month for her and her parents, David and Elizabeth Flannery. Kate had been accepted into the preveterinary medicine program at South Dakota State University in April. Officially, her emphasis of study would be Animal Science with a minor in Wildlife and Fisheries.

The family had driven to Brookings for a day visit to the campus for the first time in late June. Other than her paternal grandmother, who as a young woman taught high school English in Chicago, Kate would be the first person in their family to attend college. Both parents harbored some apprehension about her move away from home. They trusted their daughter completely and were confident she would be safe; but still, to them, Brookings held dangers not even dreamed of in the tiny village of Dupree. Even though Kate was a South Dakota rancher's daughter—strong, lean, and independent— there was always room for worry. From Kate's point of view, she had proven herself many times over and there was little reason for parental concern.

On the fifteenth of September, a few days after Kate turned eighteen, they had returned to the campus with most of Kate's possessions piled into the back of Dave's pickup truck. The three of them transported everything from the Ford to her dorm room before lunch. A few blocks south of the university they discovered The Pheasant, a former gas station and café, now gussied up to be one of Brookings' top dining spots. They ate enormous burgers and French fries slowly and quietly, delaying as long as possible the inevitable, painful goodbyes.

"Tell me your classes again," her father said, trying to fit his country mind around a college girl's academic schedule. He had been a rancher all his life, successful and respected in the Dupree community, but knew little of college academics. His realm consisted mainly of cattle, horses, difficult weather, hard work, long hours, and caring for his family. His PhD was in taming the land, calloused hands, barbed wire, and driving cattle to market.

Kate reached into the back pocket of her jeans and pulled out a folded paper. She smiled at her dad. "English 101 is my first class, three hours a week, Monday, Wednesday, and Friday. It's with Professor Michael Marks."

Dave interrupted. "More English? I thought you wanted to be a vet. You've already read every dang book in the Dupree library and half of Rapid City's. How much English does one person need to know?"

Beth reached out, rested her hand on her husband's thick arm. "Hon, English is required for everybody who goes to college. It's part of the curriculum."

"Okay," he said, shaking his head. "What else?" He toyed with the rim of his cowboy hat resting near his plate. Beth had strict family rules about taking your hat off at the table.

"Math 102. College algebra. It's also a three-credit class. Dr. Arlys Bundt." She looked at her dad. "Should be easy. Math was my favorite class in school."

"Mine too," he said, an easygoing grin tugging at his lips. "So long ago I've forgotten most of it. Only use algebra and geometry when I'm building something. Trig wasn't required then."

"I hated algebra," Beth said. "All those symbols gave me a headache. I think I got a C minus, the only low grade I got in high school." She flashed a dazzling smile at her husband. "But I can bake a cherry pie, charming Davie."

Dave laughed. "You betcha. Best pie crust in all of Ziebach County. You've got the blue ribbons to prove it. You can also draw a pretty picture. But, C minus ain't low. D minus is low. And I got my share of those. Most of those D's probably should have been F's, but I squeaked by on my charming personality" He flashed a wide grin at two of the three women he loved most in life. His mother, eighty-three-year-old Susan Flannery, had declined to make the trip from Dupree.

"Yeah, right," Beth said. "I've heard a few stories about you in high school. Quite the charmer."

Dave smiled and some rare color came to his cheeks. It took a lot to embarrass Dave Flannery. Eager to change the subject, he turned back to Kate. "Two classes all you got?" he asked. "Sounds way too simple for the 2016 valedictorian of Dupree High School. What are you going to do all day? Shoot pool?"

"I have two more classes, Dad," Kate said. "Doc Walters told me to start off the first semester easy so I won't feel overwhelmed at the beginning. He says a lot of kids take too much and aren't ready for college level classes. I guess quite a few can't hack it and eventually just give up or flunk out."

"Sounds right," Dave said. "Start slow and build your confidence. Good advice. I'm glad you and Doc Walters are buddies. He's got more brains than most people in this world."

"I have a four hour Biology 151 class with a lab, and a Vet 103 Intro to Veterinary Medicine class. It's a one hour elective." She looked at her parents. "I can't wait to get started. I know I'm gonna really miss you guys, but I've been wanting to go to college for so long." She paused, glanced at her mother.

Beth smiled, "You'll miss Chris too." Kate and Chris had been best friends through high school. Their relationship had deepened the last half of their senior year after they had gone to the Senior Prom as a couple.

"Yeah, I guess," Kate said. Toward the end of the school year, after Kate had been accepted to college, tension started building between the two. Chris, uncertain of his future role in her life, voiced concern she would meet somebody else in college and never come back to Dupree. She had reassured him she was going to college to study and earn a degree in Veterinary Medicine, not search out a husband, but Chris seemed unconvinced. A touchy, invisible barrier had grown between them.

"I heard Chris plans to go to state trooper academy over in Pierre," Dave said. "That's what his dad told me the other day."

Kate's blue eyes softened. "It's his dream, Dad. His grandfather was a trooper and now his dad is too. I was hoping he'd try something else, maybe not so dangerous, but he's got his heart set on it."

"Chris is smart and sweet," Beth said. "By the time you're through vet school he'll probably be sheriff of Ziebach County. Law enforcement is an honorable profession. You don't need to worry. He'll be waiting for you every time you come home from school."

Kate remained silent. She really liked Chris, but . . . whatever the future might hold, she wanted to keep her options open.

Dave looked thoughtful. "I know it's still a long way off," he said, "but someday I'm gonna need some help running our ranch." He stretched his arm across the table and touched his daughter's hand with his fingertips. "Sorta hoping you'll be the one, or your husband, or one of your daughters or sons. I want our land to stay in the family forever. It's been good to us Flannerys for a long while."

Kate turned her face away and stared at something invisible out the window. The distant future, a time when her father would be unable to run the ranch, was not something she wanted to consider. A lump formed to her throat. Her parents looked at each other, knew it was time to say goodbye.

Dave stood up, peeled a five-dollar bill out of his jeans pocket and laid it next to his plate then put on his hat. He smiled big at his college girl. "Stay out of the well, Kate Flannery."

It was a special farewell. *Take no unnecessary risks*, it meant, among other things. He walked around the table, hugged his daughter for a long moment. He looked at his wife. "Let's go home, Beth. Be gettin' dark soon."

Kate walked through the scanner at the entrance to the library. A sleepy-eyed librarian looked up and smiled as Kate passed by. The chilled air took Kate by surprise and she quickly zipped her hoody up to her throat. Standing alone on the library steps, she slipped her cell phone out of her jeans pocket. September had been balmy by South Dakota standards. But now, three weeks into October, the September t-shirts and shorts had disappeared, replaced by sweatshirts and long pants.

There were three text messages: one from her mother, one from Chris; and one from Orville Hampstead, a red-tailed hawk who five years earlier had helped save her life when she had accidentally fallen into an abandoned well. The phone's screen dimmed in the fading light. Jagged movement from above caught her eye and she glanced upward toward a light pole. Only then did she realize it was snowing. She pocketed her phone and hurried toward her dorm.

"I was starting to wonder where you were," Amy said. She was in her normal position, stretched out on her bed, head propped up on a pile of pillows. Book in hand, she swiveled her legs and sat upright on the edge of the bed. Amy Mitchell was a solidly built, pretty girl with long dark hair. She had been born and raised in Sioux Falls, far more of a city girl than Kate. Amy was a business major, and she and Kate had hit it off from the very first day together as roommates.

"I'm getting hungry."

"Me too," Kate said. "Why don't we order a pizza or something?"

"I'll call," Amy said. "Pepperoni, okay?"

Kate moved across the room and sat opposite Amy on the one soft chair in the room. It had been Kate's grandfather's favorite, and after he died she commandeered it as her own. Whenever she curled up in it to read she felt his peaceful presence. "Sure. Pepperoni is my fave. Did you know it's snowing?"

"No way," Amy said. "In October? Too weird." She moved to the room's only window and pushed the blinds to one side. "Wow. It really is. I love the snow."

Kate looked again at her phone and opened the message from Chris. **Hey. Miss you lk crazy. Washed my trk today. Driving to Pierre tomorrow. Registering at academy. Hugs and stuff.**

Kate smiled as she read his note. She was tall and slender, an offshoot of her parents.

Growing up, Kate had worn her blond hair in braids until junior high school. Since then, and all through high school Kate wore her hair short in a cute athletic look. But, immediately after graduation she had allowed it to grow out, and now it touched her shoulder tops. A week before college started Beth and Kate drove to Rapid City on a shopping spree. Before leaving for home, her mom had maneuvered a reluctant Kate into an upscale beauty salon called Purty Gurls to have it cut and styled.

Apparently the young men of Brookings, South Dakota approved. Wherever on campus Kate walked, heads turned. The product of Irish and German ancestry, she was fair-skinned, her hair, eyebrows, and eyelashes a soft buttermilk. In bright sunlight her eyes faded color, but in shadows they were Crater Lake blue. From her father she had inherited a quick wit, a relentless work ethic, and determined cheerfulness, even when things weren't going her way.

Kate tapped in a message. **Snowing here. Freaky. Studied all day. Roads could be slippery. Be careful. Hi to all. More hugs and stuff.**

Amy paced the small room, cell to her ear. "Binnewies Hall. Yes. It's connected to Larson Commons. Ring the bell. I'll meet you in the lobby. Amy. Eight bucks, right? Okay. Bye." Amy looked out the window again. "I can't believe it's snowing so hard. I don't remember it ever snowing in October. Global warming must be kicking in." She looked at Kate. "The pizza will be here in fifteen minutes. Do you have any money? Five each will cover it."

Kate pointed at her desk. "There's a five and some ones by my computer." She turned back to her cell and opened her mother's text. **Hi. Cold and snowy here. TV news says 5 inches by morning. Dad's worried about the stock. Gramma's feeling better. How's school? Love, Mom**

Amy pulled a sweatshirt down over her jeans. "Is two bucks enough for a tip?"

"Plenty," Kate replied. "We're college girls, remember? Try not to fall in love down there."

Amy giggled. "Actually, he sounded kinda cute on the phone. Be right back."

The door closed and Kate replied to her mother. **Hi, Mom. School's fine. I like my classes. Amy is fun and really nice. Snowing here too. Good about Gramma. Tell Dad hi. Love you.** She hit the send button and immediately opened the final message.

She smiled as she read Orville's tortured text: **Hi Kate college girl. Cold this day. All hawks in cruel. You study what? Owen fly Sioux Falls. Annabelle terrible worry. Mother fever. Orvie.**

Kate had grown used to Orville's less than perfect English. She marveled that he communicated as well as he did, and his ability to type a text message with his talons blew her away. Kate knew Orville's son Owen was quite brainy, but also suffered from the poor vision he'd inherited from his dad and grandmother. Snowing the way it is, Kate thought, Annabelle has every right to worry.

Just then the door opened and a beaming Amy walked in, pizza box in hand. "That there was one handsome cowboy," she said. "I'm gonna be eating a lot more pizza from now on."

Kate laughed, Orville's text message temporarily forgotten. "If it snows all night do you think they'll cancel classes tomorrow?"

Amy had a mouthful of pizza. "Nah," she mumbled. "Not in South Dakota. Direct meteor strike? Maybe." She laughed. "C'mon girl, before I eat this whole thing."

Kate frowned. She remembered Orville's text. Something in her mind clanged an alarm bell.

Why in the world, she wondered, would Owen fly over two hundred miles to Sioux Falls?

. . . or those born of deformity in the dim light of a cold and dripping morn. And the most wretched of these curses—to live one's life groping in darkness, never to witness the leaves of autumn . . .

THEY WERE, THESE HATEFUL CROWS, VIGILANT, famously clever, and patient beyond even cold, lifeless stones.

Crows are born bullies. Their hearts carry no real intent to kill; their aim is merely to harass, intimidate, and enforce an invisible territorial line. Yank some feathers—draw a dram of blood—cow those who dare enter their space. Send a strong message—*No Trespassing!*

Four days earlier, just as the tallest buildings of Sioux Falls had appeared on the horizon, nine black marauders attacked the class from the rear. A startled cry from the rear of the formation alerted the teacher, and she had instantly peeled off from the point. Furious at the cowardly attack, her beak and talons bared, Chawla Ride had surprised and challenged the black raiders with the ferocity of her defense—a teacher protecting her students. Mindful of their strict training, the formation of young red-tails had flown on without their point.

Chawla Ride had hurled herself fearlessly at the assailants. The crows tried to regroup, to present her with a solid, impenetrable defense. But she was too powerful, too expert in her maneuvers, some of which the crows had never before witnessed. They did not realize they were matched against one of the best flyers the Advanced Flight Academy had ever produced until much too late. When she had transferred as a graduate student from India, she was already a notorious acrobat in the air. She never boasted of it, but anyone with eyes could only marvel at her strength and skill, a powerful ballerina dancing on air.

Chawla Ride, gold wing bangles flashing in the late afternoon sun, engaged her enemy with reckless abandon, born of complete confidence in aerial combat technique. She raked black feathers with sharp talons; buried her beak in the chest of one, the soft-feathered throat of another. Shocked at seeing two of their comrades plummet to earth and unable to defend against such fury, the remainder, cawing loudly in their cowardice, turned tail and fled.

Good they did, because it was in her final delicate joust—the complex Dread Licorice, a lethal twisting maneuver taught only at the A. F. A. in Pierre—that Chawla felt the sinews of her left wing tear away from her shoulder bone. At first, pumped full of adrenalin, she failed to recognize how severely she had injured herself. It was not until later, when she struggled to resume her position at point, that she realized how much damage had been done. She was pleased she had driven off the pests, but disappointed with herself for resorting to a tactic known to be risky. At the Academy her flight instructors had insisted student flyers reserve Dread Licorice only for the most extreme attacks—"Life and

Limb Maneuvers"—as they were called. In fact, since her graduation five years earlier, Chawla had never once felt compelled to utilize Dread Licorice, even during a run-in last year with a belligerent eagle twice her size.

Despite the increasing pain in her wing, she managed to lead the flight safely into Sioux Falls, albeit at a slower pace. Ms. Ride immediately sought treatment. The doctor assigned to the competition bound her wing to her chest; she was given ice, a painkiller, and told to rest.

When he finished placing her wing in a sling, the doctor said, "You're fortunate the bone did not snap, but the muscles are severely sprained. Whatever else you do, do not attempt to fly for at least ten days. These types of injuries take a long time to heal."

She accepted the doctor's treatment and advice, knowing full well she would have to fly back to Dupree in just three days' time. Did the learned doctor imagine she would allow her students to fly two hundred miles home alone, with hostile crows, owls, and eagles about, while she convalesced in Sioux Falls? She refused even to consider such an option.

"Thank you, doctor," she replied through a gritted beak.

At dusk, the crows, nearly a thousand strong, gathered in a grove of sycamores just west of Sioux Falls. After an hour's discussion, the crow's leader, Polgar, spoke at great length of disgrace and revenge. Polgar, distinguished from her clan by a single white feather shaped somewhat like a writer's apostrophe adorning her otherwise coal colored chest, had inherited her position of leadership from her father, Genghis.

Polgar's only living relative was her son Trafalgar. He was a huge crow, famous for his nasty disposition. Perched menacingly at her side, he too carried the white feather on his chest. The crimson sun, sinking in the west behind Polgar, reflected the raging fire of hatred in her dark brown eyes.

"Can someone explain to me how it is possible," she began, "for nine crows to be overwhelmed by a single red-tail hawk?" She paused for effect. She knew no one in the gathering would dare offer an excuse. "Two of our brothers have been slain and seven others driven off."

Elders Langan and Ung-Yong, perched nearby, broke into hoarse caws of disgust.

"Cowardice shames us all. My mind refuses to accept this defeat, and revenge overflows the dam in my heart," Polgar said. "We cannot tolerate such humiliation. We will bide our time, and when opportunity allows we will seek our vengeance. Our superior intelligence will prevail."

Her powerful words drew a bloodthirsty roar of approval from the audience.

"Red-tails pride themselves in their vision. Oh, how they boast of their eyes! They fill their poetry with cheap rhymes—*eyes, pies, guise, skies*. Their songs and poetry reek of it." Polgar flapped her thick wings several beats for emphasis. "How many more times must we endure hearing and reading the nauseating, contrived cliché: '*Eyes like a hawk*'?"

Polgar's odious caws thundered now. "This red-tailed she-wolf of the skies must never fly again. I demand she be bludgeoned to the ground, pinned down, and her eyes torn out. I want her left sightless. Let her beg to be killed. We will not grant such kindness. Her whimpers for death shall go unheeded. The brother or sister who brings her eyeballs to me at this place will be rewarded with everlasting honor." Polgar dipped her frightful head with excitement. "Who among you is brave enough?"

A thousand pairs of black wings flared open, and an explosion of raucous caws filled the darkening sky. Each voice claimed the treasure to be theirs alone.

"The red-tail's eyes are mine!" they shouted.

Polgar, pleased with the response, paused, refilling her bottomless reservoir of hate and anger. The black horde surrounding her dipped their heads in silent agreement. "I want her left alive and naked on the ground, her feathers torn out, never to grow back. Let the lowly ants feast upon the drops of blood clinging to the roots of her feathers. They can drag her lifeless feathers off for decoration in their underground lairs. Do not dare to eat of her flesh or you dishonor yourselves. Soon her living carcass will stink worse than lifeless carrion. The ants alone may gorge upon those empty eye sockets and lick them dry."

A roar of dark approval erupted.

"Our scouts tell us the red-tails are now perched in the largest oak in Falls Park. Information has been gathered. There will be a flying competition on Friday and Saturday. On Sunday she will lead her students home. We will lie in wait. Patience for now, revenge soon enough."

Polgar opened her massive wings, caught air, and was gone. Behind her the sky reverberated with the terrible din of inflamed hatred.

Chapter Four

. . .a single tree standing solitary on the prairie cannot resist the fierce October winds, but a deep-rooted grove, trees thriving side-by-side, branches intertwining, brace each other up against the gale.

THREE HOURS OUT OF SIOUX FALLS, JUST SOUTH of Cuthbert and almost directly over Twin Lakes, Oliver peeled out from the rear of the formation. He accelerated past Noah, Casey, Riley, and Caroline, and nudged Owen out of the second rank. On the other side of the formation, Gabe powered past Isabella, Sophie, Ben, and Sven to replace Emma. Oliver and Gabe formed up behind Rowdy, while Emma and Owen drifted back as replacements on the trailing edge.

The wind had been steady in the group's face the entire way, and the three front flyers, taking the brunt of its force would become exhausted much more quickly than the others. From the ground looking up, the second formation's appearance as it continued west was:

Rowdy

Oliver Gabe

Noah Quinn Sven

Riley Sadie Cork Carter Ben

Casey Ian Chloe Parker Daisy Sophie

Caroline Olivia Mandy Logan Eli Jack Isabella
Owen Lily Brady Emma

The three-hour rotation system for long flights, developed in ancient times, helped alleviate the mental and physical toll of exhaustion. The last row in the phalanx, flying with protection from the wind, could husband their strength and remain fresh to fend off attackers.

The real problem was that Rowdy, flying at the very tip of the blade through a brutal oncoming wind the entire distance, had to endure twelve hours of continuous, exhausting flight.

At the three-hour mark, just as they sailed past Twin Lakes, Rowdy signaled the others of the need for rotation by accelerating sharply, climbing five feet and then leveling off. The packed formation instantly followed his maneuver and the rotation was promptly completed.

A human, standing on flat ground with no obstacles in between, can see a large object— say an elephant wearing a necklace of blinking red lights draped around its neck—at a distance of three miles. The curvature of the earth prevents a six-foot tall human with normal vision seeing objects more distant. However, someone standing on a mountain on a dark night can see a candle's flickering flame thirty miles away. Even more astonishing, on dark and clear nights, humans can see the Andromeda galaxy from two point six million miles away.

Scientists believe a red-tailed hawk can see eight times more clearly than humans. An ancient legend in the South Dakota red-tailed hawk community claims they have been granted exquisite vision so they might "see around the bend to eternity."

As Emma drifted back to her new slot at the rear of the formation, she couldn't resist the urge to look behind them in the distance, hoping to catch a quick glimpse of Ms. Ride. The students were well aware of their teacher's injury, and they cared greatly for her safety. Flying alone over unfamiliar terrain is always risky business, and a solo flyer easily becomes a target for hungry eagles or rapacious owls. Already weakened and unable to fly at top speed, Ms. Ride would be less able to defend herself. If forced to ground she would become easy prey for a great horned owl, red fox, raccoon, or coyote.

Emma stared hard, but she was unable to discern even a scintilla of movement five miles directly behind them. All was inert. Gray, thick clouds hovered just above their flight path and the distant background, also an artist's wash of indistinct gray, blurred her vision, making the colors and shapes dissolve together. Concerned, Emma accelerated and tucked herself in tight beside Rowdy.

"I can't see Ms. Ride behind us," she said. "Should we circle back?" Emma was surprised how much stronger the wind was at the point. Flying in row two had been strenuous enough, but now she noticed Rowdy's ride was significantly more difficult than hers had been.

"We cannot go back," Rowdy answered. There was an unusual terseness to his speech. "She ordered me to lead—no stops, no hesitation, no time to spare. The weather worsens. We must stay on course. As long as Chloe can maintain the pace we will not pause."

"But," Emma protested, "Ms. Ride may be in serious trouble. You know her strength. She would not lose sight of us if she could help it." She paused, hoping Rowdy would offer up a solution.

When he did not respond, she said, "I'm willing to go back and check on her. Flying with the wind at my back will make it much easier." She blinked her greenish gold eyes rapidly to clear the ice forming in the feathers edging her eye sockets. "She's our teacher, Rowdy. We can't just leave her. Abandonment would dishonor our class."

"Will you disobey your Point?" Rowdy roared. He turned his head slightly and glared at his classmate. He loved Emma, as he loved all members of the class. The concept of loving had been welded with an intense flame into his mind and heart by his parents, teachers, and elders since the day of his birth. To red-tails the only alternative to love was death, a boundless void between. "Would you put all of us in jeopardy over Ms. Ride? She is prepared to protect herself against any force." A rare trace of impatient anger, one Emma had never heard before, spiced his voice. "Have you forgotten her agility in the air? Nothing with wings over South Dakota dares challenge her."

Emma remained silent, her graceful wings matching beats with his shorter, thicker ones. She knew she should move back to her assigned rotation position in the rear. She risked punishment for even challenging the point flyer. Flying beside Rowdy put the entire formation out of balance, slowed them all, and distorted his navigation.

"I must ask you, Rowdy: if our teacher were at point this very moment, and you or I, or any of us, became weak or ill in the flight, would she continue on and allow her faltering student to drift off alone into almost certain death? Ponder that, my Point."

By challenging her point's authority, Emma had stepped over the stringent line flight protocol demands. She went on. "I think she would not. She would send the strongest fliers back to keep company, to assist, encourage and protect. I am certain she would send you, or Owen, or me, or all three of us back to aid a struggling one. Think you not? Did she not inform you Chloe is ill and may need to fall back? Should we not love our teacher as much as we love each other?"

"I am forbidden to leave the point position," he replied. His voice softened, difficult to hear in the onrushing wind. "You know our protocol as well as I."

Shards of icy rime caked his entire face from beak to eye, giving him the appearance of a grizzled geezer hawk peering up from his deathbed.

"Take Owen with you. You two are our strongest flyers. I dare not risk anyone else. If she is still aloft she will be at our altitude. Fly exactly as we came. If you do not come upon her in fifteen minutes, I order you, under her authority, to turn back and rejoin us. If you find her, she will instruct further and you will obey. Your absence puts us all in grave danger, Emma. We are much weaker without you and Owen. Be brave. Be swift. Weigh the circumstances well. We cannot and will not turn back to search for you."

With those sobering words, Emma moved closer, and placed the side of her beak gently against his. She held it there for the customary five heartbeats, then, with a swift swish of her tail feathers, she elevated three feet, and dropped back beside Owen.

She spoke loudly against the rush of wind. "Leave rank," she ordered. "Rowdy has ordered us to go back and check on Ms. Ride. We have but fifteen minutes to locate her. We must hurry." In a flash she nudged against Owen, casting him adrift.

The two young flyers did not hesitate. They lifted their wings, rose and wheeled above their classmates. A moment later, headed back the way they had come, Emma accelerated, and taking advantage of the tail-wind became the rounded shaft of the arrow. Owen fell in mere inches behind, flying in the vacuum her body created. With the helping wind pushing them, the two courageous soldiers, their lives in grave jeopardy, but unwilling to leave their injured teacher behind, sped into the uncertain light. The remainder, led by one even braver, surged toward home and the everlasting safety stored within the family circle.

Chapter Five

. . . and some will plant fields, minister to the ill, or sell goods in distant markets, while others will build shelters—but All will talk, and read, and write. The hardships wrapped themselves around us, owned us, but there was no other way.

KATE DID NOT SLEEP WELL. DURING THE NIGHT, the wind intensified and the sound of its howling groans against the dorm's window and the roof above had awakened her once, twice, a third time. When her alarm clock buzzed at six thirty her eyes felt puffy, her mind unrested and dull. But she refused to give in to her weariness and craving for more sleep; she threw back the covers and glanced across the room. Amy, a mossy covered log in a deep and silent forest, did not flinch.

Kate hurried to the window, the cold floor uncomfortable to her bare feet. She peered out. Even in the early light, the landscape below was blindingly white. An hour earlier the wind had finally stopped its relentless pressure and calmed its ferocious self. All was eerily calm.

After a quick shower Kate dressed, choosing warmer garments from her meager wardrobe. She gathered her study materials, shouldered her backpack, and prepared to leave.

"Amy," she called. "It's ten past seven. I'm going now."

The log refused to budge. Kate walked to the edge of the forest, shook her friend's shoulder. "You have a nine o'clock. Get up, you bag of bones."

There came a rough, muffled sound of disbelief. "I don't believe you. Go away. Leave me be." The log came alive, rolled over, shielded its eyes against the morning glare. "I hate Mondays. They should be unconstitutional."

Kate laughed. "Good luck," she said. "Coffee at ten thirty at Java City?"

"God willin' and the creek don't rise," the log replied.

Ten minutes later Kate had created a pristine path through the snow from Binnewies Hall to Java City. The coffee shop opened at seven thirty, giving her just enough time for a bagel and a latté before her English class took up at eight. With a plastic knife she spread cream cheese on the warmed bagel. Her cell chirped. For a moment longer she continued decorating her breakfast. Satisfied with the preparation, she took a bite of bagel, then a quick sip of latté. Finally, she opened her phone. It was Orville again. Instantly she remembered she had not replied to his previous message. This morning's text was more direct, but still mystifying. **Owen not home. No one know. Class miss to be. Tell me best. Orvie.**

Kate tried to sort out Orville's convoluted language. She glanced at her watch. She still had fifteen minutes to make it to class. Chewing on a bite of bagel, she puzzled over his message. Not wanting to be late to class, she wrapped the bagel in a napkin, threw her bag over one shoulder and grabbed her coffee cup.

Professor Michael Marks stood at the door of the classroom. Tall and thin, near the middle of his fourth decade, he was dressed casually in blue jeans and a red and black checked flannel shirt. His hair, trimmed short, had grayed around the temples. Under his nose loomed a thick silver hedge.

When Kate entered the room he smiled. "Morning, Kate Flannery," he said. "Glad you braved the storm."

She managed a quick smile. "I try not to let weather slow me down," she replied. "Dad always says, 'Weather don't count for much. Just get after what needs to be done.'"

"I like your dad's attitude."

Quickly she found a seat in the front row. There were eight or nine other students scattered in the first few rows. Normally forty or so would be in attendance. She took a bite of bagel and pondered Orville's message.

Tell me best? she thought. The overriding concern seemed to be his son Owen was not home. But if he'd flown to Sioux Falls, he'd be in Sioux Falls. Wouldn't he?

"Morning all," Dr. Marks said. He grinned at the sleepy contingent from the front of the room. "We're a few head shy of a full herd today. A guy up in Seattle told me don't fork hay for a whole herd if only a few show up, so today's class is going to be a bit on the abbreviated side. I won't tell anybody as long as you guys don't rat me out."

The class laughed. Their eyes widened, anticipating the happy prospect of a short class. Dr. Marks intrigued them. They knew he had a PhD in American and British literature and had graduated near the top of his class from Cornell University, but he seemed almost too informal and cheerful each day. Some wondered if he took himself seriously enough. They expected college to be drudgery. They couldn't imagine such a well-educated man acting as if college English was mostly fun and games.

"Got a question for you." He paused, went face-to-face, made eye contact with the herd. "Anybody here not own a cell phone?" He buried his hands deep in his front pockets. He grinned and waited, rocked back and forth, heel and toe in what appeared to be serious work boots, then pointed to an upraised hand.

"Liam. Are you admitting you don't own a cell phone?" A look of disbelief clouded Dr. Marks' face. "What planet are you from?"

The class swiveled toward the alleged Alien. Liam sat alone in the fourth row. He smiled big with dazzling white teeth, bright blue eyes, and a blond bushwhack of wild hair. "Planet Manitoba, actually. No cell phone, smart or otherwise," he said. "No one in my family owns one. But if I saw one I'd recognize it."

A guy sitting off to one side mumbled, "What about a comb? Recognize one of those?"

Two or three people snickered, but Liam and the professor seemed not to notice.

A girl frowned and whispered, "Smartass."

"I'm happy for you, Liam, but somewhat astonished," Professor Marks said. "Can you give us a snippet of background?"

Liam smiled even wider, sat up tall, enjoying the sudden spotlight. "Sure. I'm from Manitoba, Canada, way up north, along the lake. My parents home-schooled me. My dad is a fisherman in Lake Winnipeg. I've got two sisters, both younger. Mom used to teach English in Winnipeg, but now she's a pen and ink artist."

"Do you think your life has been shortchanged by not having access to a cell phone?" the professor asked.

"Not at all. I had a great childhood. My sisters and I grew up without any telephone service, television, or indoor plumbing. My dad loves hockey so all of us, even Mom, played hockey when the pond froze over. We had tons of books and board games. We played outside almost every day, even in terrible weather." He shrugged his shoulders. "I don't think rural living has hurt me any. Moneywise we aren't rich, but family wise, we're royalty."

Kate thought Liam looked familiar. It came to her. He was the lone figure she'd noticed sound asleep on a study table at the library yesterday afternoon. *Handsome.* Her young heart stalled, skipped a beat. The image of her boyfriend Chris popped into her head, and she closed her eyes, sucked in a deep breath. *I've got to get over him. He doesn't own me.*

"I doubt it's hurt you much," Marks said. "Cell phones are definitely a convenience, but not owning one has also enhanced your life. Glad you're here, Liam. So glad you're here. Your presence in this classroom, validates what college is all 'aboot.'" His mimicry of the Canadian pronunciation made a few of the more alert students giggle.

"That someone with your background has meshed here with the rest of us lends a whole different perspective on how to live well in a modern, and in my opinion, overly electronic world. We humans have been communicating with each other since the beginning of intelligent life on this planet." His voice was softer now, more serious. The herd leaned forward, eager to sip of this Cornell man.

"To humans, talking to each other is of paramount importance. We absolutely must tell each other how we feel, what we've seen, what we plan to do. We love each other through sounds, words, and sentences. We build stuff using ideas formed of words. We buy and sell using words. We dream. We look to the future. Imagine your life for a moment if you can, without a cell phone in hand. Think of your family and friends back home. The sound of their voices reassures you. Their texts inform you. Their humor tickles you. Their despair ushers rivers and lakes to your eyes."

He walked to the wall of windows, turned his back on his students. Peered out. Grasped for perspective. Saw the world fresh. He spun around, his voice powerful now. "I wonder how our friend Liam informs his parents and sisters and friends way up north how much he loves and misses them. How he paints a picture for them of the buildings, walkways, and trees of South Dakota State University. Or how beautiful the girls in his Monday morning English class are."

The class laughed.

He stepped close, eyed them as colleagues rather than underlings. "Today as you brave the cold and piled snow, think deep on the importance of communication in our lives. On Wednesday morning when you return to this classroom at this same dreadful hour of the day, we will discuss this matter of human communication more fully." He paused. A few glanced down, intimidated by his powerhouse gaze. "Any questions?" He searched their faces for doubt, disagreement. Gave them time to form a rebuttal. None came forward.

"I assume you're still reading *The Odyssey*. It's one of our world's most precious pieces of literature. Given the extra forty-five minutes you've gained this morning,

I would expect you to make some progress. You, friends, are amidst your own life's odyssey. These college years are like no other, and I'm delighted you're here." He let his eyes find every face. "Okay then, get thee gone, and don't let the weather slow you down. It's a mere impediment, nothing more. One more thing, if you haven't already done so, introduce yourself to Liam on your way out. He knows stuff the rest of us can only guess at."

Dr. Michael Marks, a long drink of water, walked briskly to the door, extended his big hand as each student passed by. "Thanks for coming," he said to each. "Take care. See you Wednesday." The young professor's presentation, front to back, had lasted fifteen minutes.

Chapter Six

*. . . and in the narrow, piss reeking back
alleys of the great cities of the world, you
will sometimes encounter thieves—or
worse—lurking, waiting for the innocents
to blunder into their webs.*

MBUSH. THEY CAME AT HER FROM ALL SIDES, A
jarring cavalcade of black darts.

Unable to maintain a pace of even twenty miles per
hour Chawla had slowly drifted farther back, eight miles
or so. She finally lost sight of her students. She was confident in Rowdy's ability to lead them home safely, but
as the morning wore on and she slowed even more, she
began to consider her own chances of survival.

Hawks' hearts do not contain a chamber reserved for
fear. Each day's dawn is cherished. They understand it
very well could be their last. A hawk must kill in order
to stay alive—the other side of the equation—they too
might be killed.

Chawla, slowly became aware her growing fatigue,
inexorable pain, the forceful wind, biting cold, and
blinding snowfall might force her down. She knew if
grounded alone, under these weather conditions and her
weakened state, she would be in an extremely precarious
position. She did not fear it nor rue it; she merely knew
it, and accepted it.

The first one took her completely by surprise. A black-feathered Kamikaze slammed into her from above, hitting a glancing blow to her back and momentarily taking her breath away. Not designed to be hammers, a bird's bones are hollow, their bodies filled with air sacs allowing them to be buoyant in the air.

Attacking in silence was unusual for crows, never shy about announcing their presence. Loud caws of intimidation have long been one of their sly strategies. They filled Chawla's airspace. The air around her was black with them, an inkblot; the serpentine hiss of their wings was the only sound.

In rapid succession Chawla's body was bludgeoned again and again, until she lost count, a boxer's punching bag at the gym. She made no attempt to ward off the blows, instead absorbing them as best she could, concentrating all her efforts on remaining airborne.

Strange, she thought, they drive me down with collisions instead of slashing at me with their beaks. She almost chuckled at the thought: Where are their brash voices today? Have they finally learned silence is golden?

She had experienced countless crow skirmishes with small groups in the past, and had never considered them a serious personal threat. To her and all red-tails, crows were not murderers but merely harassers. They were but loud momentary nuisances, no more fearful than a curious hummingbird—not a hawk's true foes—the great northern horned owl or the mighty eagle. With those two mortal assassins, she always fought for her life.

But, this time there was something different in the crows' tactics. She was used to their earsplitting caws of insult, and thick snapping beaks; those she could deal with. Always before, as soon as she neared the edge of their territory they would be satisfied, tire of the game, and drift away.

But now she was being pummeled from all sides. They hurled themselves into her body, forcing the air from her lungs and knocking her from side to side. Each impact caused her to drop a few feet of altitude, and their sheer numbers prevented her from moving from a neutral posture into an aggressive, attacking one.

Realizing their intent was to drive her into the ground, Chawla made the fateful decision to escape by climbing into the snowy atmosphere above. She felt certain they would not follow her above a thousand feet. She knew crows are low-level scavengers, not high flyers, and she felt her only chance to elude them was to climb. Abruptly, with a piercing squeal, concocted of pain, anger and defiance, she forced her wings to carry her into a vertical Up the Elevator Shaft ascent, difficult enough to perform even when not being struck repeatedly by black asteroids and suffering the pain of a throbbing wing.

Chawla's foes, for an instant or two, seemed mystified by her sudden change of direction; but as soon as they realized her intent, they adjusted their strategy to attack on a horizontal plane, striking her from the side. A moment before she had been a lumbering cargo plane losing power and going down—now, through sheer willpower—she transformed herself into a launched missile. Because of her weakened wing she labored to gain the velocity she needed to sustain vertical ascent. At the Academy she had been taught an axiom of flight: at a certain point, if airspeed is not sufficient, gravity will take control and slowly rotate the flyer face downward and hurl them into the ground—a deadly aeronautical stall.

She glanced at her wing watch. When the crows first appeared, she had been flying at an altitude of four hundred and fifty feet. After suffering dozens of their Kamikaze strikes she had been knocked as low as one hundred feet before she started her climb. She was now flying blindly through thick clouds at seven hundred feet, ascending directly toward the universe, perhaps beyond.

The weaker crows began falling back as she passed eight hundred, and for the first time she heard and interpreted their frightful caws. Though not fluent, she knew enough of their language to decipher their shouts of desperation. *Stop her. Don't let her escape. Revenge is at hand.*

At nine hundred feet, the falling snow became her friend. The higher she climbed the thicker the snow curtain became, and the crows' vision, as well as her own, became more and more compromised. It was as if she were flying in the center of a fluffy cotton ball hounded by a pack of ruthless wolves.

The alarm on her watch sounded at one thousand feet; she was serene now, almost unconscious in the never-ending bombardment of soft and beguiling snowflakes. She was vaguely aware of three dark shapes, two flanking each side, and the third trailing just behind; she realized their voices contained new elements—hollow desperation and grinding fear—tones one never heard from the obnoxious crows raiding overstuffed garbage bins on the ground. Her watch sounded a second alarm, two beeps of warning, and she knew she had just passed one thousand one hundred. She closed her eyes. Composed herself. Clamped her beak tight. It was almost over now. They would leave her be—or she would die.

She felt a beak grip one of her legs and then the other; and she knew she could not bear any more weight. It was time. She resigned herself, relaxed; two would die with her.

Chawla folded her exhausted wings tight to her body, let her head go limp and droop backward; her body slowly rotated upside down, and began the vertical descent, serenity fast upon her.

A third assailant, an instant too late, cried out in despair, "Give me your eyes. I must have your eyes." A black hooded crow with a white insignia on her chest slashed wildly with her beak at Chawla's face hoping for disfigurement at least. Chawla made no effort to defend herself. The power of gravity wrapped itself around her, became her armor.

But Polgar, terrified of the height and speed, could do no harm, and was left behind.

She was upside down now, falling headfirst; the strap of Chawla's wing holster loosened and slipped off. It contained only her cell phone, pictures of her parents back in India, and a small jewel studded purse.

Polgar jabbed at the strap with her beak, tasted expensive tanned leather, clamped on it, savored it, and claimed it as her own magnificent trophy. Still unsatisfied, Polgar called out again and again. "Rip her eyes out!"

Ah, their game all along. The corners of Chawla's beak quivered for a brief instant, a shadow of a grin. *They covet my vision.* She giggled, a young fledgling again. Her joyful spirit danced wildly, sensuously, around an ancient fire, its sparks illuminating a dark sky. The flaming pyre, beside a wide river far away in India, awaited her swift arrival home.

The two anchored crows, trailing above, hung on to Chawla's legs, stubborn in their grim suicide pact; they'd rather die than admit defeat; and so Mother Earth's most powerful child, Gravity, gathered all three in her welcoming arms. Faster and faster they fell, a trio of fly-ers welded together by hateful circumstance, plunging headlong into pale oblivion. An eternity passed by in a few seconds, then a soft explosion in the snow. No movement. Silence. Three lonely raindrops called back home.

High overhead a dark shape paddled off, cawing loudly, a purloined leather treasure dangling from her chiseled beak.

Chapter Seven

. . . and just as the sun surrendered to the western horizon they came to the river, wider here, running fast, but not so deep. He had carried his grandmother, toothless now and unable to support her own weight, on his back for three days—the family's rule, not his. His young legs, still strong, would have gladly carried her another three. Kneeling, he laid her gently on the cold ground, bent and kissed her forehead, whispered kind, and reverential words. He turned, followed the others into the current; midway, water to his waist, he made a mistake, looked back; she lifted her wrinkled hand, a slight movement at the wrist . . .

THE ICY SLEET BEGAN TO SOFTEN INTO TINY unique cushions of snow. The frozen pellets of rain, like flinty kernels of heated popcorn, fluffed themselves, and caught in the currents, began to drift downward more slowly. The horizontal slugfest with the wind lessened, becoming a gentle pillow fight.

Emma stared through a vertical curtain of white amidst a gray background. Flying at thirty she knew they would backtrack a mile in two minutes. In the fifteen-minute window Rowdy had allowed for the search they would fly seven and a half miles before she must turn back. She had set the timer on her wing watch the instant they left the formation and kept close observance of their speed, altitude, and direction.

Swiveling her head, she spoke loudly into the rush of chilled air. "Owen, glue eyes to ground. I will navigate. Double-check my course. Keep us true."

Owen knew his reply would be lost to Emma's ears in the rush of wind. He accelerated slightly, bumped her tail feathers with his head, once, and then again. His actions relayed the unspoken messages: *I understand. I will do as you have instructed.* He dropped back a few inches, tucking in behind and slightly inside her flight profile; he became her shadow. He cast his eyes down on the accumulated snow, his eyesight strained to catch even slight depressions. Owen wasn't sure exactly what he hoped to see, but assumed he would notice anything out of the ordinary related to his teacher's disappearance. He hoped at some point they would meet Ms. Ride head on, and the three of them would then continue the long journey home together.

They flew silently, a tiny blade scissoring through the slender braids of white cotton falling about them. Emma marked at five minutes, then ten. Fourteen. In the final seconds, her heart became heavy with despair. She could not face the abandonment of her beloved teacher.

Every atom of her existence rebelled against such a cruel thought. *Where was Ms. Ride?*

When her wing watch beeped at fifteen, she dove without hesitation to ground. She had not planned to do so, but her heart forced her to rebel against her training and defy Rowdy's instructions. She landed four feet above the white carpet on the remains of a fallen tree branch, old and brittle in death. Owen, a snow crusted statue, plopped down and perched beside her.

"Fifteen minutes behind and now even more," she said. "Where can she be?"

Of all the students in the junior class, Owen was considered by his classmates and the faculty to be the most thoughtful. He loved math and science. He studied the finer points of aerodynamics and excelled in advanced flight maneuverability to the point he often frightened his classmates and instructors. They knew he was nearly blind in bright light and yet he dove and spiraled and climbed with borderline recklessness, often alarming his worried classmates. Despite his visual handicap, Owen was considered one of the three best flyers in the class. Behind his back, many in the school pointed a wingtip his way and shook their heads in admiration. The older red-tails in the community sometimes compared him to his father, Orville, and to the legendary RT Boyd Higgins, a superb flyer in his day.

"I believe Ms. Ride is either hunkered down on the ground or she has turned back to Sioux Falls," Owen said. "We have flown true and she would never allow herself to fly off course."

"I agree," Emma replied. "Somehow though, I doubt she turned back. Her pain would have to be unbearable for her to abandon us."

She studied the sky, twisting her head about. "What if she were forced off course?"

"It's possible I suppose," he replied. "But it would take a huge eagle or owl to force her to modify her flight plan.

She has moves our predators have never seen. I'm almost certain she'd die before she'd allow herself to be dragged off course."

Emma turned toward Owen. "My thought was because of excruciating pain, she neglected her navigation, a small miscalculation, gone unnoticed. Of all the possibilities, which do you think is most likely?"

"Very difficult to say," Owen replied. "What you imagine is possible, but I think her wing has failed, too painful for her to fly. Going back to Sioux Falls would hurt just as much as going forward to Dupree. If she's on the ground the weather is protecting her from predators. My opinion is she's down."

He opened his wings to shake off the accumulating snow, fluffing his feathers against the encroaching cold. He twisted his goggled head to face her. "We must return to our class now or we also will die in the snow. The temperature is dipping, my watch registers twenty-nine degrees, and our strength will fail us if we continue to fly alone. When our eyes freeze shut we are done." There was no hysteria in his voice; he spoke matter-of-factly, as if nature alone would judge and decide the matter.

Emma's golden eyes flared, recoiled in angry disbelief. "You would abandon your teacher, Goggs?" For the first time, in her exasperation, she used his nickname. "You would let her freeze to death alone? Feel the teeth of a coyote bite into her throat? No cheery companions in her final hour? Are you so heartless?" She hissed the poisonous words.

Again, Owen's words were blunt; he shrugged off Emma's rage and disappointment. "It is not our fault. We have done our best to locate her. Don't blame yourself or me for this calamity." He opened one wing and gently placed it on Emma's shoulders. "We did not cause her to become injured or lost."

Emma, angrier still, shook off his attempt to comfort. "No," she said, her eyes boring into his, "we did not cause it, but she became injured protecting us. I'm certain she awaits rescue. We must try everything to save her. It is our sworn duty."

She calmed herself, then in a lilting, almost poetic voice, recited the *Prairie Winds School of Flight* motto posted above the entrance to the school: "Sareem Tay Karlit, Sareem Shay Sokeer, O'sareem, O'sokeer" *To Try—And To Succeed—Our Mission. To Try—And To Fail—Still Honorable. Not Trying—Dishonorable.*

"Agreed," Owen replied. The shape of his eyes, barely visible behind the goggles, were rounder than standard for a red-tail, and were not canted downward as evolution for hunting prowess has provided; also his eyes were located more toward the front of his face like headlights on an oncoming automobile. In fact, Owen's eyes most resembled the eyes of his maternal grandfather, an owl who was ruthlessly murdered for sport in Minnesota.

Owen moved his goggles down, let them dangle from his neck, and trained those oddly misshapen eyes on his companion.

"There is still hope, Emma," he said with great tenderness. "We can be reasonably certain Ms. Ride is on the ground somewhere between this point and where we turned back in our search. I've scanned the ground from four hundred fifty feet, but noticed nothing unusual. I propose we turn back toward the safety of our class, but fly a mere twenty feet above the ground."

He paused, ruffled his tail feathers. "The glare of the snow compromises my vision somewhat, but with my goggles, my vision is adequate; my eyes peering straight ahead allow me better depth perception than even yours. If I fly arrow tip I will see obstacles you might miss, while your panoramic vision gives you a fuller sweep of the terrain below. I promise I will not fly directly into a tree trunk, though we might brush a few branches here and there." Despite their desperate situation he let out a giggle, the unusual tinkling sound of ice cubes tumbling into an empty glass.

"If you scour the ground," he continued, "it is almost certain we will find her. If we do not locate her within fifteen minutes, we can be certain she has flown off course or turned back. If she's off course, it's doubtful anyone will ever locate her remains." The unspoken message contained deep within his eyes comforted Emma. "Even in the face of such an enormous loss, we have not dishonored ourselves, our classmates, or our school."

"To fly so low is risky business, to the max," Emma said. She fully appreciated the dangers of such an undertaking. "Trees and boulders loom. A collision will be fatal at thirty."

She reached out, touched his shoulder with her wing tip. "Never mind," she said. "You fly better than any of us, and in failing light your eyes are much superior to mine. The world has always been full of danger, and so it is today. We must fly at thirty or we will never catch up to Rowdy. He will not wait nor return for us. I will scrape the snow with my vision; you must weave the way." Her tone was supportive now, no longer accusatory. "Not a moment to waste," she declared. She opened a wing, gestured ahead into the woods. "We must fly like the snake, not the arrow. Be twisty, Goggs."

In an instant Owen raised his goggles, secured his helmet's chinstrap, and was airborne;

Emma, eyes fastened on the glistening white carpet below, flew a mere inch behind his red-streaked tail. The twosome sped low and fast. They were hunters now. The navigator, goggled up, stared straight ahead into the gloom of approaching night; fearless, he set the pace, and plotted the winding path.

Chapter Eight

. . . and when young men and young women mingle, share food and laughter, a peculiar electricity, unfamiliar to physicists, is often passed between them—a type of magnetic force that defies scientific measurement or explanation . . .

NOT WANTING TO TRAIPSE CLEAR BACK TO THE dorm and with time to kill before her next class, Kate decided to return to the Java City coffee shop. She found an empty chair at a table facing a large picture window, fogged up by the shop's warmth. It had started to snow again, huge feathery flakes. Kate placed her backpack on a chair and hung her coat over another chair back; for a moment she lingered, seemingly mesmerized by the graceful motion outside. There was a folded copy of the morning *Brookings Register* on a nearby empty table and she claimed it as her own.

Kate got in line at the counter. The shop was unusually crowded for a Monday morning. Apparently other professors had also abandoned ship early. Just as Kate placed her order and started to walk away, Liam came through the door. Without thinking, Kate waved and smiled. When he smiled back she said, "Hi, Liam. I was in Dr. Marks' class with you. I'm Kate. I've a table over there." She pointed across the room. "You can sit with me if you like."

"Great," he said. "I'll be over in a minute. I need a cup of tea."

Two minutes later Liam smiled and sat down. While they waited for the food to arrive, Liam looked at the front page of the *Register*. "Untimely Artic Blizzard Strikes. Up to seven inches of snow surprised most of the Dakotas and extended into western Minnesota yesterday. High winds and freezing temperatures will remain through the week. In many places roads are closed and the power is out. The governor urges everyone to stay home except for medical emergencies." Liam paused while two bagels, a coffee, and a cup of tea were delivered. He glanced up at the waiter. "Thank you. Much appreciated." He clipped his words close in the Canadian manner.

Kate offered Liam a shy smile, one suitable to pour on a waffle. She liked his soft-spoken, polite manner. Though she had been pretty much going steady with Chris for the last year of high school, she often dreamed of a bigger world filled with all sorts of interesting people. "I can't believe this weather," she said.

Before Liam could respond, Kate's cell rang, an upbeat snippet from "Louie Louie." "My mom," she said. "Excuse me." She stood up and walked toward the door. "Hi, Mom. Did you guys get any snow last night? We got a ton here."

There was a long silence. "Orville stopped by this morning? What did he want?" Kate moved into the hallway, leaned against a wall. "The whole junior class didn't come home? Is it possible they stayed in Sioux Falls another night? Ms. Ride wouldn't risk flying in a snowstorm, would she?"

Kate peeked in the door at Liam, elbows on the table sipping his tea and leafing through the newspaper. "Did Orville call Ms. Ride?" There was a short pause. "Maybe her cell is out of power and she couldn't recharge it." Another pause. "Flight school students aren't allowed to carry cell phones." There was a long silence. "Orvie can't fly down to Sioux Falls in this kind of weather. That's crazy."

Kate listened while her mother filled in the gaps. "I'll call Chris," Kate said. "He can talk to his dad about it. Maybe the sheriff's office can trace Ms. Ride's cell or something. Okay. Call me back if you hear anything. Love you. Tell Dad hi. Bye, bye."

"Anything wrong?" Liam asked when she returned to the table.

Instead of answering, she said, "I'll tell you a hard to believe story. Five years ago, when I was twelve, I accidentally fell into an abandoned well. I was trapped there overnight. Nobody knew where I was. About a week earlier a red-tailed hawk had crashed into our house and broke his leg. We took him to the vet, and my grandmother and I took care of him until he could fly again."

She glanced at Liam, looking for signs of skepticism or worse. "His name is Orville."

Liam seemed amused. "Did you name him or is Orville his real name? Interesting name for a hawk."

"It's his real name. His parents named him after Orville Wright, you know, one of the pioneer plane inventors."

Liam's eyes told her nothing. He took a nonchalant sip of tea as if falling in wells and being rescued by a hawk named Orville were everyday occurrences.

"Okay," Liam said. "Interesting story so far."

"Well, my parents were gone for the weekend and my grandmother was home alone. When I didn't come home from the fishing trip, she put Orville in my dad's truck and drove out to the river. By then it was almost dark. Grandmother got confused and accidently drove into the river. She had to walk three miles back home in the dark.

"In the meantime, Orville discovered me unconscious at the bottom of the well. It took quite a while, but eventually Orvie's flight school instructor, a hawk named RT Boyd Higgins, organized the senior class of flyers and they tried to pull me out with a rope, but I was too heavy. Not long after, my mom and dad and some sheriff guys came along and built a winch. I told you it's hard to believe."

Kate smiled at Liam. "I know it sounds really peculiar, but there is a red-tailed hawk flight school near where I live, and this year's junior class and their teacher flew down to Sioux Falls last Thursday to compete in a state flight school competition. Everybody thought the weather would be fine. Well, on Thursday the weather was fine. The competition was Friday and Saturday, and they were supposed to fly back home on Sunday. Then the blizzard hit. The hawks haven't arrived home yet and no one has heard from them."

"How would your mom even know about them being missing?" Liam asked. "They usually don't put missing bird stories on the evening news."

His question seemed sincere. "Orville, the hawk I've just told you about, is married to Annabelle, and, well—their son, fledgling, whatever—Owen, is in that class. I've known Owen since the day he hatched, and he's a very good student and excellent flyer. Anyway, Orvie flew over to my parents' home this morning and told my mom about it. She called me just now to let me know that Orville and Annabelle and all the hawks are upset and worried."

Liam smiled over his teacup, a quizzical expression. "Can we back up for a minute?"

"Sure," Kate said. "What?"

"In the first place, why did Orvie crash into your house? Hawks have the best vision in the world. Was he texting while flying, or what?" He flashed a skeptical grin.

Kate giggled. "Real good question. Orville's grandmother married an owl. A bit unusual I know. Orville's mother apparently inherited an owl's DNA for her eyes, and neither she nor Orvie can see very well in sunlight. It was a real bright day and he flew through my mom's clothesline, caught a wingtip, and flipped himself into our house."

"So now he only flies at night?" Liam asked.

"No. In bright light he wears these really cool goggles to protect his eyes. He can see fine during the day as long as he's wearing them. And at night, when most of us can't see worth beans, he really cooks it. He crashed before anyone, even his parents, realized he was nearly blind during the daytime. His son Owen and some of his other children have to wear goggles too."

"And Orville can speak English?" Liam asked. A wry grin tugged at the corners of his lips.

"They teach English as a second language at the flight school. All South Dakota red-tails learn how to read English, but very few hawks speak it much. Their beaks aren't really compatible to our sounds. Orvie, and his former flight instructor from school, Boyd Higgins, are probably the two best speakers of English in their community. Higgins solves two English crossword puzzles every day. Anyway, most people don't ever get close enough to a hawk to have a conversation. Red-tails are actually very shy."

"And most humans are quite wary and skeptical," Liam said. "I'd really like to meet Orvie. I don't remember if I mentioned it in class today, but I'm majoring in *Wildlife Management*. I believe all animals have incredible abilities, much greater than we humans imagine."

Kate smiled, her eyes and lips creating a dazzling harmony. "That's exactly what I believe, and why I want to be a vet."

"The snow storm probably forced them to land and wait it out," Liam said. He took another sip of tea. "Hawks are incredible birds and there's no doubt they've survived lots worse conditions than these. Their DNA is linked to the dinosaurs so they've been around a long, long time. Once the snow stops they'll probably take off again and be fine."

"I hope you're right," Kate said. "Their teacher is from India. She was an exchange student at the Academy of Advanced Flight in Pierre a few years ago. I know she won all kinds of honors while she studied there. I think she earned her Master's too, and then after graduation, when Boyd Higgins retired, she was offered his job at the school near where my parents live." She paused a moment, thought of something. "I wonder if her cold weather skills are up to par? I mean India doesn't have much snow, do they?"

Liam laughed. "Are you kidding? Not much snow, along the coast and in the interior, but the Himalayas run through the north of India. There's plenty of snow and cold weather there. And surely she had cold weather survival training in Pierre. She'll be fine. I'll bet they're all sitting around a campfire somewhere, probably toasting marshmallows on long sticks."

All of a sudden none of it seemed very serious. Liam's honest acceptance of her experience with hawks had taken some of the danger and worry out of it.

Kate's phone burped again. She scanned the text message. "I hate to be the bearer of bad news, but all classes are cancelled for the rest of today and tomorrow." She grinned at Liam. "See how useful these cells can be?"

"Way cool," Liam said. "I'm going to the library." He stood up and shouldered an enormous backpack. He ran a big hand through his untamed hair. "If there's any way I can help with the hawk situation let me know. I'm on the first floor in Bison Hall. Otherwise, I guess I'll see you Wednesday in English class. I'm looking forward to it. The professor is fun."

Kate brought a hand to her forehead. She felt too warm. Had she held a mirror up to her face she'd have seen fire racing across her cheeks. Where is Bison Hall? she wondered. She turned her head toward the door, hoping to catch another glimpse. No Liam in sight, but just then, her roommate, Amy, walked in. She waved at Kate, pointed at the coffee line.

Kate waved back. She had lots to share about a certain new friend from Canada.

. . . and let the names of those precious young ones who fall be etched in smooth stone, orderly rows side by side, remembered forever . . . and surround this sacred place with sheltering trees and glorious flowers of every possible color.

JUST PAST NOON, NEARING THE HALFWAY POINT of the flight, six hours into it, the class approached Mac's Corner in Hyde County—nothing but a gas station, three-table café, and grocery store—a minor oasis beside a desolate country road. It was here they had rested and gleefully shared pizza on the flight to Sioux Falls just four days earlier when the weather had been clear and an almost balmy fifty-five degrees. Ms. Ride usually allowed them an hour on the ground: a chance to chat, eat and refresh their strength. There would be no pleasant rest stop today.

Rowdy had not wavered in speed or direction, but as the snow thickened from above he had gradually been forced to lower their flight elevation from four hundred fifty feet down to three hundred. His watch beeped at six hours and he initiated the second rotation as before. From the rear rank Lily and Brady accelerated past the others to replace Oliver and Gabe in the second row behind Rowdy at point. Owen and Emma's spots remained open at the rear.

Rowdy
Lily Brady
Noah Quinn Sven
Riley Sadie Cork Carter Ben
Casey Ian Chloe Parker Daisy Sophie
Caroline Olivia Mandy Logan Eli Jack Isabella
Oliver Gabe

When humans run the famous endurance race called a marathon, they generally form a large clot at the starting line, with the younger, stronger, faster, more confident or foolish runners leading the way. As the run continues, the slower runners, often called joggers, slowly fall back to a comfortable pace they hope to maintain over the entire terrain. By mid-point some have been slowed to a walk by blisters or inadequate training. At the finish line, exhausted stragglers are often more than two or even three hours behind the front-runners.

All members of the Prairie Winds School of Flight had been selected out of the regular Iron Lightning School For Hawks near Dupree at age two because they had demonstrated superior wing strength and strong intellectual capacity. There were no joggers here.

At two hundred miles of continuous flight, moving as a single unit encrusted in white, the class appeared as a feathery ghost wrapped in a deathly shroud. The twenty-two miles per hour pace was easy enough for all of them, but after almost nine hours without food or rest a few were beginning to feel the light-headedness of advanced exhaustion.

In the last half-hour the wind had shifted and increased as the storm intensified; instead of striking them straight on from the west, they were now being buffeted from the north, and despite Rowdy's best efforts to stay true for Dupree they were a hundred yards off course, blown slightly to the south. Rowdy had no way of knowing which of his classmates behind him were still strong and which were growing weak. He kept faith Chloe and all the others could keep pace.

Rowdy's exacting line of flight took them about fifty miles northeast of Pierre, the state capital. Other than their starting point, Sioux Falls, it was the only large city they would be near on the entire trip. In another ten minutes, he knew they would pass almost directly over the tiny historical railroad town of Blunt in Hughes County. Worry over how tall the county's grain elevator and silo complex might be nagged at him. He knew some of these rural towns' farming structures approached a height of three hundred feet.

All red-tails are trained to never fly in darkness below three hundred feet, specifically because of the danger silos and grain elevators pose. Each year a handful of hawks, flying blindly in the dark, barrel into one of these concrete structures at twenty to thirty miles per hour with disastrous results. In these near whiteout conditions, Rowdy's vision straight ahead was limited to about fifty yards, a distance they covered every three and a half seconds.

He checked his watch again and again, not trusting his vision to steer him safely past even huge obstacles like a grain silo. He feared becoming disoriented by the unrelenting snow and his own growing fatigue. He worried too about the possibility the tenacious wind had gradually inched them into danger. To see more clearly, he slowed and led the formation down even closer to the ground.

At an elevation of two hundred seventy-five feet, twenty-six wing watch alarms sounded in unison, indicating extreme danger. Rowdy peered anxiously into the gloom for any hint of structures—any faint outline of shadowy darkness indicating an obstacle—but still the convoy flew on. Lily and Brady bumped him, alerting him they were flying too low, afraid he was asleep at the wheel. He fluffed his tail feathers in their faces indicating he was alert to the danger. He knew they were less than a half-mile from Blunt. His heart raced as he subconsciously braced himself for a possible collision. Other than aborting the flight and leading them to ground, there was nothing he could do. One degree above blindness, they flew on.

Two minutes later they were safely past the town and out over mostly open prairie again. Rowdy allowed himself a sigh of relief. *Only three hours to go.* He knew once they crossed the Missouri River near Mission Ridge it would be smooth flying home to Dupree.

His mind wandered then, wondering what had become of Ms. Ride, Emma, and Owen. He had every confidence in Owen and Emma, certain they had located their teacher and were escorting her along somewhere behind them. He was not particularly surprised they had not rejoined the class, knowing Ms. Ride's injury was probably too severe to fly even at twenty-two.

Each flyer knew they were on the final leg now and gathered comfort and strength from each other. It mattered little to them that the soft feathers around their eyes were crusted with frozen ice, their wings growing heavy with accumulated snow. Their young and power-ful hearts, buoyed by the knowledge their arduous trek was nearing its end, beat firmly, producing the tremen-dous heat necessary to power the wing.

Their watches beeped in unison at the nine-hour mark and the flight's final rotation began. Just behind Rowdy, Caroline replaced Lily while Isabella nudged Brady aside. The others fell neatly into place.

Exactly forty-seven minutes and nine seconds later, as they neared Okobojo Point, the blade hit Rowdy first, severed a wing and sent him spinning off into space. He did not utter a sound.

Caroline shrieked just as the monster bit into her torso, flinging her away in a lifeless heap.

Isabella and Noah, struck at the same instant, were dead before they hit the ground.

Quinn sensed the whisper of death as it hissed past, but he miraculously slid by, untouched.

Sven swerved, but not soon enough. The next blade slashed him in half, killing him instantly.

Amidst the chaos, Riley and Sadie unleashed their shrillest voices, screamed the warning:

Klliintt! Dive! Dead heroes, both. Clutching each other in a final act of friendship they spiraled downward, their last heroic words already uttered. Above them utter chaos reigned.

Cork caught a glancing blow, fluttered helplessly downward, his youth cut terribly short.

Chloe, Parker, and Daisy fought the adrenalin, refused to panic and followed their training.

According to the standard red-tail hawk flight manu-als, the immediate response to this particular warning dictated a brave maneuver called Isaac's Apple; it calls for a vertical dive with wings tucked tight to their bodies. Those who attempt it fall as suicidal stones. The danger lay in the fact they were only two hundred seventy-five feet above ground with little or no chance to pull out of such a precipitous dive. The manual protocol states: **NEVER** attempt Isaac's Apple below seven hundred feet. Side by side, the three terrified hawks dove hard toward the ground.

Lily and Brady, flying at the trailing edge of the formation had perhaps a fraction of a second more time; they attempted to escape by reversing into the rarely used, and ultra-difficult Back Door maneuver. No chance. Both were struck.

A few others, frozen in abject terror, unable to react, simply flew straight ahead into the slashing apparatus. All died silently, their voices frozen in their throats, their bodies chopped to smithereens.

The murderous rampage had taken less than ten seconds. Quinn had felt the deadly blade swish by, a hair's breadth margin between tomorrow and eternity. Behind him he heard cries of surprise and agony as his classmates were struck and sent spiraling to the ground. Even with the sounds of the dying resounding in his ears he maintained the course. Rowdy, Olivia, and Isabella flying directly in front of him had disappeared in an eye blink; they were there and then they were gone—their only trace a fine spray of warm blood on his face. A hundred yards past the carnage, unable to comprehend what had just happened, he slowed and waited for others to join him, but none did. He hovered, uncertain of what he should do.

Surely I'm not alone. Quinn's mind denied the truth even then. *It cannot be.* He circled back to aid his fallen classmates. He turned sharply into a wide arc and rapidly descended. He dared not confront the invisible blades again. He leveled off at fifty feet and flew past the base of the tower. His friends, all those he'd spent his childhood with, lay scattered below, most motionless—obviously dead; others twitched weakly in their final throes.

He landed softly, walked among them, offered comforting words and encouragement to those still breathing. He flung himself down on those past help, whispered soft words of everlasting love and affection; he stained his feathers with their blood, and made promises he could not keep.

He lingered an hour or more—time meaningless now, oblivious to the cold and falling snow. All movement on the nightmarish landscape ceased, all sounds too, and the relentless snow, driven by a strong north wind, inch by inch, buried them all.

Quinn tried time and again to take a count. He knew there were twenty-eight students in their class. His mind, reeling in horror and despair, had forgotten that Owen and Emma had gone back to aid Ms. Ride. If all had died he should count twenty-seven bodies, but each time he attempted to count his mind would stumble and lose the number. The grisly task overwhelmed him; his mind refused to perform the simplest arithmetic. He finally arrived at twenty-two, but he couldn't be certain. The oncoming darkness and falling snow mingled with his revulsion, creating a blurred sense of reality.

Trance-like, he muttered incoherently. "Where are the others? Where can they be?"

For several minutes he stood, a feathered statue in the snow; he swiveled his head slowly from side to side. Unable to comprehend the calamity he said, "They must be here."

At last, hopelessly muddled, Quinn took to the air; it was pitch dark now and he knew his own chance for survival depended on finding shelter for the night. A mile south of the killing grounds he came upon a small creek lined with cottonwood trees, their autumn leaves sagging under the weight of the heavy snow. Beside the creek were the remains of an untended apple orchard. He sailed in low and found refuge under the canopy of drooping, snow-laden limbs. He perched on a thick branch of the largest cottonwood; the trunk shielded him from the wind, offering comfort in the night. He fluffed his feathers to create insulation, shook the wet snow from his wings, and hugged himself as best he could. A frantic hunger took hold, gnawed at his ribs. For an hour he shivered uncontrollably, chilled by the air and the surreal images of his lifeless classmates. Finally he slept.

Snow covered the murder scene, a pristine white linen tablecloth spattered with warm frothy blood, feathery body parts, and motionless corpses at a dinner party for twelfth century drunken royals. The guilt-ridden snow, not wanting to be branded an accomplice, tried to conceal the monstrous deed; it continued to fall silently. Towering high overhead, oblivious, the murderous wind turbine licked its bloodthirsty lips and generated on.

. . . and when others, more desperate than ourselves need help, are we to turn a deaf ear or look the other way as if the voiceless wind alone called out?

Kate's cell quivered and sang, "Louie, Louie, Me Gotta Go" when Orville's text arrived. **No home yet. Me go look. Orvie.** Kate glanced at her watch, ten thirty-seven. A comforting cup of tea by her side, she'd been reading *The Odyssey* in her grandfather's chair since their return from Java City. She placed a tasseled bookmark.

Amy stirred from her nap, traveling on an odyssey of her own somewhere in dreamland where handsome pizza delivery-men lined up ten deep at her doorstep. "What's up?" she mumbled.

Kate thumbed her phone—a short **Be Careful** reply. "My red-tail friend is going to search for his son Owen and the missing class. They still haven't returned. I know their teacher and she is really, really dependable. I'm certain she'd inform someone at the school if they were having serious problems. It just doesn't make sense."

Amy rolled over on her side, faced Kate and yawned. "How would she notify anybody if they're marooned somewhere between Sioux Falls and home?"

"All the teachers fly with a cell phone. They carry it in a leather holster under their wing."

"Well, why hasn't she called someone?"

"Exactly," Kate said. She stood up and walked to the window. The snowfall had stopped and brilliant sunshine glared from above and below. "If no one has heard from her she must be unable to use her cell. Maybe it malfunctioned. The battery could be dead. Do cell towers function in such heavy snowfall?"

"I have no idea," Amy said. "I thought they always work. Do the students carry cells?"

"Yes, but they aren't allowed to bring their phones to school." Kate sighed. "Their parents must really be worried. I know my mom and dad would be way frantic if I didn't come home from a school field trip and no one called them."

Amy sat up on the edge of the bed, yawned. "Is there anything we can do?"

"The only thing I can think of is the snow must have forced them down somewhere between Sioux Falls and Dupree. They live outside every day of their lives, so they know how to survive in any weather. But, if the teacher's phone isn't working there isn't much anyone can do. I imagine most of the roads are impassable and even if we had a car we couldn't go search for them. It's just huge wide-open space between Sioux Falls and Dupree, so it's not likely we could find them anyway."

"Maybe Liam, the guy you met for coffee this morning, has a car," Amy said. "He could put chains on and we could go search."

"It's over two hundred miles from Sioux Falls to Dupree," Kate said. "My dad drives it three or four times a year. But hawks fly in a straight line, the shortest distance from point A to point B. They don't follow the roads. We'd never find them driving the roads."

Amy stood up and stretched, pretty even when disheveled. "It's almost lunch time. Lets go to the library. You said Liam was going there, right? Let's see what he thinks. Then we can all go to lunch together. But first, I need to cute up."

They found Liam sitting in a corner by himself. He was reading old *National Geographic* magazines. He smiled up at Kate. "Long time no see," he said. "Who's your friend?"

Amy held out her hand and smiled. "I'm Amy, Kate's roommate."

Liam stood up, and engulfed her hand, the old-fashioned gentleman. "Hi, Amy." He looked at Kate. "What's up?"

"It's about my hawk friend, Orville," Kate said. "His son's class still hasn't come home. Orvie texted me a while ago. He said he's going to go look for them. I'm getting really worried because their teacher should have called by now." The girls sat down on either side of Liam.

"I'd be worried too," Liam said. "They were supposed to be home Sunday and it's almost noon on Monday. And the teacher hasn't called? Something is seriously wrong."

"Don't mean to pry, but do you own a car?" Amy asked. "If the roads are okay maybe we could help locate them."

"I had an old beater Volkswagen bus up in Canada, but I sold it to help pay my tuition. I'm not on scholarship or anything, and my parents can't help much. I rode my bike here. Sorry."

Amy's eyes widened. "You rode a bike clear from Canada?"

"Yeah. Northern Manitoba. No bigee really," said Liam, an unmistakable happiness in his eyes and voice. "I've taken longer rides."

"I doubt a car would help a whole lot anyway," Kate said. "Hawks don't follow the roads."

"Just a second," Liam said. "Let me get my road map. He fished into a faded blue backpack and pulled out a carefully folded South Dakota map. He smiled. "When you don't have access to electronic maps you use old school. He pushed the stack of *National Geographic* magazines aside and opened the map on the table. "Okay." He put a fingertip on Sioux Falls. "Where's Dupree?"

Kate leaned over the table. "Way up here in Ziebach County right beside Highway 212."

She placed her finger on the spot. My parents' ranch and the hawk community are real close to Iron Lightning, a Lakota Sioux community. It's just a few miles from town."

"Let's draw a straight line from Dupree to Sioux Falls," Liam said. "Can I borrow your triangle for a minute?"

Kate and Amy laughed. "Yeah, right," Amy said. "I must have left mine in the dorm."

"No problem," Liam said. He grabbed a *National Geographic* and using the spine as a straight edge drew a line with his pen between the two locations. "There's your most likely route. We're sitting quite a-ways north."

"There are hardly any roads," Kate said. "There's not much out there, period. It's mostly empty ranch and farmland. If they were forced down, there's no way anyone in a car could help them."

"Not necessarily," Liam said. "People live in some pretty remote places. I grew up in a tiny place called Pine Dock, Manitoba right on the western shore of Lake Winnipeg. There are some people living there, but they are few and far between. And there are hawk colonies just about everywhere. Maybe if your hawks sent out a distress call other red-tails would help them."

"I guess that's possible," Kate said. "But I was hoping there is some way we could help," She dabbed at her eyes with a tissue. "Orville and Annabelle risked their lives to save me. I thought it's my turn to help them."

"Do you guys have a snowmobile?" Liam asked. He grinned, his face alive with mischief.

"Parked out front," Amy said. "No helicopter though." She nudged Liam with her shoulder.

Liam smiled. "I grew up driving a snowmobile. They'll go dang near anywhere and the new ones are quite fast. If we can borrow or rent a snowmobile we could follow their flight route clear to Dupree." His teasing eyes turned serious. He looked at Kate. "Like I told Dr. Marks this morning, I don't have a cell, but I'm sure your phones have a GPS. Much more accurate than my compass."

Liam drew another horizontal line straight from Brookings just south of Highway 14 until it intersected with the first line near Mac's Corner. He studied the map. "Where our lines meet is just about half way between Sioux Falls and Dupree, a logical spot for them to stop and rest. I don't know how fast a red-tail can fly in near blizzard conditions, but probably only twenty or thirty miles an hour." He started to calculate on the margins of the map. "If they averaged about twenty-five miles an hour, the entire flight would take just under twelve hours. Do you think a hawk can fly that far without stopping to rest?"

"They are really strong flyers," Kate said. "They all were selected out of regular school because of their flying ability. If they left Sioux Falls Sunday morning as soon as it was light and flew all the way without stopping they would have been home sometime late in the afternoon, maybe five or six."

"Remember though, it was really cold and windy yesterday," Amy said. "Flying when windy and snowing would make it even more difficult."

Liam looked puzzled. "I doubt it was snowing when they left Sioux Falls or their teacher wouldn't have risked it, and she would have contacted the school. The fact she didn't makes me think she thought they could make it home safely. Along the way though, the weather worsened and eventually they were forced down somewhere."

"But where?" Amy asked. "If they weren't too far out she would have turned around and gone back to Sioux Falls, her most sensible option."

"Exactly," Liam said. "And apparently she didn't go back. So they're most likely somewhere beyond the mid-point, west of where our lines intersect. If we start at the point of intersection and navigate a straight line west from there to Dupree I think we'll at least have a chance to find them."

He slid his index finger across the map, paused, and then looked up. "If my roommate will loan us his pickup, and if Highway 14 is open, we can drive as far as Highmore. Our best bet is to leave the car there and rent a snowmobile. From there we go south for nineteen miles on 47 until we hit our line just north of Mac's Corner." He looked at Amy and Kate. "Do you guys have sleeping bags? Doubt we can do this in one day."

Both girls nodded their heads in the affirmative and exchanged looks.

Liam looked at his watch. "It's almost noon now. If we hit McDonalds for lunch on our way out of town we should be able to make it to Mac's Corner before dark. Are you up for some adventure?"

"Definitely," Kate said. She looked at Amy.

"I'm all in," Amy replied, a dreamy quality in her voice.

"Bring some money," Liam said. "We'll need gas and food." His eyes danced a rocking tune as he surveyed the two. "I'm 'bout broke."

Chapter Eleven

. . . and if men die of their adventures, so what? They have only followed the path already arranged before they were even born. Why should others risk their lives to save what the laws of nature have ordained?

OWEN KEPT THE PACE AT THIRTY; HE ZIGZAGGED around tree trunks, telephone poles, farmhouses, and barns. His vision was compromised due to the dazzling snow, but darkness was fast approaching and the oncoming outlines of the various objects were sufficient for him to avoid collisions. He flew with absolute precision, moving two feet to the left to avoid a small willow trunk, then instantly correcting two feet to the right once they were safely by. The two of them zoomed over the landscape, one a keen-eyed searcher, her eyes to the ground, the other an intrepid navigator, eyes glued straight ahead.

They were about three miles east of the small community of Wessington Springs in Jerauld County when they passed over Firesteel Creek, appearing to Emma as a narrow ribbon of dark water flowing between two heaping banks of snow. A few hundred yards farther they came upon a crudely built horse corral, a mountainous barn, and a small frame house established in the center of a large meadow. It was dusk now and the home's windows emitted shining lights—small beacons of warmth and hope in the hostile gloom. They sailed past the home's steep pitched roof, swerving at the last instant to avoid the brick chimney; sparks from the fireplace flew upward like bottled fireflies set free.

A quarter of a mile past the ranch Emma noticed a leaning fence post line supporting three strands of sagging barbwire at the edge of the clearing. As they passed by, Emma's eye caught a whisper of movement near the base of a fencepost; two dark rocks also poked partially through the snow. Her mind instantly deciphered the vision: a lost field mouse struggling to find its nest in the accumulated snow. Her hunting instinct immediately rejected the thought—movement too disorganized, too random in an ordered universe. It was clearly out of place. They were already fifty yards past the sighting when she accelerated up beside Owen.

"Turn," she shouted. "I saw something. Follow me."

Emma banked hard to the left into a tight arc; her companion reacted and stayed close on her tail. She slowed and floated, extending her talons and landing with a powdery thump on the snow beside the fence post and dark rocks. "Two dead crows," she muttered. "Dead crows and nothing more."

"Not long dead either," Owen added. "Their warmth lingers." He moved his goggles down to his neck, surveying the sky above them. "Trouble lingers still. It's very difficult to kill a crow." Emma moved closer. Her eyes widened. A quarter of an inch of feathery gray wing tip protruded from the icy snow; it twitched and gave a slight shudder—alive still, or merely a feeble movement in the wind?

"It could be," Emma said. Desperate talons and beaks dug into the snow. A hawk's wing took shape in the hollow. A single gold bangle appeared, then another, Ms. Ride's trademark jewelry.

"It's her," Owen cried. They ripped at the snow with new strength, beaks used as chisels and scoops. The body appeared lifeless; her eyes and beak were frozen shut.

Emma placed her beak directly on Ms. Ride's nares, felt a tiny puff of warm air being exhaled. "She's alive," she shouted. "She's still breathing. Hallelujah!"

Owen quickly burrowed his head under his teacher's stiff body, braced his legs on uncertain snow and lifted with all his might. His talons dug in, found frozen dirt, the solid foundation he needed. Emma joined the task and burrowed next to Owen; they strained against the unseen icy forces holding their teacher down. A moment later, two sets of youthful ingenuity and strength combined to pop Ms. Ride free of her frosty tomb.

"The crows," Owen murmured. "They weighed her down and pulled her out of the sky." The two lifeless crows, her final tormentors, clung to Chawla's legs.

Using their beaks as levers, Emma and Owen carefully pried the crows' beaks open and freed Ms. Ride's legs from their deathly grip.

"The barn," Emma cried. She pointed with a frantic wingtip across the meadow. "We've got to get her out of this snow and warm her."

"Roll her over onto my back." Owen snugged his goggles over his eyes and tucked his wings tight to his body. Then he lay face down in the hollowed-out depression— the robbed grave—until his back was level with the surface of the snow.

Emma, using herself as a miniature bulldozer, dug her talons into the snow, pushing Ms. Ride's body until their motionless teacher nestled atop Owen's back. "Open her wings," Owen said, his voice muffled by the snow. "So she doesn't roll off."

Emma carefully pulled Chawla's stiff wings open on either side of Owen. "Okay," she said. "Can you catch air with such a heavy load?"

Owen had often heard his father describe the moment when a class of student red-tails had attempted a Power Climb to lift Kate Flannery, who weighed ninety-eight pounds at the time, out of a deep well. Frantic to save Kate's life, Dr. Spud Richfield, the Prairie Winds School of Flight's superintendent, had calculated each student would have to lift their own weight plus two and a half pounds each of Kate's weight. The task had proved to be too strenuous for such young wings and hearts, and despite their Herculean effort, Kate had remained trapped and unconscious in the well.

Owen knew an adult female red-tail weighs close to three pounds and the last time he was weighed at school he was just a few ounces over two pounds. He calculated he needed strength enough to lift five pounds. "Piece of cake," he said, using one of his father's favorite English expressions.

Owen braced his legs under him, took three sharp breaths, and slowly rose to a shaky standing position. Emma, wings extended, helped balance the load. The scene was reminiscent of a World War II rescue mission deep behind enemy lines with a soldier hoisting his dying comrade upon his back for a frantic rush to safety.

Standing almost erect now, Owen wobbled and nearly fell in the uncertain footing. "Is she too heavy?" Emma asked. "The extra weight may bring you both down. Let me fetch a rope from the barn. We can drag her across the snow."

"We've no time for a rope," Owen said.

Unable to help, Emma faced Owen. She repeated her question. "Can you carry her?"

Without a word Owen spread his wings, gave a preliminary flap or two to shake off the accumulated snow, and with a sharp grunt was airborne. He flew low along the fence line for twenty-five yards or more before he gained just enough altitude to clear the forbidding strands of barbwire. The barn door beckoned, yawning darkly four hundred yards away. Owen flew uncertainly, dipping and rising with his cumbersome burden. About half way across the field he felt Ms. Ride start to slide off his back. He struggled to stay airborne—only feet off the ground— but he was afraid if she fell they might not be able to get her reloaded to complete the transport. He dipped one wing, and with a mighty shrug of his shoulders his cargo seemed to stabilize again. Flying escort, Emma shouted encouragement. "Just a bit more, Owen. Be strong, Goggs."

Gliding now, just inside the door, an exhausted Owen pulled his talons in tight to his body and slid to a somewhat controlled crash landing on the barn floor. Ms. Ride, jolted by the impact, slid off, and lay motionless. Owen lay on his back, wings spread, gasping for air.

"Help me, Goggs," Emma called. "We've got to get her out of the chill. She pointed a wing tip toward the darkened side of the barn. "We can search the stalls for something to wrap her in. But first, let's move her out of the doorway."

Where Ms. Ride lay, about four feet inside the barn, a powdery covering of snow had drifted in and partially covered a narrow concrete slab; in the dim light Emma could see a bare dirt floor, cold, but safely out of the wind and snow. Owen gathered his strength and staggered back to his feet; still breathing hard, he hobbled over to where Ms. Ride lay.

"Grab a leg," Emma said. She gripped one leg as gently as possible in her beak just above the talons, and Owen did the same. Walking backward, they carefully dragged Ms. Ride's seemingly lifeless body to the far side of the barn. Behind them, almost hidden in the failing light, a horse whinnied; another nervously stamped its hooves— whether curious or frightened, they couldn't tell.

"This will have to do for now," Emma said. "I'll stay with her. Go find a covering. And take your goggles off, will you? When you wear them inside, you look silly. It's plenty dark in here for you to see."

Owen, stung by her thoughtless remark, moved his goggles down, and unbuckled his chinstrap. Muttering to himself, he wandered off toward the back of the barn, his vision almost perfect within the dim structure.

A few minutes later he returned, dragging a ragged saddle blanket in his beak. They managed to lay the blanket out flat and slide Ms. Ride onto it. Then they turned her on her side, her back toward the wall. Emma lay down behind Ms. Ride and offered her life, a living engine of warmth: she spread her wings, folding them as best she could around her teacher's stone-cold body, and cuddled tight.

Owen carefully wrapped them in the blanket, a cozy double cocoon, leaving only their faces peeking out. "Are you okay?" he asked.

"I will be once she starts to thaw out. Bit cold at the moment."

Owen leaned weakly against the blanketed mound. "What else needs be done?" he asked.

"Survive the night," Emma replied. "Rest for the morrow, come what may. No doubt more crows lurk nearby. We need to be careful."

Somewhere in the distance a dog barked. Two horses toward the back of the barn shifted their feet; company for each other, their sides touched, sharing the warmth.

Owen removed his helmet and goggles, and surveyed the barn. He noted its dilapidated state—the sagging timbers, open spaces in the walls. Slowly he gathered enough stray bits of straw and hay to fashion a nest. He built it as close to Emma and Ms. Ride as possible, hoping some of his body heat might help them survive the night. He burrowed in, covering himself completely. He lay on his back, and closed his eyes; silently, his beak barely moving, he prayed for his teacher's recovery, and his classmates' safety. Prayed for strength, courage, and guidance on the morrow. Gave thanks for his vision, his wings, his parents, and Emma. His helmet and goggles. Done. He yawned. Felt the hunger gnawing. He turned on his side, faced away from Emma.

"Emma," he called.

"Go to sleep, Owen," she said.

He giggled. "That blanket stinks. Enjoy the aroma."

"Goodnight, Goggs." Deep affection swirled in her voice.

They slept.

Chapter Twelve

. . . and sooner or later, a child, casting off the mantle of childhood, will defy her parents, go against their will, and face the consequences.

THE PICK-UP TRUCK, AN OLD BEATER FORD rescued from a tow truck auction, quaked at even the slightest bumps in the road, but the heater blasted plenty of warmth and extra noise. A long jagged crack from top to bottom marred the windshield on the passenger's side. Kate and Liam filled the gas tank at a Shell station, and themselves at McDonald's before leaving town, paying with Kate's credit card. Highway 14 heading west out of Brookings, plowed earlier that morning by the state department of transportation, presented a ribbon of gray stretching endlessly through an undulating sea of white. The snow had stopped for the moment.

Amy had made a tactical mistake. When she called her mother to outline the adventure her mother flew into a tirade, and demanded Amy not go. "I'm still a child to her," she told Kate.

Kate had decided she wouldn't call her parents until the trip was well underway. *No sense worrying them for nothing.*

It's one hundred sixty-seven miles from Brookings to Highmore," Kate said. "According to my phone it's a two hour and fifty-two minute drive. We left McDonald's at one, and it's now two fifteen. We should be about half way there—another hour and a half or so."

Liam laughed. "No way. Your phone is way off. We're averaging about thirty miles an hour, conditions what they are. The road's slick and the tires are bald. We'd probably be safer and faster on skateboards."

While at McDonald's Kate had sent her mother a text: **With a friend on way to locate Prairie Winds class. Driving west on 14. Snow stopped, road okay. Don't worry.**

A moment later a reply: **Dad says too dangerous. Pls stay home. Annabelle called. Orville has gone to search. More snow expected tonight.**

Kate sat quietly, riding a pensive shotgun. Back in the school library the plan had seemed a fun and reasonable way to locate and help Orville's son Owen and the others. Now she wasn't so sure. Finding a small group of hawks in the vast South Dakota prairie suddenly appeared close to impossible, if not insane. She'd known Liam for less than a day. If Amy's parents, and her own parents felt it was too risky, then maybe it wasn't sensible. Her normal reaction in junior high and high school had always been to argue a bit, and then follow her parents' advice. But she was a college girl now. Shouldn't she be able to judge these things for herself? She believed people should offer help when help was needed.

The truck rattled along through the small communities of DeSmet, Manchester, and Iroquois. The truck seemed to be the only vehicle on the road, rarely passing an oncoming car. Kate fiddled with the radio, but produced no music or news—just an ocean of static. "We might as well be on another planet," she said. "This radio is worthless." She scrunched herself against the door.

Fighting the road racket, Kate raised her voice, "Hey Liam," she said, "maybe this isn't such a good idea. It's too big out here. We'll never find a small band of red-tails. What do you think?"

"Up to you," Liam said. He glanced across at her, but she was staring out the side window at a bleak farmhouse perched on a low rise beside the road. The house was framed by two ancient shade trees and surrounded by a huge plot of pumpkins—a horde of orange swimmers' caps breaking the surface of churning white water at the start of a summer triathlon. A large jack-o-lantern leered back at her; it perched nonchalantly on the top step of the porch, grinning hideously at the few who dared venture by.

"If nothing else, it's a harmless adventure," Liam said. "They've already cancelled classes tomorrow so we won't be missing anything at school. Red-tails have been on this planet almost forever, and they've adapted to all the extremes the world offers. It's probably riskier for us than it is for them." He smiled widely, showing straight white teeth. "I'm fine with whatever you want to do."

Kate frowned at her own uncertainty. She had always been bold, almost fearless. She said, "Why don't we go at least as far as Highmore before we decide? If things don't look good we can turn around and drive back to Brookings. There's supposed to be a bowling alley and steakhouse in Highmore. We can eat dinner there."

"Fine with me," Liam said. "If this beast of a truck keeps running."

Kate closed her eyes, leaned her head against the cold window. "I hope so," she murmured. She trusted her father's judgment in all things, and it made her uneasy knowing she was involved in something he deemed too dangerous. Just now, hearing Liam confirm her father's concern about undue risk, had deepened her uncertainty, but she couldn't shake the feeling the hawks needed their help.

She felt a sharp pang of guilt, wondered what her boyfriend, Chris, would think if he knew she was riding on a slippery country road with a college guy she barely knew. Even though three feet of empty space gaped between them something kept drawing Kate closer to Liam. When riding with Chris in his truck she would always ride tight to him, thigh touching thigh, her left hand resting lightly just above his knee. Her face flamed at the thought.

"Highmore it is," Liam said. He took a deep breath, gripped the wheel and stared through the dirty windshield. "We'll decide forward or backward from there. Relax, girl."

Kate suddenly wished Amy were sitting beside her, a teasing and joking companion, and a bulwark against her growing anxiety. *Have I put myself back in the well?* She stiffened with the memory.

A moment later a feathery snowflake brushed the windshield and disappeared. Then another.

. . . and when the facts are gathered, sifted through, and examined, there remains but one more need. Someone must be blamed.

AT NINE O'CLOCK, OWEN'S FATHER, ORVILLE, started calling. One of the first on his list was RT Boyd Higgins, a former flight instructor at the school. (All South Dakota red-tails use the initials RT.) Higgins was retired now, but stood out as one of the pillars of the red-tail community.

"Something has happened to Chawla Ride's class," Orville began. "Something bad."

For a moment Higgins did not reply. He knew the class had flown to Sioux Falls for the competition, but had given it little thought. It was an annual event, one he'd participated in with his classes for many years. When he retired it was Chawla Ride who had replaced him on the faculty. He knew her well, thought very highly of her, and considered her to be one of the best young teachers in the district. "What do you mean?" he asked. "What's happened?"

"I don't know," Orville said. "They should have been back here this afternoon before dark. We waited and waited, thought for sure they'd show up. You know, the weather and all."

Higgins drew in a big breath and glanced at his wing watch. "Did Chawla call anybody at the school?"

"No. Most worrisome. She's always been dependable, and if they were gonna be late she'd have called and at least left a message for the parents. I've called around some and nobody's heard from her. I've a real bad feeling, Boyd."

"I understand," Higgins said. "Tell you what. I'll call the superintendent right now. I'll bet anything she called him. Either way he needs to call a meeting and let all you parents know what's going on. Fair enough?"

"Okay," Orville said. "I know a lot of parents are worried. Call me right back and let me know what he says, will you? Annabelle and I can call all the parents and let them know too."

"Of course," Higgins replied. A cold chill made him shudder as he tapped in the number.

Less than an hour later, Dr. RT Spud Richfield, school district superintendent, spoke to the red-tail parents and a few other concerned hawks from a low platform hastily set up in the flight school's cafeteria. "The last time I heard from Ms. Ride was Saturday afternoon when she informed me the class had won second place in the competition, all was well, and they would leave Sioux Falls for home right after breakfast on Sunday morning."

He paused and listened to the anxious murmurs. When it was quiet and all eyes were fixed on him again, he said, "I'm positive she followed her plan, but the extreme weather change may have taken her by surprise somewhere along the way. I have every confidence in her navigation abilities, but apparently the weather worsened to the point it became unsafe to fly. When we hired her four years ago, she was considered the best female flyer in all of South Dakota. Everyone here has experienced flying in fierce snowstorms. Wind driven snow can be blinding for any of us."

Many in the crowd nodded in agreement. The snowfall was unusual for October, but common to their lives. Everyone in the room had survived snowy flights.

"No doubt when Ms. Ride judged it unsafe to fly she led the students to ground to seek shelter. All of our teachers are trained to put student safety above all else." He cleared his throat, and fluffed his graying feathers.

With the school custodians gone home for the night, the furnace was off and the cold was seeping in through the many cracks and crannies of the aging building. "I'm positive she would call me if she could. The only explanation I can offer you is her phone must have malfunctioned. I've called her at least twenty times in the last four hours, and all of my calls have gone directly to her voice mail. Even so, I'm optimistic she and the students are safe and will be on their way again as soon as the snow stops falling and morning light arrives. That's all I have to share with you at this time. Please go home, stay warm, and surely we'll all celebrate back here tomorrow when we see them approaching the school."

A wing shot up and a loud voice called out. "Dr. Richfield. Have you notified the Hawk Patrol Squadron in Pierre the class is missing?"

"Good question, Dan. I called headquarters about five hours ago as soon as I felt the class was overdue. I spoke with the base commander, Major Lance Trapp, who happens to be a friend of mine from when we both flew with the Silver Wings Commando Group years ago over in Albuquerque. I explained the entire situation to him, and it's his opinion, as it is mine, Ms. Ride has taken the class to ground, found shelter, and is merely waiting for the weather to abate. His sincere thoughts are with us and he believes our young ones will be home safe and sound early tomorrow afternoon. Any other questions?"

A pretty hawk standing near the front raised a tentative wing. "Dr. Richfield, do you know if Ms. Ride flew point?"

"I assume so, Nancy, but I'm not positive. It's customary for our teachers to fly point on long flights not specific to training. My guess is she was at point. The only reason she wouldn't be is if she were incapacitated in some way, and she appointed one of her stronger flyers to the point position. I know your son Rowdy has flown point, and I believe Owen, Emma, Quinn and several others have as well. But, in such difficult weather conditions I think it's safe to say Ms. Ride was at point.

"Anyone else have a question?" Dr. Ridgefield surveyed the crowd.

A burly, dark feathered hawk toward the back growled, "Why'd you even send 'em clear to Sioux Falls this time of year? Just for a little flying contest? Ridiculous if you ask me. It's way too risky and a big waste of time. Hell, the weather around here is always unpredictable. And another thing, Ms. Ride may be a top flyer, but she's a foreigner. She don't know squat about flying in a South Dakota blizzard. Anything happens to my Lily, there'll be hell to pay."

Dr. Richfield tried his best to smile in a very delicate situation. "First off, Gary, the weather caught everyone off guard. On Thursday morning when the class left, the flying conditions were almost perfect—blue skies and sixty-two degrees. The forecast for the next five days was for more of the same. The weather service was completely fooled by the storm."

He cleared his throat. "Also, our school has competed in the Sioux Falls October Fly competition every year since I've been here, going on twelve years now. We're proud of our school and our students. They may not beat all those big city schools, but every year they're among the most skilled young flyers in the state. This past weekend our sons and daughters out performed the best students from Rapid City, Pierre, and Sioux Falls. As far as I'm concerned that's a great accomplishment. True, Ms. Ride was born in India, but she was tops in her class at the academy, the fledglings love her, and I have every confidence in her ability to bring them home safely."

The superintendent checked his wing watch. "It's getting late. We've done all we can for tonight. Let's go home and try to get some sleep. If I receive one scintilla of information about their whereabouts I will personally notify each of you immediately. I appreciate your patience and understanding."

There was a small wave of murmured disgruntlement, but for the most part the parents seemed to accept Dr. Richfield's explanation of the situation, and realized the school had done all they possibly could for the time being.

Owen's parents, Orville and Annabelle, stood alone off to one side of the crowd. Like the others, they too were bewildered about the class disappearing, but still held supreme trust in Dr. Richfield and Chawla Ride. With nothing more to be done before morning they flew the short distance home, climbed into bed, and held each other tight.

Long after the assembly had winged away, a lone figure sat motionless. RT Boyd Higgins did not have a son or daughter or even a grandchild enrolled in the school. But several parents in the gathering had been former students of his. He had attended the meeting out of concern for the safety of the class and their teacher.

He had listened carefully to Dr. Richfield's explanation, and weighed the superintendent's words against his own accumulated years of flight and teaching experience. The explanation soothed and comforted him, and yet a sense of foreboding about the lack of communication from Ms. Ride lingered and tormented. Higgins knew Chawla personally, and absolutely trusted her skill as a teacher and flyer. He was convinced something completely unforeseen had happened.

Finally, shaking his head as if to clear the cobwebs, he fluffed his feathers against the chill, and stood up. He knew his wife would disapprove, but he had already made up his mind. At first light, he would fly his own mission. He had no other choice. He needed to know they were all safe. With a sigh, he gathered his strength and headed for home. It was far past his bedtime.

. . . and the trouble with fibs, mild decep-
tions, white lies, and such, they take on a
life of their own, and like untreated car-
buncles, swell and puff up with the poison
inside until they can no longer be con-
tained and burst, a splash of dishonesty,
staining the lips forever.

CARLETON D. REESE, A TALL, THIN MAN WITH A rascal of a gray moustache, leaned patiently against the counter at Country Machinery Rentals in Highmore. Locals called the store the CMR. Around town, where he had lived his entire sixty-one years, Reese was known simply as "Cot." If he wondered what two young people were doing renting a snowmobile an hour before closing on a cold, snowy Monday afternoon he kept the question to himself.

He glanced at his watch and then at Kate, who was filling out the rental forms for the Yamaha snowmobile and ski-cart. "Are you sure this can't wait 'til mornin'?" he asked. "Be pitch black out there in another hour or so. Riding snowmobiles is kinda dangerous after dark. Don't recommend it."

Kate glanced up and smiled. She started to speak and then thought better of it.

Cot studied Liam across the room. He shifted his feet, and folded his long arms across his chest, almost a defensive posture. Wasn't quite sure what the boy was up to. "We open up again at seven-thirty tomorrow morning. It would save you some money too."

"I think we'll be fine," Liam replied. "It's a straight shot down 47 to Mac's Corner. It's only nineteen miles or so. And there's hardly any traffic on the roads. We drove over from Brookings this afternoon and only passed two or three cars the whole way. Shouldn't take us more than an hour to get to where we're going, a place called Lazy Creek." Liam was examining an antique tractor. "We'll camp somewhere along there for the night."

The man looked skeptical. "Forecast is calling for five to six inches more snow tonight. We've got two or three motels in town here, or I'll let you camp for free in the yard overnight if you want. Nobody will bother you. Start south first thing in the morning. Be lots safer. You got proper gear, a good tent and stuff? Gonna get real cold before the sun comes up again."

"Yes, sir, we do," Liam replied. "I've done a lot of camping up north in the snow. Shouldn't be a problem at all."

Kate signed her name, and pushed the rental agreement along with her credit card across the counter toward Cot. The man reminded her of her Dupree School social studies teacher, Ken Bender. On the last day of school before graduation, he had signed Kate's yearbook: *In a thousand years of teaching school, you're the best student I've ever had, Kate Flannery. I'm expecting great things. Keep in touch, and don't for a minute ever forget Dupree. We're small on the map, but just as big-hearted as anywhere else in the world. Once your teacher for a year—now your friend, forevermore. K. D. Bender.*

"You don't mind if we camp here?" Kate asked. The showroom was warm and she had taken her parka off and laid it on the counter. "On the front lawn?"

"Don't mind at all," Cot said. He ran the card. "I sure wouldn't want my daughter riding a snowmobile down highway 47 in near blizzard conditions. I really think you'd be better off sleeping here or getting a motel. Probably quit snowing by morning."

Cot took off his green and yellow John Deere baseball cap and rubbed his forehead with a thick finger, revealing a thin covering of sandy colored hair. "Lazy Creek is just a dribble. As creeks go it ain't much at all, and far as I know there's nowhere along there to camp. No park or campground, nothing really. Used to fish some there when I was a boy. Me and another kid would take a lunch and ride our bikes down there. Doubt there's a fish left in it now." He took his cap off again and laid it on the counter. "Maybe you could camp in the front yard at Birch Church, right there by Mac's Corner convenience store. Pretty sure they wouldn't mind none. Just about everywhere else you'd be on private property. I'd invite you to come stay over to my place, but I live eight miles outta town in the opposite direction from where you're headed."

"Hey, Liam," Kate called. "Maybe we should sleep here tonight and leave in the morning. We have permission to camp here." She looked at Liam, not to seek approval but to study his face.

Liam approached the counter. "Doesn't matter to me," he said. "I'm good either way. But, I'd really just as soon get going." He shrugged his shoulders. "At least get as far as Mac's Corner."

Cot slid the receipt and a pen to Kate for her signature. He stood up tall, looked at Liam. "You ever drive one of these machines before?"

Liam laughed. "Yes, sir. My dad taught me how to drive one when I was seven or eight years old. The mail-man wouldn't deliver up our little dirt road, so one of my chores was to drive three miles into town every day to pick up our mail. When there wasn't any snow, I'd ride my bike."

Cot didn't look convinced. Less than a year earlier a man and his wife had been killed just two miles outside the town limits when they drove through a rancher's barbed wire fence at seventy miles an hour. As a volunteer fire fighter, Cot had been one of the first on the scene. The images of the carnage still kept him awake some nights. "Do as you please," he said, "but you're welcome to camp out front. I own the property, and nobody will bother you." His eyebrows arched, *C'mon kids, do the right thing.*

Liam smiled at Kate. "I'm ready to go down the road if you are."

"Well, I guess," Kate said, without conviction. "We'd better get started before it starts to snow any harder."

Cot gave Kate a sharp look. "You tell your folks what you're doin'?"

"I called 'em a couple hours ago. They're fine," she said. The fib stung her and she blushed, her eyes shiny with it.

She backtracked. "Well, a little worried I guess. Snow and all."

Liam said, "I wrote my mom a letter last week when it was still nice out. They trust me. I've camped out by myself all over Canada."

"Being self-reliant is one thing," Cot said, "but people sometimes overestimate themselves." He stared hard at Liam. "Specially young men."

"My parents worry about me," Kate interrupted. She shrugged her shoulders. "Always have." She turned to Cot. "Thank you so much," she said. "We really appreciate your offer, but I guess we'll get going."

"You're quite welcome," Cot said. "Might want to eat before you head out of town. Bowling alley over on Main Street has some right good eats. Go there at least once a day myself. Nice people run the place. Known 'em all my life."

He held out his hand to Liam. "If you change your mind, young man, just come back and pitch your tent out there." He gestured with a chiseled chin toward the front entrance. "Visitors are always welcome here in Highmore. Otherwise, we'll see you right back here before closing tomorrow. Five o'clock. Your truck'll be fine right where she sits."

"Thanks," Kate said. "We really appreciate your help. See you tomorrow afternoon sometime."

She stuck out her hand, closed the deal. "Appreciate your concern, sir," she said. "Don't worry about us. We'll be fine."

Kate pulled on her parka, grabbed Liam's sleeve, gave it a tug. "I'm starved," she said.

"Let's go eat." She pulled him toward the door.

"Be safe now," Cot called. He walked across the room, watched them through the plate glass windows.

Kate and Liam quickly unloaded the tent and two backpacks into the ski-cart hitched to the Yamaha. The last person to rent the cart must have hauled freshly cut wood in it, the cart's bed still rich with the tree's perfume. Cot Reese had patiently gone over the safety and operation procedures with them and though Kate had only ridden in a snowmobile a few times in her life, she seemed satisfied Liam could handle it. To demonstrate, Liam had driven around the yard twice in a wide circle while she and Cot watched.

With a practiced flick of his wrist Liam fired up the big Yamaha. It gave out a deep-throated roar of raw power. He gestured to Kate. She clambered aboard and fastened the chinstrap of her helmet; she wrapped her arms around Liam's waist, and quickly they were gone.

Cot walked back to the counter, opened the cash register and took out a small ring of keys, some cash, and a few checks. He turned to the paneled wall behind him, grabbed his heavy wool coat off a peg, and flipped the light switch. The showroom went dark, but outside, two floodlights mounted above the door sprang to life, illuminating the walkway and parking lot. He locked the door and hurried toward his pick-up, his heavy footsteps crunching loudly in the carpet of snow laid down over gravel. He lifted the windshield wipers, took a couple of long-armed swipes at the windshield with his arm, cleared off an inch of fresh snow. "Dang kid," he muttered. "There's a boy who thinks way too highly of himself. Ought to know better."

Twenty minutes later when he turned into his own driveway he caught sight of his wife, Barb, standing at the kitchen sink window. He knew she'd been anchored there for ten minutes or more, making sure he made it home safe.

When he closed the front door behind him, and the cold draft caught her, Barb shivered. "Brr," she said. "Glad you're home, Hon. Dinner's on the table."

She studied his face. "What's wrong?"

"Oh, nothin'. Just a fool college kid and his girlfriend got me worrying a bit. Wouldn't want our Emily camping overnight alone with him. Don't quite trust him somehow."

Chapter Fifteen

. . . and when the ship's survivors surfaced, they sputtered and gulped, pawed at the water, kicked with desperate legs. Anything to live another minute.

IT WAS DEATHLY QUIET. UNSETTLING SO. SOMEtime past midnight the falling snow had ceased. The temperature dropped still more, creating a glazed crust over the desolate landscape. The wind, perhaps ashamed of its role in the mayhem, spoke only in whispers. The tower loomed high above, its three blades barely spinning in the morning breeze, no more than a child's breath against the flame of a first birthday's candle. Gradually the sun poked through the cloud cover from the eastern horizon, sending brilliant flashes of red, orange, and gold dancing off the sharp edged spinning guillotine above.

The remnant of the Prairie Winds School of Flight junior class lay mangled and scattered around the monstrous structure. No movement. No moans. No muted whimpers of agony. Small snow-covered mounds protruded here and there. A gravel road, featureless in the piled snow, ran fifty yards distant from the base of the turbine. Another half mile farther sat the indistinct shape of a modern home surrounded by shade trees.

By eight o'clock it had warmed sufficiently for the icy crystals forming the crust to begin melting. Small drips formed, and ran. Overhead, slivers of blue sky were pancaked between layers of gray clouds.

A few minutes after nine, Lily wiggled free of her frosty white blanket. When she'd heard Riley and Sadie's cries of alarm she'd had sufficient time and wits to follow the dictates of Isaac's Apple and dive straight down into oblivion. In fact, a microsecond before the top of her head hit the ground, she had lurched upward with every ounce of wing strength she possessed. She still plowed into the snow at almost sixty miles per hour, but not quite at such a steep angle. At impact her skull had absorbed a terrific blow. She was slowed just enough by the cushion of snow to survive the collision. Stunned and unconscious for several minutes, maybe longer—her body lay sealed in an icy grave.

It was then Death called out to her. First it flirted, and then courted her. Death beckoned with a bony, featherless wing. *Do nothing, friend Lily,* Death whispered. *You are safe with me, dear Lily,* Death cooed. *Come to me, my darling Lily,* Death coaxed.

Lily awoke and struggled, freed herself of the ghastly embrace. Death and darkness lurked below—light and life beckoned from above. Her wings, pinned tightly to her sides were useless. She wiggled from side to side, managing to turn upward; using her beak, she chiseled away at the snow. Lacking a rope to pull herself up, Lily utilized her beak like the strong fingered rock climber digs her powerful fingertips into the tiniest cleft, trusts her strength, and advances the climb; just so, Lily strained toward the light.

The snow was not packed here; it remained light and fluffy, and she was able to draw enough air into her nares from the minuscule cushioned pockets to keep from suffocating. Slowly she inched upward until her beak finally protruded into the air. The tip of it exposed, she could breathe freely now, but she was so exhausted from her struggle she fell asleep. And sleep, no matter how welcome and needed, is often the precursor to death. With no merciful nurse to help her to stand and walk the corridor, she inched closer to the last door, the black and final place. Snow continued to fall, perhaps unaware it buried desperate gasps for life.

Before she slept, Lily wondered if the twirling blades had killed everyone else. Perhaps, she thought, others were also determined, even now pulling themselves toward the surface.

After an hour's nap Lily emerged again; when her head popped free she blinked her eyes against the eastern sky. She twisted from side to side hoping to catch a glimpse of her classmates. Seeing no movement, she tried to free her wings. Impossible still. She opened her beak, sent a plea to the wind: "Kiree! Kiree! Kiree!" *Please! Please! Please!* If there were a red-tailed hawk within a half-mile, she knew help would soon arrive. The mute and motionless forms just under the surface, mere bumps in the snow, remained silent.

Lily began to swivel herself, trying to create space below the snow's surface. Despite not having eaten for twenty-four hours and being almost paralyzed by cold, she was fueled by a haunting feeling of dread for her missing classmates. She fended off such horrid thoughts from her conscious mind.

Slowly she emerged and began to fear the predator. She was cemented in place; unable to defend herself with her talons, she made easy prey. If a starving coyote discovered her, she would become a helpless dandelion under the lawnmower's blades. Again, she banned from her mind all negative possibilities. Her right wing slipped free. She used it as an oar, scraping at the snow. A moment later, her left wing popped out. She opened them wide, tested their strength against the air. With a tremendous shake of her body she sprung free of the snow, and stood on wobbly legs. For the briefest of moments her heart soared; she rejoiced at being alive.

No more than an eye's blink later she plunged into despair—alone—so terribly alone. Her shoulders trembled in the cold and a quaking shiver came hard upon her and she tottered, her mind dazed. She glanced at her wing watch. The second hand still moved.

What day is it? she wondered. She backtracked. *We left Dupree on Thursday. We competed Saturday and Sunday. No! The competition was Friday and Saturday. We left Sioux Falls Sunday morning, Ms. Ride at point. No! Rowdy at point. Where was Ms. Ride? She flew behind. How long have I been trapped beneath the snow? Is it Monday morning?*

Her mind reeled with the enormity of it all. She glanced again at her watch: ten fourteen.

She looked up, cringed at the scythes puttering overhead in the morning breeze. Understanding the destruction battered her senses, too horrible to consider. High overhead, beyond the blades, thin patches of brilliant blue slipped through uneasy, dark gray clouds.

A familiar sound clawed at her ears. She swiveled her head like a traffic cop at a busy intersection. She blinked her eyes to make certain she was not dreaming, or deceased. Nothing moved. Even the wind held its breath.

A voice too faint to locate sung out, pleaded. She tried her own voice, but the sound coagulated in her throat. She opened her wings wide, stretched them. Attempted to respond again. It was a raw sound, not her voice at all. "Trroom. Reets. Reettts." *I am here. Where are you?*

"Trroom." *I am here.* The sound directed Lily's gaze away from the turbine's column toward the almost invisible road. Her eyes scanned the snow, caught a miniscule movement. The tiniest tip of a yellow beak protruded, quivering in the snow. A puff of warm air rose, a tiny cloud of life.

"It's Lily," she said, as if to convince herself she still lived. "I'm coming," she called.

Not yet trusting her wings, she waddled toward the sound. Subtle recognition came to her. Could it be? Oliver—the class poet? Happiness melted her heart and words of joy tumbled out. "Oliver! Classmate! Friend! Bard!"

Lily furiously excavated the snow still covering his head. His eyes remained shuttered, sealed by ice. She continued digging and within minutes Oliver was freed from his icy tomb. Lily nudged him to his feet, murmuring his name all the while. He stood blindly on unsteady legs, a newborn against the wolves.

Lily had always been naturally shy with her male classmates, but now a stronger force than reticence gripped her heart, and guided her actions. Casting her modesty aside, she aggressively embraced Oliver; she wrapped her wings completely around him, and pulling him tight, offered the comfort of her heart's roaring furnace. An upright, clumsy bundle, they toppled over onto the snow. Neither young hawk laughed or giggled.

This was not a playful tumble on another happier day during school recess.

"Oliver," she whispered. "You must live. Be strong. Help will come."

His eyelids strained and bulged against the frozen seal, but would not open. "Am I blind, Lily? I only know your voice. Let me die if blindness has struck me. I don't care to live if I can never fly again."

Lily rebuffed his weakness, and reassured him. "Your body protected your eyes against the snow, Oliver. I'm certain you will see and take flight again. Be patient."

Where are our classmates, our friends?" he asked. "Is Ms. Ride here? And Rowdy? Where is our point, Lily?"

"I dare not know," she replied. "My mind forbids thinking on it." She rubbed her beak on his. "Every atom of my body mourns, but I know not why. Just share my warmth, Oliver, and live."

A fierce roaring sound approached. Lily looking toward the road, caught the words *Range Rover* amid a rooster tail spray of snow. Lily lifted a wingtip in hopeful supplication. A large figure, hunched over the steering wheel did not look right or left. Gradually the noise receded and all was quiet.

Lily and Oliver, survivors of the night, held each other in chilled silence. The cold, ruthless in its embrace, courted them both. An hour later, errant snowflakes began to dust their bodies. More snow seemed certain.

Chapter Sixteen

. . . and grandfather, his voice still resonant, said, "For every bully born there are a thousand gentleman, kind in nature, soft of speech, and clear of eye. They stand up for those who cannot stand for themselves."

OWEN AWOKE WHEN THE SUN'S SWEEPING RAYS peeped over the sill of the world's eastern window and rudely invaded his envelope of sleep. For a moment he was disoriented, but when he looked up to see slivers of sky peeping through holes in the roof and heard the deep creak of water-stained rafters groaning under the weight of the accumulated snow, the memory of his predicament became clear. He stood and brushed loose bits of straw from his head and body. He opened his wings, once, twice, and with several shakes, fluffed himself against the cold. His head swiveled about, taking stock of his surroundings.

He noticed the various apparatuses common to farming and ranching—the looming shape of a heavy tractor, coils of ropes, lengths of chains, bales of stored hay, and various hand tools hanging loosely, suspended from big nails pounded into the water stained stud walls. The barn door entrance gaped wide, revealing a thick, pristine covering of snow covering the ground just outside.

A few feet away Ms. Ride and Emma were still wrapped together. Using his beak Owen carefully pulled back one corner of the blanket, exposing Emma's face. Her eyes were open and she whispered, "Help me up. We need to check on Ms. Ride."

Once unwrapped and on her feet, Emma leaned down and held her ear tight against Ms. Ride's chest. She looked up at Owen. "Her heart is loud. She feels warmer now." Emma flashed a tight smile. "Help me cover her."

They managed to rewrap the blanket around Ms. Ride's body. Together they rolled her from her side to her back and then to the opposite side, hoping the movement would help make their teacher more comfortable and perhaps stir her awake. Chawla's eyes, however, remained closed, and her breathing shallow.

"One thing we've forgotten," Owen said. "Her cell phone. I know she always flies with one."

"She took our picture just before we left Sioux Falls," Emma said. "But, I didn't see her holster yesterday when we first found her. Perhaps it fell off when she and the crows struggled before they crashed into the snow. Will you fly back to the fence and search for it? Her cell could save us."

"Of course," Owen replied. Despite the dire situation, he allowed himself a chuckle. "I'm glad I have my goggles. The sunrise is bright off the snow this morning, blindingly so."

Emma opened her beak with a slight twist, a female hawk's version of a cute smile. "Would you have me go in your place, Goggs? Are you afraid you will get lost and not be able to find your way back to so large a building as a barn? Are you really so blind?" She giggled at the stricken look on Owen's face.

"No, of course not. I just meant . . .oh, never mind. I'll be back in a moment." He swooped low out the barn door toward the fence. Landing with a soft thump near the spot where they had excavated Ms. Ride, Owen looked about. The dark, frozen bodies of the two crows stood out, reminding him danger could be near.

Even with his Maui Jim goggles protecting his eyes, the bright sunlight made it difficult for him to glance skyward, so he concentrated on locating Ms. Ride's holster. He and the other students had admired it many times before, handcrafted by a rogue company in Maine from the same leather used to manufacture major league quality baseball gloves. Ms. Ride always referred to it as her Batter Up holster. A specialty gun outfitter in Rapid City carried a nice supply of the size required to fit a hawk's wings and their miniature cell phones.

Except for a few of the hard-core, old-school red-tails, most of the adult hawks wore holsters on their daily flights—hunting missions, visiting town, or when calling on friends. Besides cell phones, the hawks found the holsters quite useful for carrying small amounts of food, money, or important documents. Just in the past few months, young hawks had also taken to toting their cell phones wherever they flew, except to school where they were banned. The older hawks snickered at the proliferation of phones, often commenting with mockery—*those who carry cells would rather talk than eat.*

Owen hoped Ms. Ride's holster and the loop of leather strap would be close at hand. He began to further excavate, widen and deepen the hole they had dug yesterday. He hammered at the crusty top layer with his beak, then used his talons to sweep the chunks to one side. Nothing. He had paused momentarily to catch his breath when a dark shadow struck from above. His concentration at task on hand and his lack of careful vigilance had given his foes the immediate advantage.

Knocked off balance by the surprise strike, Owen tumbled head over teakettle. As he scrambled to regain his feet he was Kamikazed—flattened by the impact. He heard heavy wings above him beating furiously. Like the blinded Cyclops of *The Odyssey*, Owen staggered about, woozy from repeated blows.

His instinct of course was to fight. Engraved in Owen's heart was the absolute certainty he was more than a match for any crow. But how many had set upon him? Unable to see clearly because of the bright light reflecting off the snow, he tried to estimate by the sound of their beating wings and darting shadows. He knew instinctively crows feared his talons and beak, and none would be so brave as to test him head on. Were there five? Or ten? Or more?

Owen's school studies assured him crows never attack a hawk to kill. Their harassing maneuvers are almost always territorial in nature and seldom end in death or even serious injury. They merely detest and will not tolerate trespassers. And yet here they were, violently in his face. Were his textbooks incorrect? Owen had no spare time to consider such scholarly issues. His adversaries forced his hand—kill or be killed.

He turned, beak upward, unsheathed his talons. His flailing wings searched for air, caught, and lifted him. "Treepteedeet," he sang out. *Bring it on!*

Chapter Seventeen

. . . of course there are differences between men and women. If not, there would be nothing in this world but barren rock and fire and wind and water.

THE STATE HAD GRADED A TEN-FOOT WIDE TRAIL beside the road, used mainly by ranchers to move small herds of cattle safely from pasture to pasture without having to use the highway. It wasn't a smooth and flat roadway, but the snowfall had filled in the smaller holes and gaps, easing out the rough spots. The two adventurers, bundled against the fierce cold, sledded south alongside Highway 47. Their single headlight illuminated the trail in a bumpy, rollicking way, like a flirty moon pulled by unruly tides. Despite the recklessness inherent in youth, Liam was a seasoned and surprisingly cautious driver, choosing the safer but slower path beside the road rather than traveling the road itself. Snow was falling heavily now; the absence of the reflecting moon and distant starlight created poor visibility on the road and made passage there risky to the extreme.

At the restaurant they had studied the map again and plotted exactly where they would intersect the class's supposed flight path, about two point four miles north of Mac's Corner. They settled on a plan to pitch the tent beside the road, sleep until the sun woke them, and then, as closely as possible, follow a direct line northwest toward Dupree. It seemed sensible enough, but Kate, a rancher's daughter, knew large land parcels were almost always fenced to keep livestock in.

"What about the barbwire?" she asked. "Most of the land is private property and will be fenced off. And creeks? How will we get across?"

"No problem," Liam said. "We just zip around all obstacles. I would never cut a fence. If we can't get through, we'll have to figure out a way to skirt the property until we can get back to our correct line. It's the same thing with the creeks. Ranchers and farmers have to cross their land too, so there has to be a safe route." He grinned. "Solving problems makes it more fun."

It was an easy enough and reasonable sounding solution, but Kate was left with some uneasy misgivings. Liam however, seemed oblivious to any difficulties. They might as well have been on a carefree joyride in a '57 Chevy convertible cruising down Main Street looking for some Saturday night action.

Except for a restless waitress who spent most of her time peering out the restaurant's front windows at the deserted street, they had the place to themselves. Two days of heavy snow had buried the roads, making the town appear almost uninhabited. While they ate, Liam entertained with stories of growing up in the Canadian wilderness. He was a captivating storyteller, and Kate was drawn close, enjoying his fountain of humorous, self-deprecating experiences.

An hour later, with their bellies full, teeth brushed, and bladders drained off, they settled into the snowmobile in the deserted restaurant parking lot. Just before walking out the door Kate had sent a text message to her mother: **Everything OK. Love you.** She switched the phone off, wanting to conserve the battery as much as possible. It was six-thirty-five, Monday evening.

Overhead, the sky was blotted black with the night's ink; the usual spectacular display of the Milky Way star system was hidden, reduced and condensed to a never-ending supply of feathery diamonds floating silently to earth. The Yamaha purred through town, riding the centerline until they reached the main intersection where 47 turned south toward Mac's Corner. Almost immediately Liam pulled off the road and onto the side trail, slowing to make sure the trailer followed properly. Their equipment handled the terrain without a hitch; in less than an hour Liam braked to a stop near a small bridge where Lazy Creek flowed under the road. Over the years, construction and bridge maintenance crews had widened the area as a staging place for their heavy equipment; to the young adventurers it seemed a fortuitous place to spend the night, a safe distance off the road and out of harm's way.

They climbed stiffly from the machine and stood unmoving, two blunt statues in a darker world. They removed their helmets and shook out their hair. The temperature had fallen even more and a slight wind had picked up, sending their vaporous breaths plunging into the night. Just to one side and fifteen feet down the bank from where they stood, they could hear the steady soft gurgle of flowing water, a natural and soothing cadence repeated from the beginning of time.

Kate yawned, and holding her helmet in one hand, stretched her arms high overhead. "Okay," she said, "we're here. Now what?"

Liam turned back to the cart, and fished in his backpack, extracting a large flashlight. He handed it to Kate. "You're in charge of the torch," he said. "We need a level spot about ten feet square to pitch the tent. Time for the Manitoba Stomp."

"The Manitoba what?" Kate asked. Liam was full of surprises, but she was willing, and game for most anything.

Liam laughed. "It's a dance we snow campers use to pack snow. No music, and no rhythm necessary. It's a fine blend of the waltz and playing Hop Scotch. I've even seen Christopher Walken do it on Facebook. C'mon Kate, dance the stomp. It'll help warm us up. Put your hands on your hips and do the Manitoba."

Kate laughingly followed Liam's bizarre stomping style, sort of a combination zombie shuffle and country western line dance. Soon they had a large square area packed down. When Liam was satisfied with the foundation he led Kate back to the cart where they unloaded their packs and the tent bundle. How they had managed to pack themselves and all their gear into a snowmobile and a tiny cart was a testament to their youthful ingenuity.

Liam's well-used camping equipment was sparse, designed not for cosmetic appeal, but for simple utility and easy transport on a hiker's back; it was the kind of gear never featured in an REI catalogue, but it had been road and weather tested during his long bike ride from Manitoba to Brookings. When he pulled out the groundcover, Kate wrinkled her nose. "Ugh. Smells like stinky armpits."

Liam laughed. "You're much too kind. It smells a lot worse, but it'll help keep us warm and cushion the tent floor."

Kate illuminated the campsite, while Liam laid out the tent, poles and lines. Once the tent was standing, Liam pounded in the extra long ground stakes with a small hammer. The tent's structure, though not pretty, presented a good, serviceable shelter. Liam sat down in the entrance and slipped his boots off. "Hand in the pads and bags. I'll organize the interior before you crawl in. It's going to be a tight squeeze because it was designed as a one-person tent, but I think we can make it work."

Kate passed the rest of the gear to Liam. A moment later he stuck his head out. "Not exactly the Ritz Carleton, but nice and cozy. He smiled up into the flashlight beam. "It's going to be cold at first, but your body heat will warm your sleeping bag fast and keep you comfy all night. I recommend, from past experience, putting your boots inside your bag way down at the bottom. Just wipe all the snow off first." He held up a tattered, small brown towel; sometime long ago, in a previous life, perhaps, it had been white. "Use this to clean the snow off so your boots won't freeze."

He opened his backpack again and produced a small battery powered reading lamp. "Just a minute." He ducked back inside the tent, and placed the lamp at the far end; it cast a pleasant warm glow throughout the interior.

Kate was impressed. "Nice," she said. "Almost dorm cozy."

"One more thing," Liam said. "It may seem contradictory, but the less clothing you wear, the warmer you'll sleep." He grinned up at Kate. "I promise not to peek if you won't." The darkness hid her deep blush.

"Where do we go to the bathroom?" she asked. "I really have to pee." On long hikes and fishing expeditions while growing up she had used nature's accommodations many times; she was familiar with the procedure, but had never gone before in the snow.

Liam dug into his seemingly bottomless pack once more and found a flattened partial roll of toilet paper and handed it up to Kate. "Anywhere but the creek," he said. "The fish don't appreciate it. Take the flashlight with you. I'll wait here."

With a certain amount of apprehension Kate wandered off away from the road to complete her toilet in the darkness. Holding the flashlight in one hand complicated the matter somewhat, but she managed.

"Don't fall in the creek," Liam called out. "Not good."

When she returned Liam was buried deep in his down bag on one side of the tent, only the tip of his nose and a small tousled patch of blond hair visible. He had folded his jeans, shirt, and parka neatly at the foot of his bag.

Kate crawled headfirst on her knees into the tent. Sitting on the end of her sleeping bag, she removed her snow-caked boots, and wiped them down. As Liam had instructed she pushed them to the bottom of her bag. She zipped up the tent door and sat cross-legged. She put the flashlight on top of her small black camper's pillow so her half of the tent was illuminated. The tiny reading light also added to the pleasant glow.

She sat for a moment, unsure of what to do. Her jeans, at the ankles, were crusted with snow and soaking wet. Quickly she slid them down and off. She folded them as best she could and placed them at the foot of her sleeping bag.

She glanced at Liam, motionless beside her, his face turned away. She scrunched herself up and into the sleeping bag, but remained sitting up. She sat there a moment longer, then abruptly turned off the reading lamp and the flashlight. She unbuttoned her shirt and slipped it off. The cold hit her bare shoulders and she shivered. Quickly she undid her bra and placed it under her pillow. She put her shirt back on and buttoned it up.

Kate cocooned deep into her sleeping bag, and zipped it nearly to her chin.

"Liam?" she said. "Are you asleep?"

"Not yet. Getting there."

"Thank you."

"For what?"

"Being a gentleman."

"Thank my dad."

"Why?"

"He taught me to always respect Mom and my sisters. He thinks all women are roses."

"I'm more of a sunflower."

"Go to sleep, Kate."

"Thank you, Liam's Dad," she said. "Your son is a good guy."

"Kate," he said. "It's late."

These were soft whispers of trust and understanding passing between them, colliding in the darkness, and building a bridge.

"Night," Kate said. "I'm glad you're here. Are you warm yet?"

"I'm fine," he said. "Fun day."

Kate did not respond. She yawned in the dark, closed her eyes. Felt safe beside him. The soothing sounds of nearby water seeking a lower place, and a long day of travel lulled her away. Shadowy thoughts—unbidden and unremembered—settled comfortably upon her.

Snow continued to fall.

Chapter Eighteen

. . . and there will always be those in the community, both men and women, seemingly stronger than the rest, who when they hear the siren's cry must throw back the covers, pull on their jackets, and rush to help.

ORVILLE, IN ADDITION TO HIS NORMAL CELL phone holster, always filled a second auxiliary wing holster to the brim with Raptor Flight Mix, a hearty blend of various seeds, nuts and dried fruit chunks, put together by his wife, Annabelle. He much preferred fresh meat, but in the hunting intervals he often snacked on Annabelle's concoction. Whenever she inquired about his supply, he'd say with a smile, "Keep it coming, babe. A hawk can never have too much to eat."

She could only shake her head and laugh. "'Tis such a silly, nilly hawk I've married."

Orville added a small medical first aid kit containing bandages, tape, scissors, and a tiny tube of antibiotic ointment. It was a clumsy load and would slow him down, but he wanted to be prepared for whatever he might find. He had waited most of the night for a call from the school before finally falling into a restless sleep long after midnight. Unbeknownst to him, as a safeguard against hunger, Annabelle had packed a peanut butter and jelly sandwich well hidden beneath the small down sleeping bag he always carried for winter flights. Ready now, he grabbed his tinted Maui Jim goggles hanging by their Velcro strap from a brass peg near the front door. Orville's vision, like his son Owen's, was compromised in bright sunlight, and he also relied on a fine pair of custom made goggles to fly safely during daylight hours.

"Are you sure you have enough food and water in your belly to fly so far?" Annabelle asked. "It might turn out to be a more difficult flight than you imagine. The weather report for later today is not favorable. I dread the thought of you getting caught in a blizzard." Putting on a brave face, she looped his favorite white scarf around his neck and deftly tied it off.

"Handsome," she said.

Orville managed a playful grin at his lovely wife. Even under such serious circumstances his eyes reflected steadfast boyish mischief. "I'll be fine, babe. Never worry about the world beyond our control. Owen and his classmates will be home soon. I won't be deterred by foul weather. Besides, you know the weather newscasters always elevate the conditions worse than need be."

Her husband's words were strong and confident, but contained a rare tone of worry. At the door, in farewell, she watched as he pulled his brown leather flyer's helmet over his head and snugged the Velcro chinstrap. She hugged him tight, unable to argue more.

"I'll call you as soon as I locate them," he said. "I can't wait any longer." Blinking into the bright sunrise still emerging low in the east, he perched on the ledge of their home; then he pulled his goggles down over his eyes, laid his beak upon hers, held it there for five heartbeats, and then, without another word, opened his tremendous wings and was gone.

Annabelle stood and watched him climb, clutching her robe at the throat to ward off the terrible chill. The home's deck faced east, and as Annabelle watched him scramble to cruising altitude, she shaded her eyes with a wingtip; almost blinded by the molten blaze on the horizon, she whispered a solemn red-tail prayer: "Feereeri ri rueet." *Make known a sure path for the one I love.*

Orville was prepared to fly the entire two hundred miles to Sioux Falls if necessary, but he sensed he would intercept the class much sooner. He believed poor weather conditions had forced the class down, and they had simply taken cover for the night. He was also confident once it was light enough to fly safely Ms. Ride would coax the students from their shelter and they'd be on their way home once more.

He had one nagging worry: why hadn't Chawla Ride notified the school? Orville knew she was a superb flyer and extremely trustworthy. She was required by the school district to carry a cell phone, yet she hadn't used it. Something untoward had prevented her from calling. But what could it be?

During the first few minutes, his wing muscles, still warming up and burdened with the extra weight, Orville lumbered along to gain the altitude necessary for the best possible surveillance of the snow-covered ground below. The clouds had scattered sometime during the night and he could fly at precisely six hundred-fifty feet, where he leveled off and began his most efficient, energy saving wing-beat, a rhythm he could sustain all day long if need be. Overhead and to the south the sky was clear, but barrel-shaped, ominous dark clouds lurked to the north. Just east of Dupree he noticed a small dark figure flying about a mile ahead. By its silhouette he was certain it was another red-tail, probably heading off for an early morning hunt.

Orville, flying at exactly thirty-seven miles per hour, slowly approached the other hawk from behind. As he closed to one hundred yards, Orville smiled with recognition at his former flight instructor, RT Boyd Higgins. Since his retirement from teaching five years earlier, Higgins had taken to wearing a distinctive black beret. Orville sent out the standard air greeting of recognition and friendship: "Kriiiteelee." *Hello my excellent friend; no troubles here, and may none burden your wings.*

The shape ahead wobbled at the sound, turned his head to see who tailed him. A moment later Orville was alongside. "You are up much too early to hunt," he said. "How far must you travel for your breakfast? Are there no rabbits left in Iron Lightning?"

Boyd Higgins grinned across at Orville. Approaching eighteen years, Boyd appeared the statesman, his head feathers much grayer now than when he'd patrolled each day in a Prairie Winds School of Flight classroom. He wore the beret rakishly tilted to one side, snugged tight just above his eyes. He and Orville shared two unique bonds—the unbreakable one between former student and teacher—the other as co-participants in a daring rescue attempt of Kate Flannery five years earlier, and the two had remained close friends over the years.

"I let others much younger than I do the hunting," Higgins said. His eyes were hooded, mere slits against the onrushing wind and brilliant sunrise. "My forté is the eating." His face turned serious. "No, I imagine today we're traveling the same lane. I'm off to find Ms. Ride and our fledglings, as far as Sioux Falls if necessary. The clouds to the north portend more snow, and it's imperative they return home today. Another night spent in the open without proper cover could be disastrous."

Orville swiveled his head north, eying the ominous clouds. "Don't worry, my friend, our mission is the same, and we will make fine company," Orville replied. "It's good to have pleasant comrades on long journeys of uncertain outcomes. My son Owen is with them. As you might imagine Annabelle and I are quite anxious for his safety."

They flew another mile side by side without speaking. Boyd Higgins broke the silence. "If we are to fly together, you must slow down. I'm a geezer now and you'll soon wear me out at this pace. I'm gasping already. Can we fly at my thirty-two instead of your young hawk's thirty-seven? Another mile and I'll fall out of the sky for sure."

"Of course," Orville said. "I should have slowed without being told. Worry makes hurry as my dad often says."

Higgins glanced at his companion. Able to breathe easily again, he said, "A journey of unknown outcomes, you say? I'm positive we'll find them. There must be no other result."

"I agree," Orville replied. "I fear though, something is amiss with Chawla Ride, and perhaps the weather is not through toying with us just yet. Those clouds are full of trouble."

Higgins said, "I'm positive we will find our lady hawk soon enough. One thing we sometimes forget is how precious students are to their teacher. Chawla has been their shepherd and would never abandon them without first giving up her own life."

"And the reverse too," Orville added. "If she has suffered some mishap, they will never desert her. Even at their own dear expense."

. . . and many things in this world are foul and cruel; we push them aside, too ugly to consider in daylight, ignore them as if they do not exist. And yet our sleeping mind dredges them up from the depths, where the bins of terrors dwell; and from the safety of our feathered pillows we are chilled by creeping visions, swatted over the head with them. We cannot escape because they are hidden, encrypted in our DNA.

MISTER GEPPETTO, THE MASTER WOODCARVER of Pinocchio, could not have created a better instrument of aerial death than a red-tail hawk.

Learned scientists inform us about one hundred forty-five million years ago, near the end of the Jurassic Period, an unknown reptile somehow became airborne. Imagination alone brings us to a life or death chase, a jagged cliff, and a desperate leap into space, webbed arms flailing at the air. The first known bird, *Archaeopterx*, still had teeth. Though winged, it had scant feathers. No doubt it was a ferocious foe, both in the air and on the ground. It lived in a world of constant terror, and contributed greatly to it. Its fully feathered descendants live today as raptors.

Owen attacked. He had never killed out of hatred or rage. Nor had he ever killed in a cruel manner. Killing was his business, all raptors' expertise. No thought of self-defense entered his mind. His eyes, normally a soft golden green, became tinged with the red of blood lust. Millions of years of killing had prepared him for this moment, and he embraced it.

The South Dakota red-tail creed forbids killing beyond need, indeed *kill only out of hunger* stands as the one inviolable pillar of their constitution. Red-tail hunters are permitted only to gather their daily bread—but when assaulted the sacred laws are washed away. A red-tail's DNA dictates the action. Black feathers flew and spurts of blood stained the snow as Owen ripped and shredded and tore. Coarse caws—*Death is upon me*—filled the air, a mournful symphony. Owen heard and understood, but this was not about mercy. They had dared attack him, and now they would pay a heavy price at the checkout counter for their impudence.

Soft thumps of writhing black bodies littered the ground beneath the combat zone. A few, seeking revenge even in their death throes, called out to their comrades to tear out the villain's eyes, but crows' beaks and minds were not built for such precise surgery. Evolution has swept crows down another, much wider DNA path. Their bodies evolved as bulky, heavy black lumbering transports, their voices loud and threatening, big wings and massive hearts to power the load, but simpering cowards in brutal combat. Instead they became crafty wolves in mauling packs.

This was the bold and foolish Long Hair—General Armstrong Custer—marching his soldiers against fifteen thousand years of Cheyenne, Sioux, and Arapaho hunting skill at the Battle of the Little Big Horn. General Custer defended his country's land stealing politics. The Native Americans fought only for survival.

These warriors were the descendants of ancient men who harbored courage enough to cross the ocean on a treacherous glacier formed land bridge from Asia. These men and women knew *Death* by his first name; they shook *Death's* hand every day. They looked *Death* in the eye and never flinched. They were married to *Death's* cousin—*Hardship*. They went days without food, slept in the open, broiled under the sun, shivered at night under thin blankets. With tears not yet dry they buried their wives, children, and elders in stony graves.

Toward the end of the battle, after Long Hair lay mortally wounded, many of his soldiers threw down their guns, raised their hands in surrender, and pleaded for mercy. None was given. The Native Americans exacted revenge born of years of lies, broken treaties, promises never kept, and maltreatment at the hands of the white man; they took no prisoners.

At school, Owen had been taught these human histories, and eagerly absorbed them. He learned them, and yet remained indifferent to them. They belonged to other tribes and clans. He did not yet realize how all living creatures are linked in perhaps the darkest way—survival.

Though vastly outnumbered, weak from hunger, and rapidly tiring, Owen fought the onslaught. Air has no corners and the crows could not box him in. Owen's maneuvers defied the crows' sluggish thick-beaked mugging attempts. These crows were amateur murderers, cunning and clever, yes, but also clumsy, unstudied killers. Their only strategy was to overpower Owen with blunt force, sheer numbers. They pummeled him with their bodies and slowly drove him toward the ground.

His talons gripped the snow; his beak stabbed and ripped viciously as they suffocated him with their heavy wings. He was knocked over backward and pinned to the snow under a black-feathered comforter of crows. They pecked viciously at the strap to his goggles, attempting to rip them from his face. Unwilling to die just yet, he slashed upward with his talons and kept their beaks from his eyes.

A moment later, just as a new horde of crow replacements descended in a smothering black wave, Emma, hearing the commotion, arrived to aid her classmate. She joined the fray, a relentless fury, and the crows dropped in a torrent, heavy black raindrops from a smoky cloud. Two red-tails against ten crows, a hundred; it mattered not. If need be they would all die this day.

Minutes later, Polgar, observing the hopeless massacre from afar, screamed a piercing retreat call; the remaining few crows turned tail in speedy escape. Polgar's own heart, powered by fear, lent strength to her wings, and speed to her flight. In an instant Owen was back in the air; though one hundred yards behind, he zeroed in on the crow leader, and calculating her cowardly path, aimed himself; he took her in mid-air with his talons, gripping her glossy back below the wings, and forced her to the ground. She was helpless now, pinned, her wings open wide on the snow.

"Mercy," she pleaded, her voice weak. "Please grant mercy. We meant no harm." Her simpering caws were but weak, breathless gasps now. "We only sought to protect our nests."

"You meant no harm?" Owen roared. "You and your worthless gang of garbage chasers knocked our teacher from the sky and you meant no harm? You would have my eyes and you meant no harm? You, the tormenter of all who inhabit the air or walk the earth, forfeit your life today. There will be no mercy."

Owen's talons closed on Polgar's head; he slowly forced her head back, exposed her throat; he took his time, swiveled his head to see who watched; with a sudden viciousness born a million years earlier, his beak drilled deep, found a river of warm blood, held her until she went limp. Finally he released his grip, stepped back, his duty done.

"Where is your cleverness now?" he hissed at the motionless corpse. "Where are your cowardly brothers now?" His tired wings caught air; he circled once to be certain; satisfied the deed was complete, he hurried back toward the barn, Polgar's blood still wet on his beak.

A black-feathered witness hiding silently high in a nearby tree cawed softly to her mate. "Did you see the white feather on her chest?" she asked.

"It is none of our affair," he replied.

"Coward." She spit out the distasteful word. "You know it was Polgar as well as I."

"Leave it alone," he said. "We'll be asked why we did nothing to defend her."

"No," she said, her voice laden with disgust. "Her son Trafalgar will know his mother's fate before sunset. Feed our young ones. I'll be home in the morning."

Chapter Twenty

. . . for some, marriage and its usual ante-
cedent, love, are fragile platforms, built
on nothing more than whispered prom-
ises and candlelight dreams, flowers and
tender kisses—just as likely to dissolve as
to flourish.

THE RANGE ROVER ROARED UP THE SLIGHT incline toward the turbine, its engine working hard, but not straining. It followed the tire tracks it had made an hour earlier. As the car passed again, Lily, almost completely buried by fresh snow, opened her eyes, raised her head, and fluttered a stiff wing, a futile, desperate gesture for help. Two hours later, terribly wounded and chilled to the hollows of her bones, she would never move again.

Charles Bakken, his cell phone glued to his ear, peered through the windshield; he took no notice of the small bundle of desperate feathers and flesh fluttering a wing for help beside the road; his spacious home, insulated against the weather and warmed by the fruits of the earth, was obscured from the driveway by a steep rise and remained out of sight.

"We've been married almost two years," he said. "In Seattle, but we lived in Chicago for a year and a half." He listened. "There was no pre-nup. She never asked for one, and I didn't offer. I wasn't going to be trapped again." There was a long pause. "We moved to South Dakota about six months ago." The car crested the final hill, slowed on the level. Bakken pushed the garage door remote and waited.

"What the hell does 'equitable distribution' mean? I'm not going to give her half of everything. She gets nothing, understand?" He maneuvered into the garage, settled the big Rover next to the Benz. "I've lost three million dollars in the last year. I'm not giving her a penny of what's left."

He turned off the key and the big machine went silent. Bakken stared out the windshield at his workbench and a wall filled with neatly arranged tools.

"Who decides what is 'fair'? I've earned every damn dime. All she brought from Seattle was her clothes. Listen to me. That's what I'm paying you for." His eyes moved to the rearview mirror, watched the garage door close behind him. "Okay. I'm home now. Call me when you've got it sorted. I want out of this damn marriage. It's gonna happen one way or another. The Chicago money is all gone. What's left nobody needs to know about. It's all mine."

Claire Bakken busied herself in the spacious kitchen preparing a simple toast and coffee breakfast. She was a petite woman of Scandinavian stock, very fair skinned, with light blue eyes and natural blonde hair. As a child growing up, her father sometimes lifted her off her feet, kissed her forehead, and called her his "sweetest of all sweetnesses." She had matured into one of those women who sometimes cause others to wonder why God would pour such beauty into one female mold instead of measuring it out more evenly in all. Claire's only obvious concession to the passage of time was a pair of stylish oval shaped frameless glasses. She called them her "John Lennons."

At a few minutes after eight, she was still in robe and slippers believing her husband would be gone the rest of the week on business in Pierre. She looked forward to having the house to herself, listening to music, enjoying long chats with her daughter on the phone, and reading one of the many library books she carted home each week from the Pierre library. For the next four days she could relax, knowing there would be no arguments or angry outbursts. Her marriage was in tatters, held together by the flimsiest of threads.

Chuck Bakken had been married before and divorced—twice in fact. He had found Claire, and she had found him, on the Internet, a galaxy-wide Laundromat bulletin board for lonely singles. Claire's first husband, much too young, had died six years earlier of pancreatic cancer. She had mourned deeply and properly for five full years before she felt the need for male companionship again. She was a careful, educated, cheerful woman of fifty-three who prided herself in confident self-reliance. She had always worked, and enjoyed her engineering position at Boeing.

Regarding men, she hadn't needed to search the Internet. There were hordes of Seattle men who would have been more than willing had she made it known she was looking. But more out of curiosity than anything else, she threw a line in the ether just to see what might be swimming about. She got dozens of interesting nibbles and some sizeable bites, but she rejected them one by one until Charles D. Bakken intrigued her. He lived in Chicago, Illinois, seemed a handsome, well-educated, successful businessman.

After three months of phone calls and email exchanges, despite the advice of her two grown children and several of her closest friends, Claire had flown from Seattle to Chicago to meet the man who called himself Chuck. He had mailed her a round-trip first-class airline ticket and promised a weekend tour of Chicago. A dozen roses were also delivered to her home on Queen Anne Hill. She took the next Friday off, packed a bag, and her son drove her to the airport.

At O'Hare, Chuck met her with flowers, and led her to the parking garage to his Benz. They lunched at an exclusive restaurant. He wooed her. Made a favorable impression. As promised, he showed her the Windy City, a comfortable, luxurious tour in his car. Explained his business, and shared tidbits of his family history. Didn't mention his previous two wives. Not a word about the looming bankruptcy.

She had been impressed, but not overly so. She was already familiar with nice things. Chuck was also an engineer, an educated man—obviously successful. He owned his own company. What was more important to her, he seemed the gentleman. He was polite and inquired about her children, Seattle, her work, art, the theatre, travel and books.

When she asked about his retirement plans, his eyes lit up. "I inherited seventy-four acres of ranchland from my grandfather in South Dakota, and I'm going to build my retirement home smack dab in the middle of it." He smiled handsomely, blue eyes and even teeth. "Pure peace and quiet," he said. "No more rat race." He held his wine glass up to hers. "What about you?"

"Oh," she laughed, "I think I'm too young to retire. I enjoy my job. We build great airplanes at Boeing and I'm part of an important team there. I really haven't given retirement much thought." She looked wistful. "I'm hoping for some grandkids to come along."

"Maybe you should start thinking about retiring," he said, pleasantly. "Life is too good—and too short—to waste working. I've got enough money for both of us. You don't have to work. We can travel, see the rest of the world, and enjoy life together. I've got a big boat moored at my condo in Miami. We can cruise anywhere you please."

"I love Seattle," she replied. "My kids are there. It's where my roots are. The lakes, rivers, and trees make it an enchanting place." She giggled. "I even love the rain; the sound of it striking the windows and pounding the roof lulls me to sleep; it keeps me at peace. Perfect weather for reading." The dining room's lighting was soft; it caught and enhanced her natural beauty. Her hair and eyes glowed; her flawless skin basked in it. The shape and fullness of her lips were magnetic. Chuck Bakken and every other man in the room took notice.

He reached across the table, placed his hand lightly on hers. "Once I sell my business we can live anywhere." He gave her a closed mouth, boyish grin. "I'm not much on rain or reading," he admitted, "but I'd consider having a home in Seattle."

She weighed it all, remembered her husband, how he had loved to read, and how they had jogged in the rain together. Still. Something negligible nagged at her—the thought of living out her life alone. No exciting journeys to distant and exotic lands. Cooking for one the rest of her life. Not laughing at a man's gentle teases.

Claire discovered Chuck Bakken was a very persuasive man, and gradually she yielded to his gentle pressure. When it became obvious to her daughter, Caddi, where her mother's relationship with Mr. Bakken was headed, there was a mild confrontation between the two.

One Saturday morning at a Starbucks in the U Village, Caddi asked, "Mom do you remember what you told me when I first met Brett in college?"

"I'm sure I told you lots of things."

"Your advice was, 'Never marry a man you can live with. Only marry a man you can't live without.'"

Claire made a soft laugh. "Of course. My mother gave me the same advice when I met your dad."

"Mom, I can't imagine my life without Brett." There was a long pause while both women sipped their coffee. "Do you really love Chuck?"

"Not fair," Claire replied. "I think you're comparing Chuck to your dad. A daughter only has one father, and no one can ever replace him. Chuck is very nice. He treats me well. Could I live without him? Obviously. Just like you lived your life for twenty-two years before you met Brett." Claire took a quick sip. "But Chuck or any other man will never be the same as your dad was to me."

"I'm sorry, Mom, and I hate to say this, but Chuck creeps me out. I don't think, deep down, he's honest or nice." Caddi left it there.

Three months later, at Chuck's urging, Claire took advantage of an early retirement plan at Boeing, and they had a small wedding in Seattle. They honeymooned in Fiji like young romantic marrieds, and she was convinced she had made the right move.

Despite his early promise of living wherever she wanted, they moved "temporarily" into his Chicago high-rise apartment and she began a new phase of life. She adjusted to her new role and settled in. Fifteen months later, his financial life in shambles, they moved to the new home in South Dakota. There was no more talk of living in Seattle. He never mentioned the Florida condo or yacht again.

Bakken removed his boots and left them inside the garage. He plodded down the hall and into the kitchen in stocking feet. Without a word of greeting he went to the cupboard, grabbed a cup and poured himself coffee.

Claire, coffee cup in hand, turned. Her eyes met his. "Back so soon?" she said. "What happened?" She camouflaged the disappointment. Hid it deep in her throat, keeping it from her eyes and voice.

"Damn roads are all shut down," he growled. "Cars in the ditch everywhere. Idiots." A formidable sized man with a voice to match, he glared at Claire as if she was responsible for the road conditions. "Couldn't get through to Pierre."

"I'm sure the business can wait a few days until the snow is gone," Claire said. She raised the cup to her lips, felt the coffee's warmth and spoke over the rim. "Everybody's in the same boat. Let me fix you a nice breakfast. You don't have to work every day of the year."

"Don't tell me what I have to do," he said. "You're not my mommy."

She didn't reply. Stung by his tone, she moved to a large picture window beside the kitchen nook. She touched her forehead to the cool glass. Her eyes pooled, mirrors of disappointment and regret. A man I can't live without? she thought. More like a man I can't live with.

Outside, feathery flakes, angels' feathers, continued to fall, softening the landscape.

"Get dressed," he said. "You look like a whorehouse floozy. Don't care for cheap bimbos."

Chapter Twenty-one

. . . and whereas, in ancient times, living outdoors like nomads was certain. They were nomads. They huddled tight the fire, hands and faces grimy, teeth gapping and rotting away, wild-eyed and ragged against the cold. And yet they accepted hardship; joy resided in their faces at all times, for difficulty guided their songs and poetry, eased the cold, made them strong against the morrow.

THE SNOW'S WEIGHT HAD PARTIALLY COLLAPSED the tent during the night, and when Kate's eyes flickered open, the ceiling squatted mere inches from her nose. She lifted her head and peered about. She could see Liam's sleeping bag, rolled up and cinched; he and his clothes were gone.

She freed one arm, and zipped her bag down to her waist. She glanced at her watch. It was quarter past seven.

When Kate tried to sit up, her head touched the icy cold ceiling. It was awkward, but she managed to wiggle into her jeans while lying flat on her back. If Liam comes in now, she thought, he'll get an eyeful and a half. She giggled. Kate eyed the tent's door, took a deep breath, removed her shirt, and quickly fastened her bra—a deft act of magic behind her back; she slid into her shirt, and buttoned it; pulling her feet into wool socks; she let her sleep-mussed hair fall where it wanted. Remembering, she dug into the bottom of her sleeping bag and retrieved her leather boots, relatively warm and pliant. She anchored herself at the bottom of her bag facing the door; tightening her abdomen, she pulled herself into a V. Unhinging her knees she tugged her boots on and somehow stayed balanced long enough to tie the laces.

On her knees, Kate backed her way outside, feet first. She stood up and pulled on her jacket, zipping it to her chin. She located her gloves in one pocket and a knitted wool cap in the other. Her warm breath wafted upward, visible for a moment on her lips, then mingling and vanishing into the landscape; the sudden cold drew autumn color to her cheeks, ignited the granite sparks in her eyes.

A few feet away, facing the road, Liam had already Manitoba stomped a four-foot square patch of snow into a legless table. Scattered upon the packed down snow were a one-burner camp stove, two plastic bottles of water, and his dilapidated canvas pack. His footprints led away from the tent past the snowmobile toward the bridge. The road lay invisible, blanketed with overnight snow. Kate shaded her eyes against the glare and saw Liam leaning against the bridge railing peering at the creek below. In his hand, he held what appeared to be a coffee cup.

Kate waved, and caught his attention. Even at a distance his rugged appearance and wide smile were reassuring. He held the cup high in a morning salute, accompanied by a wide grin.

Kate pulled her cell from her back pocket and hit the power button. It hummed to life, and a flood of text message alerts appeared on the screen.

The first was a puzzling fragment from Susan Flannery, her grandmother, a published poet. Through the years Kate and her grandmother had often traded simple verbal rhymes in their daily conversation, and since Kate had left for college the practice had been continued through text messages. Grandmother had written:

Trust most your heart's dictate,
All else reject as a gilded lure.

Kate accepted the rhyme and meter challenge, a smile gracing her face as she tapped out:

To shape a young woman's fate,
Love's winding pathway, never sure.

Kate hit send, certain her grandmother would be delighted at her hurried attempt at poetry. The second message was from Chris: **Where r U? Truck stuck in drvway. Snw knee dp. Miss U crzy lots.**

She replied: **Camped nr Mac's Corner. Lots of snw. Miss U 2.**

A third text notified of a biology paper due Friday.

A reply text from grandmother arrived: **Bravo.** Kate smiled at Grandmother's approval. It crossed her mind grandmother might not approve of Kate on an overnight camping trip with a young man she hardly knew.

The last from her mother: **Orville, others searching for class. Stay warm. We're fine. Mom.**

Kate looked up from the screen. Liam, his cup held to his lips with both hands, seemed a winter postcard.

Kate typed: **With frnd. looking 4 class 2. Tell Dad I'm fine.**

She switched off the phone and slipped it into her back pocket. She looked back at the bridge. Liam dressed in jeans and a tee shirt plodded back through the deep snow toward her.

"Morning," Liam said. "Ready for breakfast?"

"Aren't you cold?" Kate asked.

"It's okay to be cold," he said. His eyes laughed before his voice did. "Growing up, my dad and I would be outside working, chopping wood or working on the house, and typical kid, I'd whine about being cold, or whatever. He'd give me this look and say, 'It's okay to be cold. No need to be warm all the time.' Dad stuck to his philosophy for everything. 'It's okay to be tired,' he'd say. 'It'll go away. It's okay to be hungry. Mom'll feed us later.' As I got older I got used to those everyday trials and Dad's simple philosophy, but I never thought, until just this moment, I'd be telling people the same darn thing." He laughed again, loud and long. "My coat is in the Yamaha. I'm fine."

"My dad's got a few of those too," Kate replied. "'Crying won't do any good. Just wasted salt water,' he'd say."

"Well, let me get some food together and then we can get going," Liam said. He kneeled down and started rummaging through his bike saddlebag, a beyond dirty gray canvas affair. "These entrees are all three months old, left over from my bike expedition, but freeze-dried food lasts a lifetime. He held up a package for Kate to examine.

"Here's a pack of freeze-dried 'Scrambled eggs, Vegetarian Bacon and Organic Hash Browns.' I've had it before and it's not too bad." He handed it to Kate. "This one is supposed to be dinner I think, but might appeal this morning:'Himalayan Lentils and Rice.' Never really tried it, but it sounds pretty good. My mom ordered all these online from REI or Amazon. Here's a culinary delight called 'Curry in a Hurry.' Might be good. The last offering this morning is 'Granola with Milk and Organic

Blueberries.' Speaks for itself." He handed them all to Kate for further study.

He poured water into a small pan and lit the burner. "Choose what you want. As soon as the water boils we can eat."

"I'll try the 'Curry in a Hurry.'"

Liam grinned. "Good choice. It's one of my personal faves. You won't be disappointed."

"I'll have the scrambled eggs," he said. "Save the rest just in case."

He frowned. "One little problem. We're a little short on silverware. There's only one fork and one spoon." He laughed. "You can have the fork. I'm pretty sure I washed it the last time I camped out."

Kate looked skeptical. "When was that?"

"When I got to Brookings for registration, around the first week of September."

"No problem," Kate said. "We can sterilize the utensils in boiling water. Do you have any more coffee?"

"Sure, lots of coffee. It's instant without sugar, but still sweet. My mom bought it online for me from Malaysia. Better than Starbucks and a whole lot less money. Just takes a minute. We'll have to share the cup."

"And the germs," Kate said with a giggle.

Liam deepened his voice, mimicked his father. "'It's okay to eat a few germs now and then, Liam. Acid in the stomach will kill most of 'em.'"

Kate ventured, "What about plates? Just one?"

Liam looked up. "No plates. I eat everything out of the pouch. Keeps it simple. Very few dishes to wash."

The snow, the teasing, and the joy of being young and strong made the coffee and food delicious. They leaned against the snowmobile, ate, shared their germs, teased, laughed at themselves and each other and took in the winter view. Kate produced a package of Oreos from her jacket pocket and they shared those for dessert, crunchy and perfect to finish the coffee.

While Liam packed up the tent, stakes, mats, and sleeping bags, Kate, as if a member of some ancient wandering tribe, carried the cup, pan, fork, and spoon down to the creek to rinse, and store away, ready for the next meal.

Soon everything was stowed into the cart. Liam spread the map out on the snowmobile.

Using Kate's GPS app on her phone and his compass, he studied the horizon and plotted the course toward Dupree across the shimmering white expanse. The whole of land designated South Dakota surrounded, engulfed, and beckoned to them.

"According to the information we have," he said, "the hawks and their teacher should have arrived home late Sunday afternoon. But, for whatever series of unfortunate circumstances, most likely the wind and cold, they never arrived. It's Tuesday morning and they still aren't home. Maybe a few are sick from the cold. Sick or injured birds won't last long out here." He waved his arm in a wide arc. "The chances of us stumbling on them aren't very good, but at least we can say we tried. We owe them an honest try." He looked at Kate. "If all goes well we'll find them soon enough and be able to help. We could even end up at your parents' place for dinner. There's a real good possibility we'll be hungry by then."

Kate laughed. "Duh. I'll be hungry an hour from now. Good curry though." She slipped her helmet on, tucked in loose strands of hair. She smiled at Liam. "Your breakfast was perfect. One of the best I've ever had. My mom's a terrific cook, and she's got lots of plates, cups, and utensils." She patted his arm.

"Just imagine," Liam said, pretending to be offended. He had finally donned his parka and helmet. "Real food served on fine crockery. Looking forward to it. Maybe you can teach me how to load a dishwasher. Never seen one up close and personal."

Kate took off one glove to fasten her chinstrap, and a moment later climbed aboard and snuggled in tight behind him. She leaned forward, put her chin on his shoulder.

"Let 'er rip," she said, her lips brushing his ear.

Chapter Twenty-two

. . . and in the end it comes down to this: water, food, shelter, love. Lacking any one of these, surely we all perish.

OWEN HAD BEEN ROUGHED UP LIKE A HIGH school boy taking on the class bully in an after-school parking lot scrap: skinned knuckles, scraped cheekbone, bloody nose. He nestled in the straw beside Ms. Ride, dizzy from combat and hunger; his goggles, splattered with blood, dangled from the Velcro strap around his neck.

Emma, ignoring her own groaning stomach and battle nicks, tended to Ms. Ride. "Please, please open your eyes," she said. She put her beak to Ms. Ride's ear. "Can you hear me?" There was no indication Ms. Ride heard wedding bells, thunder, a Puccini opera, or anything else.

Emma pulled back the horse blanket and put her ear to her teacher's chest. "Her heartbeat is strong, Goggs. But she is in another world. Will she ever come back?"

"I believe she's in a coma," he said. "It's certain her brain was rattled when her head impacted the ground. Most likely it has swollen inside her skull, but with time might heal itself."

He studied Emma. "All we can do is keep her warm and wait for help to arrive. Once the class is home and Rowdy explains what happened they'll realize Ms. Ride needs help and searchers will be dispatched."

He glanced at his wing watch. "We're almost exactly on the true flight line."

Emma gave Owen an impatient, exasperated look. "Who will find us in this barn? Do you imagine a search party will look into every barn between here and Iron Lightning?"

"Of course not," he said, taking no offense at her sarcasm. "One of us must stay to protect and comfort Ms. Ride. The other must go seek the searchers. She may remain unconscious for days, even weeks. As soon as possible she needs to be transported to a clinic for proper care. Doc Walters in Dupree would be best."

He stood on trembling legs and pointed a wing tip toward the two horses housed in the back of the barn. "It is certain someone from the house will come soon to feed our large friends. It's difficult to predict the reaction if we are discovered. If they bring a dog we will be found for certain. Be wary and stay silent."

"I'm not worried about humans," Emma said. "Most of those I've encountered have been kind. Father is acquainted with several. They always treat him well."

Owen said, "There is a girl in Dupree I trust as no other. Her name is Kate Flannery. She has opened her heart and mind to all living things. My father and mother consider her their sister. It's a mystery to me, but humans dread death even though they live many years beyond our lifespan, and yet fear drives them to be distrustful of others. To me they often seem afraid of each other. To most humans, we hawks are also *others*. Their fear of us causes them to be defensive. We must always be careful. Some humans will kill for no reason. It is a frightful, uncertain world they live in."

"Thank you for sharing your philosophy, professor Goggs," Emma said, her words tinged with exasperation. "But right now I can't think if you are right or wrong; my stomach cries out for food and we cannot survive on hay or your fanciful words. If we are to be strong against a curious dog, its master, and the cold, one of us must hunt."

Though battered and exhausted, Owen's eyes sparked with fresh enthusiasm at her call for hunting. "We hawks are not kept captive, and no one brings us food," he said. "It's not for me to judge, but our horse friends have lost their freedom to feed themselves. I'm certain it's a trade they regret. You protect our teacher. I'll hunt."

He sat up and pulled his helmet down and snugged up the chinstrap. He gave a useless swipe at his goggles with a tired wingtip and left them dangling from his neck with a weary sigh. Before Emma could comment, Owen opened his wings, took air, and swooshed out the door toward the farmhouse.

The heavy layers of snow complicated the natural hunt, but he knew the prey must eat too, and they would be about. He fought his fatigue and soared high above the farm house, barn, and deserted pasture, circling it in a wide arc several times; he preferred to hunt while flying, but his wings felt lifeless and heavy, so he landed on a nearby flat-topped power pole supplying electricity to the house. Once settled, he fastened his goggles over his eyes and despite the constant glare off the snow he could see with reasonable clarity. He scanned the ground, inch-by-inch, noting even the slightest movement.

Emma unwrapped Ms. Ride, rolled her from her side to her back, then to her other side. The teacher's wings were stiff and inflexible from the cold, and her legs had started to stiffen as well. Emma tried to open one of the wings, but it seemed welded to Ms. Ride's body. In the process, Ms. Ride's beak quaked, as if to complain of pain, but no sound escaped the vessel. Nonetheless, Emma was heartened by even a scant show of life. "I didn't mean to hurt you," she said.

It was then Emma realized if Ms. Ride, in her unconscious state, could feel pain, she might also suffer hunger and thirst as well. Emma hurried to the doorway and, using her wing tip as a spoon, scooped up a bit of snow. She hurried back to Ms. Ride and rubbed the snow along the edges of Ms. Ride's beak. She repeated the process two more times, and was delighted when Ms. Ride's beak slivered open, allowing the melting snow to dribble in.

She spoke tenderly, as a mother to a fevered child. "You're going to be okay. It's Emma. Owen is here too. The others have flown home to Dupree. It's certain help is on the way." Emma's words were optimistic, but her mind, not so much. Another night in a freezing barn might be too much for the weakening Ms. Ride to bear.

Owen fluttered in, his beak clamped on fresh meat. He landed beside Emma and dropped the prize at her feet. "You eat first," he said. "Others will be about." He caught air and vanished before she could thank him.

Emma ate every morsel and in seconds felt the knot in her stomach begin to soften, and the strength return to her body. She rewrapped Ms. Ride—kept good company—and hummed a familiar song:

> *Breeze in the treetop,*
> *Mother's gone away,*

Breeze in the treetop,
Will you stop and play?

Although Emma was unschooled in practical nursing technique she used common sense and her first aid training to shield Ms. Ride as best she could from the dreadful cold and discomfort.

A few minutes later Owen returned with more food, enough to share. They ate in silence. Emma was thankful for her goggled friend's hunting skill and kindness. Owen had no time for conversation—his hunger demanded full attention.

Outside, the wind forced itself on the land, and the sky darkened as if the lights in a packed playhouse had been turned off for the start of Act Two following a brief intermission. They ate in silence, both quiet with their own dreams.

When every scrap had been consumed and melted snow had washed it all down, Owen turned to Emma. "We have been tested by the crows, and escaped with slight wounds of little consequence. Time will heal them. If none of our attackers survived to fly back to Sioux Falls and tell the tale, then we are safe. Our bellies are full, and sleep is the best medicine of all. It will be dark soon and the storm has returned for another go. I had hoped help would come today, but it's doubtful the searchers will challenge a blizzard. We must hunker down and be patient."

"And Ms. Ride?" Emma asked. "Will she survive another night on a cold barn floor while we rest in comfort?" Her voice dripped impatience.

"Impossible to say," Owen said, "but without outside help we are stuck right here. We have few options.

Tomorrow I will be refreshed and seek help, no matter the weather. Right now I must sleep." He stood up and began preparing a bed for the night. "Tomorrow this nightmare will end."

"Why call it a nightmare?" she asked. "We are awake."

"Because," he said, "I have killed *beyond hunger* today. You know it's forbidden by our constitution. My family and I will carry the stain of it on our wings the rest of our days."

Emma eyed him. "We are protected by an amendment. Your killing was done in strict self-defense."

Owen turned to face her, his eyes filled with tears. "Yes," he replied, "but at the end of the battle I purposely murdered their leader, the one with the white feather on her chest. She was fleeing, not attacking, and I killed her anyway. I have shamed us all." His feathered shoulders quaked with sobs.

Emma opened a wing and draped it over him. "Goggs," she said, "you have been very brave today. When we get home and tell our story, none will blame you. Please don't fret so." She gently patted his back with her wingtip.

"I'll fly for help at dawn, no matter the weather," he managed.

Not certain of him, she measured his mettle. "Others have flown in blizzards, Goggs. Perhaps I can make it through."

He did not take the bait. "You are a better nurse than I. It's best you remain here with Ms. Ride. I'm certain searchers are coming, and I will intercept them and bring them here."

He fixed his eyes on Emma. "If you were to die in the storm I would hate myself forever," he said. "You saved my life today." His beak opened, but words failed him.

Her eyes glowed. A wind stronger than friendship fanned the fire contained there. "It is best as you have said." She opened her wings wide, pulled him close. Her beak touched his and she felt his coiled strength. "Thank you, Goggs," she whispered. "You were so brave against the crows. If they had killed you, they would have found Ms. Ride and me here in the barn soon after. In the morning, you will go and save us once more."

The wind snarled its fury against the barn all night long; it rattled loose boards, dodged through knotholes and cracks, delivered more snow.

Emma, snug against Chawla Ride, dreamed of her parents, her sisters, and a handsome young hawk with a quick mind and terrible eyesight.

Owen slept too, his mind and body sealed in a breathless grave, too weary to conjure even black-feathered ghosts.

The next day, the snow and the wind had settled their differences. The sun was up in the east and the clouds parted so warmth could begin to repair the damage.

After a quick breakfast Emma sent him on his way with the familiar red-tailed prayer still ringing in his ears: "Deikrrt-Deimerrt-Deisoorrt." *God grant speed. God grant courage. God grant vision.*

A red-tail's religion, if it can even properly be called one, is based on a very close personal relationship to nature. There are no formal documents or set places of worship, and all precepts and beliefs are oral, simply handed down within the community from generation to generation. Their nearest word for God is "dei." It is gender neutral and usually translated into English as "life sustainer."

Owen, feeling strong now, accelerated past the chimney top, a thin ribbon of smoke spiraling upward, contrasting its drab color with a marvelous blue sky; anticipating higher speed, he tightened the strap on his goggles; a moment later, far below, he observed the battlefield littered with the burial mounds covering the corpses of the black-feathered eye thieves; he glanced at his Breitling Navitimer—it calculated time, elevation, temperature and speed. Ms. Ride and his parents had taught him well, and the lessons of daring flight unfolded in his mind, page after page, tactics and strategy, precise movements practiced and mastered time and time again.

At four hundred and fifty feet, he became the single point of the speeding arrow, true and level.

Emma unwrapped the blanket, placed her wings around her teacher, and enveloped her. Using her beak as a mother uses her fingers over her lullabied child, she pulled the cover around them. "It's Tuesday, Ms. Ride," she said. "Help is on the way." A moment later, confident of Owen's promise, her tummy full, and radiating life's warmth, the winged caregiver slept again.

The two stabled horses, weary of the cold and inactivity, drowsed. In the distance, a screen door rattled; a dog sighed and curled itself against the morning chill.

Chapter Twenty-three

*. . . and news of a death in the family
strikes hot, molten lava against the anvil.
How could mere words ever be more
hurtful?*

QUINN AWOKE WITH A START. CONFUSED AND
shivering he looked about; his situation flooded
back with the memory of the decimation of his classmates. His mind reeled with the enormity of it all. The
sun's peeping rays toyed with the ground below him,
creating fantastic crimson-tinged crystals on the white
landscape. He leaped from his perch without hesitation and fluttered his wings, landing softly beside the
bubbling creek. His parched throat demanded water
and his empty stomach craved sustenance—the latter a
condition not so easily remedied. He dipped his head
and drank deeply. His hunger, persistent in its demands,
would have to wait. The preciousness of time denied
a hunt. The usual quarry, buried by a foot or more of
snow, hidden and warm in their burrows, ate of their
storehouses.

A moment later, his mind clearing, he rose and circled back toward the wind turbine. During the night the
snow had acted the role of a stone-faced gravedigger
and pulled a sympathetic white shroud over the remains
of his friends. At fifty feet, all Quinn could see were

scattered knobby white mounds, unmarked graves. He circled again, barely three feet off the ground. Nothing moved. All was eerily silent. Overhead a giant windmill, jousted with nothing; it rotated at its leisure, patiently awaiting the next unsuspecting flock.

He glanced at his wing watch, studied the horizon, set a true course and with a monstrously heavy heart, flew toward home.

An hour later, his young eyes saw two tiny specks flying side by side in the distant sky. Part of the student training at the Prairie Winds School of Flight includes one hour a week of shape recognition drills (Shape Rec) for the junior class. Just as military radar operators must be able to distinguish between approaching enemy aircraft and their own, so too red-tail hawks must be skilled in visual intercepts of their adversaries, mainly eagles and owls. Recently, despite some loud grumbling by a few members of the school board, the program has been expanded to also include drone sighting, identification and avoidance strategies.

Even at a distance of three miles, Quinn realized the approaching shapes were two adult male red-tails, flying wing tip to wing tip at the same elevation as his own. He felt a rush of energy to his tired wings; the surge of adrenalin pushed his speed up a notch. The figures were not yet distinguishable as members of the Iron Lightning hawk community, but he felt certain they were. Why else, he reasoned, would they be traversing the exact same route he was navigating? He checked his wing watch coordinates once more just to be certain he was flying true.

At one mile Quinn established one of the hawks as RT Orville Hampstead, his traditional white scarf streaming, goggles, and leather helmet dead giveaways. Quinn wasn't yet positive, but he thought the other RT Boyd Higgins, much rounder and with lighter colored feathers. He knew Higgins was a retired flight instructor from the school, much honored as a former teacher and legendary flyer. Orville, of course, was Owen's father, and considered one of the best flyers to ever graduate from the Prairie Winds School of Flight. Both hawks volunteered at work parties and fundraising events at the school. Higgins was also frequently invited into Ms. Ride's classroom as a guest lecturer on some of the more complicated and obscure aspects of aeronautics.

At a quarter mile Quinn slowed, but maintained altitude. His hunger and the cold had weakened him—his spent wings mere ponderous appendages barely able to sustain flight. As the flyers closed the distance between them, Quinn's ears caught the joyful red-tail greeting: "Trep Trep!" *Hello, young friend.*

Below them stood a scattered grove of eastern cottonwood trees planted as windbreaks sixty years earlier by an industrious farmer to protect his farm animals, crops, and home from the weather. Orville initiated a dive, his white scarf flowing out behind, and Higgins followed him down. Just as they settled on a slender branch thirty feet off the ground Quinn landed between them, his face a troubled mix of relief and despair.

Orville slid his goggles to his neck and undid the chinstrap to his helmet, presenting a rather bizarre image of a red-tailed hawk; he waited a moment longer for the young hawk to catch his breath. Unable to hold back any longer, Orville said, "You're Quinn Larson, Gunnar and Albjørg's son. Why are you flying alone? Where are your classmates? Your teacher?"

Quinn swiveled his body to face Orville, his eyes brimming with tears. "Catastrophe," he gasped. "All are dead." His body quaked with the incomprehensible words.

Without a word, RT Boyd Higgins opened a wing, curled it around Quinn, and pulled him tight to his chest.

"All?" asked Orville, his voice incredulous. "All dead? Everyone? How can that be?"

"Give the lad a moment," Higgins whispered. He held the young flyer tight to his body, offering precious warmth and solace against his chest. Quinn was sobbing now, the dam of pent up emotion cracked, then failed, releasing a mournful cry of anguish.

Quinn gulped for air. "A tower. We flew into a wind turbine, invisible in the white ribbons of snow. The blades chopped us to pieces. I escaped by the tiniest fraction, the whirr of metal brushing my beak." He wailed openly. "I only wish I had died with my classmates."

Orville was dumbfounded, his senses stone, iron on the anvil under the hammer. He stared at Quinn, a living ghost. His beak opened as if to speak, closed without sound. He mumbled, "Was Ms. Ride at point?" He shook his head as if the information was unfathomable. "She died too?"

Quinn, too upset to speak, quieted himself, told the story from the beginning. "Rowdy Lee Gowdy flew point. As we approached Sioux Falls last Thursday a band of crows harassed us. Ms. Ride strained her wing driving them off. The doctor treated her, but Sunday morning when we were ready to depart for home she told us her wing was still too weak to keep pace, and she could not lead us. She assigned Rowdy point."

Quinn stared off into the distance as if to see Rowdy and his classmates once more. "The snow became worse and worse. It forced us too low. The north wind, more powerful than I've ever felt it before, may have pushed us off course. I can't be sure." Quinn paused. Finally, he spoke in a whisper. "Rowdy was our best flyer. It was not his fault."

"Are you certain there were no survivors?" Higgins asked.

"As soon as I realized what had happened I circled back," Quinn replied. "When I landed among them some were still alive on the surface of the snow. It appeared a few had driven themselves beneath the snow. I walked about to see if I might give first aid. Two or three spoke to me, called out my name . . . said goodbye. But there was nothing I could do. I stayed with them. Dusk fell and soon there were no sounds, no movement, and for that I'm grateful. Their suffering was brief." He paused and shuddered. "I spent the night nearby on the limb of a tree. I flew back to the site at dawn, but all was covered in snow. Nothing moved. I walked ten minutes or more among the mounds, hoping for signs of life. There were none, so I flew on."

"Ms. Ride posted herself at rear guard in the formation?" Orville asked. Before Quinn could respond, another question erupted from his beak. "If weather conditions were so abysmal why didn't she lead the class to ground for protection?" His face filled with emotion: he glanced at Higgins. "Students should never be allowed to fly point in such extreme circumstances." A flash of white-hot anger in his eyes signaled a need to assign blame. "Turbines are only invisible on the darkest of nights. A red-tail can see a ladybug at half a mile. Such an accident should never have happened."

"Please, Orville," Higgins said. "Calm yourself. Now is not the time to make accusations. There will be a proper inquiry later. We know the weather was horrendous. Ms. Ride must have had every confidence in Rowdy's ability or she never would have allowed the class to proceed under his leadership. You know how much she loves her students." Higgins stared hard at Orville, his steely eyes rebuking him. Ruffling his feathers against the cold, the old hawk comforted Quinn.

"I didn't mean to blame anyone," Orville said, his demeanor softening. "Ms. Ride was an outstanding and dedicated teacher, and Rowdy a terrific young flyer. My son Owen often mentioned Rowdy's ability in the air." His eyes mirrored profound grief. "But the loss of so many of our young ones is unbearable."

Orville opened his wings wide, stretched, and readied himself for flight; he pulled his goggles from the top of his head to his eyes. "We must bring them all home for proper burial."

Higgins released his grasp on Quinn, leaned back and adjusted his beret, snugging it low above one eye. "Transporting them will be a most difficult task," he said. "Each will have to be carried by a heart-broken father or mother."

Higgins swallowed hard, turned toward Quinn. "Where is this turbine?" he asked. "Do you know the coordinates? We must gather everyone there."

Quinn gave a negative shake of his head. "The snow pelted me, and my mind was so numb I could not calculate the latitude and longitude from my Breitling." He looked away, shamed before his elders. "But, I remember our altitude alarms sounded just as we passed over a small village named Blunt," he continued. "It sits hard against the rail line. We flew safely over it and continued on, but we had not yet reached the river. Rowdy was locked in at twenty-two just as Ms. Ride had instructed. I estimate the killing place is maybe ten or eleven miles southeast of Okobojo Point. I can't be sure. It all happened so fast."

"I am familiar with the area," Higgins said. "My wife and I once vacationed nearby the lake years ago. But I don't recall seeing a tower. It must have been built in the last year or so. Our sky maps are updated every two years and I know for certain a turbine does not appear on them. Ms. Ride would have been unaware of its existence." He paused, looked at Orville. "Perhaps the wind altered Rowdy's course."

"It would seem so," Orville replied, his face solemn. "Wind is the greatest enemy of true flight. I speak from experience."

"I am sure Rowdy flew true," Quinn replied. He shook his head. "He knows, or . . . knew how important . . ." Sensing his verb tenses were wrong, Quinn could not finish the statement. He buried his feathered head into Higgins' chest.

"Of course," Orville said, his voice compassionate. "The air is our home and our sanctuary, but sometimes, on a mere whim, Mother Sky betrays us." He glanced with a grim face at Higgins and shook his shoulders to ward off accumulating snow. "We cannot leave the lad alone. If you will escort him home I will locate the tower and protect our fledglings from the scavengers until you and the others return. I'll call you with the coordinates."

"I see no other course of action," Higgins replied. He glanced up at the sky; he noticed it had darkened while they had conferenced. Feathery flakes of snow drifted by. "Others might be searching too. We all will meet at the killing place, gather their remains, and bring them home, one and all. Not a feather should be left behind."

Orville peered upward past the trees into the grayish sky, now beginning to fill with endless flakes of white. "The weather worsens again, but our duty is clear." He reached into his holster with his beak and speared a serving of Raptor Flight Mix. He offered it to Quinn and the young hawk's beak stretched wide. Another and another passed between them, life-sustaining currency.

"Can you fly home?" Higgins asked the young hawk. "Two hours at least. Your family worries for you."

"I am tired, but I will fly," Quinn answered, his bare words almost lost to the quickening wind; his beak quivered, unable to speak more.

Higgins turned to Orville. "Go then. Fly with speed, courage, and clear vision. Once there, stand guard and let no more harm fall upon them."

Orville tightened his chinstrap and adjusted his goggles with his wingtips. He reached out, hugged Quinn. "Be strong. Your mother needs you," he whispered. Then the tree branch trembled, the tension upon it was released and without another word Orville vanished, a valiant knight galloping into the gloom; a minute later as he climbed to altitude his heart spilled over, and his wings felt heavy, burdened with the thoughts of his murdered son.

"Owen. Owen," he mumbled, the words unable to squeeze past the heavy lump in his throat. "Papa is coming for you." Dark clouds spitting confetti roiled above him, a stiff wind fierce in his face. "Your mother, Owen. How can I inform her? She will never understand." A foggy mist formed inside his goggles and he had to pull them from his eyes.

Higgins offered gentle words of encouragement to his charge; after a brief rest, they too climbed into the desolate sky, Quinn keeping so near his wingtips brushed again and again against the old professor's.

Overhead, angry clouds bursting with snow, dropped low, dimming the light. A seam broke like a razor to a feather pillow, and the wind began to howl.

. . . and you would gossip of men and women in marriage— ah, a perfect and wonderful union—unless one or both are insane.

ON THE ARCHITECT'S DRAWING TABLE IN CHIcago the classic clapboard farmhouse porch became a wrap-around ten-foot wide walkway with a thick beam supported roof and delicately turned spindle railing. The walkway granted shade at any hour of the day as it circled the house, and all four sides bled off into sets of wide steps leading down to gentle lawns and elegant landscaping. Behind the house the walkway widened out and became a massive entertainment deck with built-in barbecue grill, outdoor refrigerator, and seating for twenty. After living almost six months in South Dakota, Claire and Charles Bakken had yet to host a dinner party. In fact, they had stopped eating their meals together and barely spoke to each other.

The original house, built in 1897 near the center of seventy-four acres of ranch land, had been gutted and enlarged to three thousand square feet of upscale modernity—electronics, gleaming tile, exotic wood floors, two fireplaces, and state of the art stainless steel kitchen appliances flanked by marble countertops and gleaming cabinets: a dream home occupied by two who were locked in a nightmare marriage.

Charles Bakken, bankrupt of one fortune and spending down his inheritance, was determined to live off the grid; he opted for solar power panels mounted on the home's sloped rooftop and a 10-kilowatt Bergey Excel wind turbine mounted on a one-hundred-and-twenty-foot tower. Together they generated ample electricity to supply the home's needs.

Claire, warmly dressed in leggings and wool coat, paused on the top step just outside the home's main entrance; she took in the snowy landscape, glancing anxiously over her shoulder to make sure he wasn't watching. The vista to the south gave her a clear view of the turbine, blades slowly rotating in the breeze. Her normal morning routine was to walk down the driveway past the tower, a half-mile or more from the house. From there she would continue a mile further to the county road to fetch the morning *Capital Journal* newspaper, check for mail, and then retrace her steps up the slight incline back to the house, a leisurely three-mile jaunt. The snow this morning at the foot of the steps was almost knee deep, and her first thought was escape would be impossible.

Before her marriage to Bakken, when she still lived alone in Seattle, her daily exercise routine had been to walk the three-mile paved path around Green Lake on weekend mornings, and after work each weekday, unless it was even rainier than usual. If the sky were drenching, she'd drive up to Northgate Mall and put in three laps there, greeting other walkers with a big smile and cheerful words as they passed by. Skipping her daily walk had, as regular as a glass of morning orange juice, never been an option.

Desperation though, is a cruel master and Claire ploughed herself across the front lawn and reached the driveway. The matted down tire tracks made for easier going, her breath swirling in a vaporous mist around her face. Before she had walked fifty yards she heard the familiar buzz of Daisy, Bakken's flying seeing-eye watchdog over her right shoulder. At first her husband had told her he sent the drone along as a cheerful companion, a friend to watch over her; he said it was capable of instantly notifying him if she tripped and fell, or twisted her ankle, or some other ridiculous and unlikely scenario.

There were four other drones in his "fleet," as he called them, as he if he were talking about the grand Cunard Cruise Line sailing out of Southampton or The Cathay Pacific airline conglomerate based in Hong Kong. These were not simple hobbyist robo-copters. Bakken, still flush with cash before the sudden bankruptcy, had purchased top quality drones, one step down from industrial grade, and an unknown number of steps below military level machines. Each weighed twenty-eight pounds and was equipped with a high-resolution video camera, grasping hooks, and laser guided ball bearing projectiles.

Perched on a specially designed landing and recharging station in the garage, Bakken dispatched them early each morning by remote control as directed by the computer in his den. He could also direct their flight via his cell phone.

The garage door, on a preset timer, would automatically rise, and one by one the fleet would stir and awaken from their cold and mechanical slumber. Each in turn would lift off and zoom out to its assigned sector. These four drones (Bakken had named them Rodeo Joe, Scout, Popeye and Batman) patrolled the seventy-four acres of his estate in short watch sequences from first light until dusk every day. Because of power source limitations each drone had to return to its landing pad every sixty minutes to recharge its lithium ion batteries. Claire's companion, Daisy, more sophisticated and a bit larger, was powered by a fuel cell and could stay airborne for just over two hours.

There were also cameras in every room except the three toilets. Initially Claire had tried to be a good sport about it, sometimes playfully pretending to stab the kitchen camera with a paring knife while she prepared dinner, or smiling and posing provocatively when she sat down on the living room sofa to watch TV or read her book. Bakken claimed the drones and cameras were just his harmless retirement hobbies, gadgets he'd been toying with for years. Claire wasn't so sure.

One night before bed about a month after they had moved from Chicago, she toweled down after her shower and walked into the bedroom where she had laid out her nightie on the bed. A tiny red light in one corner of the room came on and caught her attention. It startled her, uncomfortably so. She grabbed her sleepwear off the bed and retreated to the bathroom.

A moment later she confronted him in his den, her eyes flashing anger. "I don't want a camera in the bedroom," she said. "I'm not your plaything to spy on."

"Too bad," he said. "This is my house and I mean to know what's going on in it. My Chicago condo got broken into and it cost me a lot of money. My car was stolen out of a restaurant's high security garage downtown two years ago. I get mad when people rip me off." He leaned back in his computer chair, arms folded across his chest.

"I'm your wife, not a burglar or car thief," Claire said, her voice quaking with anger. "I have never taken anything of yours, and I don't care to be filmed while I'm dressing or undressing."

He swiveled his chair, and turned his back to her, facing the three computer monitors on his desk. "Undress in the bathroom then. Everything in this house is mine. The cameras stay."

"You don't own me, mister," she snapped. Without another word, Claire hurried to the pantry closet and pulled out the aluminum three-step ladder she used to reach high places for dusting. She carried the ladder to the master bedroom and then returned to the garage. She grabbed a hammer from its place above the workbench and returned to the bedroom. Standing on tiptoe from the top step of the ladder she swung the hammer with both hands; shattered pieces of glass, plastic, and wallboard flew off and scattered on the bed and carpet. She left everything as it was and spent the night in one of the guestrooms, door locked. They had not slept together since.

Claire, collar turned up against the biting cold, unsure of her destination, started down the drive. She ignored Daisy's incessant hum, took out her cell phone and waved it, taunting the drone. She wanted to make certain, if Bakken were watching, he noticed it. Since the bedroom camera incident she had guarded her texts and emails assiduously, suspecting her husband made every effort to pry into her personal messages.

"Hi, Mom." Caddi's voice reverberated loud and clear against the silence of the vast landscape, marred only by the sound of Claire's crunching footsteps.

"I'm coming home," Claire said, avoiding any small talk. She knew Daisy's microphone would record their conversation, but at this point she didn't care, and made little attempt to hide it. "You were right about Chuck Bakken. Mother should have listened to daughter."

"Mom?" There was a long pause. "Are you okay?"

"Right now, yes. But, I need to leave as soon as the roads open up. We've had a freak snowstorm and there's no way to make it to the airport. As soon as the road opens I'll be on my way, hopefully tomorrow, but Thursday or Friday at the latest. I'm not coming back. He and I are finished."

Claire walked with her head down, brows furrowed, concentrating on how to present the painful message to her daughter. With the phone pressed to her ear, she passed the turbine, oblivious to the unusual cluster of tiny mounds scattered at the base of the tower; she continued down the slope toward the county road.

"What's buzzing?"

"I'm outside walking. As always, Daisy is tracking me. She's a bit noisy."

"Daisy? Who's she?"

"It's a long story. I'll tell you when I get home. Have to hang up now. Hi to Brett. Love you."

"Mom? Do I need to come there? Are you positive you're okay?"

But Claire had already clipped the call, and Caddi's questions went unheard.

Claire paused, turned and looked back toward the house, except for the roof and chimneys, obscured by the hill she'd just walked down. She turtled her neck into her parka, hand still clutching the silent phone. She saluted Daisy with her free hand, middle finger up. A long way off, she thought she heard someone cutting wood with a chainsaw. She knew it was just over three miles to the nearest neighbor's house, and she marveled at how well sounds carried over the frozen ground. She wondered if she could walk there in such deep snow.

Inside, Chuck Bakken unlocked his gun case. He'd heard and seen enough.

Chapter Twenty-five

*. . . and visitors, meaning well, do come
calling at the oddest of moments, though
the beds be unmade, the floors unswept,
and dirty dishes stacked in the sink.*

EMMA WAS STARTLED AWAKE WHEN SHE FELT A
warm nose nuzzle her cheek. The Airedale's golden-
brown eyes were so close and large it seemed as if the
morning sun itself caressed her. The dog stepped back,
stretched and bowed, playfully wagging its upright stub
of tail. She reached out with a gentle paw, rested it on
the blanket. There was no threat in her eyes, only unre-
strained curiosity—the in-your-face hummingbird of
canines. Kali had never encountered a grounded red-
tail before, and a two-headed one wrapped in a horse
blanket was especially intriguing. Hoping to stir up a
reaction, she took a step back, dancing a canine version
of Michael Jackson's slick slide moves.

Emma shifted her weight to face the dog more
squarely. Her talons were buried deep under the horse
blanket, useless. She stared silently.

Kali's black nose quivered. It was covered in scars from
other less successful bouts of curiosity, but she didn't
seem to mind. Airedales are seldom prone to grudges,
willing to forgive all but the meanest of transgressions.

A young boy's impatient voice from the rear of the barn called. "Kali. Let's go. It's freezing in here. C'mon, girl."

Kali turned her head toward the summons, but curiosity in Airedales is a stronger force than obedience. She nosed the bundle again, eager to make friends. She tilted her head, and thought things over, patiently waiting for a cheerful response. Took another dance step.

Emma read the friendly nature of the dog's advances, and remained calm. Except for her sturdy beak she was defenseless. She realized she and Ms. Ride were in a helpless situation, at the mercy of the dog's good nature, and not much to be done about it. Knowing nothing of the dog's language she opted for silence, hoping for the best.

Light footsteps approached and a flashlight's yellowish beam caught the dog from behind, casting a proud dog's silhouette on the rough barn wall. "What have you found, girl?" the boy asked. "Another dead rat? Ugh. Leave it. They're full of fleas."

Kali turned, eyes alight, tongue lolling. Her keen sense of smell had already catalogued the bundled discovery and shelved the pertinent information for later investigation. The light-hearted dog bounded past the boy, almost knocking him over.

"Wait up you lousy mutt," the boy called. He pulled up the collar of his jacket, switched off the flashlight and hurried after, paying not a whit of attention to the pair of red-tails, packaged on the cold dirt floor. A moment later, except for the faint sounds of two horses nosing fresh hay, the cavernous barn fell silent again.

Emma poked her head out of the wrap and looked about. "Ms. Ride," Emma said, "are you awake?" There was no answer. "We've had visitors. Friendly enough." She stretched her neck and swiveled her head toward the barn door, gaping wide. A heavy and dark gloom brought early shadows to the entrance, distorting the time of day. "Owen will be back soon," Emma said, trying to engage Ms. Ride's sleeping mind. "I'm sure of it." She sighed. "Please don't die, Ms. Ride. We all love you and need you—you are the potter who shapes us."

In the distance, a woman's voice called out. "Jake! Lunch is ready."

Emma settled herself next to Ms. Ride. She closed her eyes. "Hurry, Owen," she whispered. Her eyes flickered open and she giggled. *Glad that dog was such a marshmallow. Not a mean bone in her body.*

Just as darkness fell an oversized crow fluttered to the ground near the barn's entrance. He craned his neck as if to see something inside of great interest. He kept his beak clamped shut, and took a tentative step; making a quick survey he bobbed his head several times. He had already inspected the fence line where so many of his clan had died the day before and was wary of the potential danger inside the barn. He hopped forward two or three times like a child at play on a brightly chalked sidewalk. He turned his head upward, bobbed it up and down again. A moment later three others settled themselves beside him. Trafalgar had selected them from fifty volunteers for their superior size and famously nasty dispositions.

They formed up, a black-feathered pack; their red eyes pierced the deepening gloom as the weak sun slid even farther west. They peered into the barn's gloom, searching for their target.

On the porch, Kali was sound asleep, curled tightly to ward off the chill. The porch's roof above, and the side of the house helped mute the cold and wind, but late October nights still tested the Airedale's thick fur coat. Even as she napped, her black nose quivered, monitoring a thousand scents—sorting, cataloging, and comparing; her folded ears twitched at each whispered sound. One ear told her Jacob was upstairs playing a video game while his younger brother, Oscar, was taking a shower. Kali's other ear sifted out a blend of TV advertising from the living room, and the hissing dishwasher in the kitchen.

Her eyes opened. In half a second she stood at full alert. Kali was not only a family guard and protector, but also a sentry to the world. She stood motionless, her starched tail trembling with anticipation over her back.

She faced the barn, but her eyes told her nothing; she leaned forward, all senses on high alert. A deep growl came to her throat; she bounded from the porch and raced lickity-split across the yard.

Just as Trafalgar's beak clamped on Emma's throat, Kali was upon him. A bird's bones are hollow, strong, but of necessity, light weight to allow for flight. Kali's powerful jaws engulfed the crow and with one shake of her head, Trafalgar's ribs were crushed and the heir to the Sioux Falls crow clan went limp, dispatched beyond life's uncertain boundary. Kali spit him out on the floor and turned back.

As instructed, the other three crows had mobbed Chawla Ride, but she was packed so deep within the folds of the horse blanket, and they so clumsy in their attack, they had not yet gotten to her eyes. They were oblivious to the fact their ruthless leader was already dead; Death, in turn, now courted them.

A bird's wings grant flight, their greatest defense; but these cutthroats, so eager to steal Chawla's vision, had their wings furled tight to their bodies. Easy prey. Each became feathery fodder for Kali's snapping jaws. In the back of the barn two horses glanced nervously over the stall's railing at the hideous sound of cracking bones.

Emma lay gasping for breath in the dirt, somewhat shaken but not seriously hurt. Kali's tongue darted out, found Emma's wounded throat. She administered a quick lick or two of a dog's standard all-purpose saliva balm. A moment later she grasped Emma's body in her tender jaws as she would her own newborn puppy; she placed Emma next to Chawla Ride and did her best to cover them both with the blanket. Not a word had been spoken, their languages too different for useful communication, but nonetheless each understood the significance of what had just happened—two racing hearts momentarily beating as one.

Satisfied she had done all her tribe commands of her, Kali turned away and returned to her post. She deposited the crows outside the barn, four lifeless heaps for the rats and ants to consider at their leisure. Kali settled herself with a contented sigh. Monitoring began anew.

Chapter Twenty-six

> *. . . sometimes amazing things occur,*
> *almost impossible to comprehend, but*
> *never discount the possibility of coinci-*
> *dences or miracles.*

DESPITE HER WORRIES ABOUT TRESPASSING ON
private property, Kate had calmed herself with the
knowledge they were on a rescue mission; sometimes
to save others, rules had to be bent. They had passed by
several isolated farmhouses, but Liam had given them all
a wide berth before swinging back to the original course.
An hour later they stopped at the crest of a small rise for
Liam to recheck the map and get fresh GPS readings.
Kate retrieved her cell phone and they got out to stretch
their legs. Overhead, blue sky radiated here and there,
though dark clouds lingered to the north.

Liam unfolded the map, shared it with her. "There's
a tiny town called Blunt just a few miles ahead," he said.
"I know we have to hurry, but most likely there'll be at
least one restaurant. We can eat a quick lunch there."

"I've been to Blunt," Kate said. "I think we ate at the
Medicine Creek Bar and Grill. I was in high school
and my science class was on a field trip. I remember a
humongous pile of fries and really good cheeseburgers."

"Now we're talking," Liam said. He took off his gloves
and refolded the map. "The river is about fifteen miles
past Blunt. That's going to be a problem."

"What do you mean?" Kate asked.

"Well, if we stay on the hawks' flight path, we'll be stuck at the river's edge. The only bridges are quite far south or north. We'll have to decide what to do when we get there."

A half hour later they crossed Highway 14 where it jogs south toward Pierre. Blunt, from Main Street to Freeland Avenue, had been ploughed earlier that morning. Though traffic was even more sparse than usual, a few cars were parked in front of the restaurant. Five or six men were scattered about at small tables and the counter; they glanced up from their coffee and newspapers when Kate and Liam walked in; a smiling waitress with an armful of plates called, "Hi, kids. Sit anywhere you please."

They gladly shed their coats, basking in the indoor warmth. Liam settled into a padded booth against the sidewall while Kate hurried off to the toilet.

When she returned, Liam had covered the table with his map. "We've got a problem. The Missouri River and Lake Oahe are straight ahead, and if we follow the route the hawks flew there's no way across. No bridges. No ferry."

"There's a bridge at Pierre," Kate said. "I've crossed there several times."

"True," Liam replied, "But, to make it work we'd have to swing south from here, and if the hawks went down between here and the river we'll miss them."

"Or," Kate said, "we can track them from here out to the river, and if we still haven't found them, then turn south to Pierre, cross the bridge and pick up their flight on the other side."

Liam smiled, pleased with her positive attitude. "Good plan, but going clear out to the river and then down to

Pierre will take a couple of extra hours at least. Remember, I promised I'd have the truck back by tonight and I don't want to miss any school unless we really have to."

The waitress, pad in hand, appeared. "I'm Debbie. Are you ready?" she asked.

Kate ordered for both of them. "Two cheeseburgers with onions, two fries, one chocolate and one strawberry shake." She looked at Liam. "Did I forget anything?"

Liam laughed. "Sounds like enough for an army, but maybe I could handle a bowl of chili too."

The waitress smiled down at Liam. "I'll have that right out for you, sergeant. If you think of anything else give me a holler. Just so you know, we've got warm, just baked this morning rhubarb pie if you're still hungry later." She slid her pen and pad in apron slots with practiced hands, and turned toward the kitchen.

Liam pointed at the map. "I'm thinking the hawk community is already searching between Dupree and the other side of the river. All those missing students have moms, dads, aunts and uncles—older brothers and sisters. They're bound to be worried. They won't sit around and wait. I'll bet the hawks have already formed a search party and are headed our way."

Before Kate could reply, a tall, well-dressed man approached their booth. He held a coffee cup in one hand. "Are you kids riding the snow mobile parked out front?" he asked.

Liam looked up and smiled. "Yes, sir. Why do you ask?"

"Just wondering where you're from. We don't get many visitors here in Blunt, especially after blizzards. Town is even emptier than usual."

"We're college students from Brookings. We camped out last night near Mac's Corner and our route took us just a hair north of town. We needed some lunch."

The man extended his hand first to Liam, then to Kate. "I'm Dave Evans, minister up at the United Methodist Church. You didn't come all the way from Brookings just for lunch did you?"

Kate spoke up. "Probably sounds crazy, but we're trying to help some young red-tail hawks. Their flight school took part in a flying competition last Friday and Saturday in Sioux Falls. We're not sure of the exact time, but last Sunday morning they left Sioux Falls and flew toward Dupree where they live. Far as we know, they never made it home."

"I've heard of Dupree. My wife went to college with the school librarian there. I think her name was Gay, or maybe Fay, not sure. How many hawks are you talking about?"

"It's the entire junior class and their teacher. I guess thirty or so, give or take. Not exactly sure."

"And you think they flew over Blunt?"

Liam put a finger on the map where he'd plotted the course. "Not exactly over where we're sitting, but no more than a quarter mile north of here. We don't know for sure, but we think they flew a straight line between Sioux Falls and Dupree."

"Let me think," the minister said, a thoughtful, bemused look on his face. "Mind if I sit down a minute?"

Kate scooted over and the man slid in beside her. "Our United Methodist and the Trinity church are both located just five blocks north of here on Lone Tree Street." He turned and pointed a long arm in the general direction out the large front window.

"Last Sunday, as usual, I was getting ready to begin my sermon to about fifteen of Blunt's faithful. It started snowing real early Sunday morning and the roads were already getting a bit slippery. Before I start my sermon I always take my wristwatch off and lay it beside my notes on the lectern so I don't run on too long. Blunt people only stay faithful for about twenty minutes' worth of sermon. Any longer, they start drifting on me or get real fidgety."

He let out a deep, hearty laugh and his eyes sparkled with considerable understanding of human nature. "Well, we'd already sung a hymn or two and read some scripture, so it was time for me to divulge a smattering of truth about the world we live in and how we South Dakota folk might best deal with it."

The waitress returned carrying a large tray of plates. Liam quickly folded up the map while Debbie dished out the food. She paused a minute to make sure the order was correct. "Anything else then?" she asked.

"I could use a warm up," the minister said, holding out his coffee cup.

"Be right back, Dave," she said. She turned and walked quickly toward the counter, a journey to the coffee pot so familiar she could have closed her eyes and made it safely.

The minister said, "Go ahead and eat. Don't worry about me. I ate lunch a half hour ago at home with my kids. Roads are all closed between here and Pierre so they didn't have to go off to school."

The waitress returned and expertly poured a long stream of steaming coffee.

"Thanks, Debbie," he said. "How's your mom getting on?"

"She's poorly, but if they ever clear the highway I'm going to take her to see a specialist over to Pierre. Doc Cole says there's nothing more he can do, and if they can't help her at the hospital we should go ahead and contact hospice." A deep sigh escaped her throat. "We were supposed to go yesterday, but we couldn't get through. There's at least three feet of snow on the ground out by our place. Kenny brought me in to work this morning on the tractor." She laughed. "Both of us darn near froze to death."

The two college students listened quietly to a pastor comforting one of his own while they eagerly consumed some fine small town burgers and fries.

Just then the cook's bell dinged, notifying everyone in the restaurant another plate of food was ready. A "hash up" call from the kitchen sealed the envelope. Debbie turned to go.

"I'll be praying for you and your family, and the road crews," Dave said, touching her hand.

"Thanks," she said. "'Preciate it." She hurried away, an important job to do, faithful in so many more ways than one.

The minister sipped his coffee, warmed his hands, considered. He waited until the plates were almost bare, understanding better than most when silence is golden.

Liam finished first. Reached across the table and hijacked a fist full of Kate's fries. Too late, Kate reacted by covering her plate with her hand.

"Keep away, you," she said.

"Dang good burger," he said. "Fries too."

The minister smiled at the young travelers. "I was getting ready to launch into my sermon when I happened to glance out the side window. I could see the snow had started up, coming down crazy and beating against the windows. Most of these folks live quite a-ways out of town and I was concerned they'd have trouble getting home, you know, the roads becoming impassable.

"They're used to snow of course. Everybody around here is, but not in October, and not driven by such a strong wind. Storm took us all by surprise. Some didn't even have winter coats with 'em, just sweaters or light jackets. I decided the best sermon I could deliver was to send 'em home, so I just said a short prayer for safe travel, and out they went."

Debbie meandered by with the coffee pot searching out empty cups. Liam raised his hand to get her attention. "I'll try a piece of rhubarb pie, if there's any left."

"You betcha," she said. "Coming right up." She started to pour another "warm" for the minister, but he covered the cup with his hand before she could deliver the heat.

"Normally," he said, "we serve coffee and pastries downstairs in our Friendship Room right after church, but all that was cancelled. My wife Gloria unplugged the coffee pot and we put everything away. By the time we got to the parking lot everyone had already vamoosed. It was snowing huge flakes and the wind was blowing darn near sideways. We were walking toward our car when I heard a rustling sound and a shadow above caught my eye. I looked up, and right over our heads flew an arrowhead.

"I've seen lots of geese flying in a V, but these weren't long-necked honkers heading south for the winter. They were hawks for sure, big birds, gray and brown, with autumn maple leaf red tail feathers. They were flying tight to each other in perfect formation, headed west. Reminded me of those Navy planes, the Blue Angels. I saw them perform once up in Seattle jetting over Lake Washington when I was still in seminary.

"When we got in our car I asked my wife, 'What were those?' 'I believe they were ducks,' she said." He laughed. "Gloria's not much on wildlife identification."

Debbie reappeared, delivered a huge piece of pie to Liam, and gave the coffee pot a questioning wave at the pastor. He declined again, using his hand as a cup cover.

"Thank you much," Liam said. "Reminds me of my mom's pie."

"Won't be as good as your mom's," Debbie said, "but it'll be a close second. Nobody's pie is as good as mom's. One thing the waitressing business has taught me—pie, meatloaf, potato salad, you name it. Mom's is always better."

Liam laughed and forked a bite in. "Yum. Good pie. Tart."

Darla wandered off in search of another coffee cup. Kate had slowed, but was still working her French fries.

Dave sipped cold dregs, grinned over the cup's rim. "I think Gloria knows the difference between a turkey and a hummingbird, but she's pretty iffy on most other birds. I let that one weakness slide though because she bakes the best cornbread in all of South Dakota. Those were definitely hawks flying in formation right over our heads. When I first glanced up, with the snowflakes banging against my eyes, I though I'd seen a . . ."

He cleared his throat and in a powerful tenor sang:

*Then I hear a voice from heaven
saying "Pilgrim it is I
Lift your head and take new courage,
lift your eyes toward the sky."
And I see a great band of angels . . .*

The restaurant fell silent, as if all sounds but the pastor's rich voice had been sucked out the chimney; some denizens, forks balanced in mid-air, swiveled in their chairs to hear the sweet song better.

"Sorry, folks" he said, with a sheepish grin and wave of his hand. "Music is to us humans as wings are to birds. It allows us to fly higher and straighter than by any other means."

His voice lowered and the restaurant quickly resumed its normal melody of knives, forks, and spoons scraping against crockery, while continued low conversations about football, the weather, troubled knees, hips, and backs resumed where they'd been left off.

"Anyway, that squadron of hawks appeared to be a," he laughed loud and clear, unleashing his marvelous tenor again, *"sweet chariot, coming for to carry me home."*

The restaurant's operation paused again, hoping for more succor against a difficult world. Instead, the minister holstered his voice, sipped gritty coffee. "On tippy toes I almost could have reached up and touched them. I thought for sure they were gonna crash into the steeple, but they swerved at the last instant and sailed right on by."

"I'll bet you anything it was them," Kate said. "Do you remember the time?"

"Church always gets out at noon, but I sent the flock home early. It must have been about eleven thirty or so."

"Just about what we calculated," Kate said. "Now we know for certain they made it this far. How much farther is it to Lake Oahe from here?"

"Couldn't say for sure because there's no road running at an angle toward Dupree the way hawks would fly. I'd guess somewhere between twenty and twenty five miles."

"Is there anything real tall out there they might have crashed into?" Kate asked.

"Not that I know of." He ran thin fingers through his hair. "A few barns, maybe a silo or two, some big ol' oak trees."

He paused. "Wait. I haven't seen it, so I don't know how tall it is, but a few weeks ago someone at church was telling me about a guy who built a wind turbine on his property. Apparently, he didn't bother to get the required building permits or have it inspected or anything; just went ahead and had it built it without telling anybody. His place must be five or six miles from here toward the lake. You might look there."

Liam finished his pie using the edge of his fork to salvage a few crumbs of crust. "Well, all I know is they're still out there somewhere, else they'd been home late Sunday afternoon or early Monday at the worst." He looked at Kate. "If you're done eating, we'd better be on our way. Locate 'em if we can and offer to help."

"If you don't mind," the minister said, "I want to pray for your safe passage." He reached across the table and took Liam's hand in his own. Kate reached out, placed her hand on Liam's, closed her eyes, and focused on the warmth radiating from the precious words.

Chapter Twenty-seven

. . . but rivers do separate people, and mountain ranges the same. Marks drawn in the dirt by men with sharp knives, or paltry stick fences may deny passage, but rain erases such lines, and nature destroys feeble fences. Soon chance encounters, shouted angry words, defiance and confrontations boil over. Maps delineate boundaries, possession, ownership—spilt blood.

THE WIND HAD PICKED UP STILL MORE; A BULLY now, it pummeled Orville from the north, blowing him a hundred yards off course with one savage breath. Dark clouds descended, enveloped him, and forced him low. His Breitling alarm sounded at three hundred feet, but he dove still lower. The temperature had plummeted in the last half hour and his goggles began to ice up; almost sightless, he flew on.

At eighty feet he brushed the top of an oak tree, sending him into a momentary tailspin. He recovered easily enough, but heeded nature's warning and decided to go to ground until the storm passed. A few years earlier as a bachelor, he would have been reckless and flown on, but now he had other responsibilities as a loving husband to Annabelle, and father to Shaw, Delta, and Fofanna; in those roles he always exercised caution, and this time, being prudent, he sought safety.

He had survived many precarious situations in his life, and this storm did not scare him one bit. Orville considered it a mere inconvenience, a hindrance to locating and transporting the remains of his son Owen and the junior class. He took a small measure of comfort in his realization the scavengers would be holed up waiting out the storm too; he felt certain the bodies would not be tampered with.

As soon as he landed he hollowed out a small space for himself at the base of a tree. He dug down until he reached the frozen turf and then laid out his ground tarp and sleeping bag. He took off his goggles, but to keep his head warm he left his helmet on, straps dangling over his shoulders. His roofless shelter was snug enough, out of the wind, and completely invisible to any wandering predators.

He pulled his sleeping bag up to his waist and fished his cell phone out of one of his leather holsters. He attempted to call Annabelle, knowing she would be worried, but the dense snow, gusting wind, and distance between him and the nearest cell tower overpowered the signal and would not connect his call.

He emptied out the other holster and discovered the peanut butter and jelly sandwich Annabelle had packed just in case of such a situation. He smiled widely. "Thanks, babe," he said. "Knew I could count on you for a special treat."

He ate the sandwich and a small pile of Raptor Flight Mix. Satisfied there was nothing more to be done until the storm abated, he lay back, pulled the sleeping bag up over his shoulders and arranged his holsters as a make-shift pillow.

Within seconds, heavy fatigue pulled him under. His sorrow fetched a time when Owen, hatched just six weeks earlier, without hesitation, had leaped from the railing of their deck into space. Orville and Annabelle, their hearts swelling with pride, had watched his brave young wings catch their first air, glide, circle back, and safely land; a wry grin had stretched Owen's beak and brought new fire to his eyes; he was so very pleased with himself.

Owen flew low and fast, a feathered bowstring stretched taut against time and distance. He ignored the unbroken white terrain below, monotonous in its simplicity of structure and color. He was certain his classmates had returned home Sunday evening and Rowdy had told the story of Ms. Ride's injury and how Owen and Emma had gone back to assist their teacher. He was positive his father would retrace their route until he came upon them—in Owen's mind, an absolute certainty. It was late Tuesday morning, a time for youthful optimism.

Food and sleep had restored his strength and he flew at a steady forty-two, close to his maximum speed. The wind, a light breeze, was neither a pushing helper nor a balky hindrance. He passed just north of Mac's Corner and out of the corner of his eye caught a fleeting vision of a gleaming church steeple highlighted by the morning sun. Though he was not religious in the same sense many humans are, nonetheless, the empty cross, a symbol of hope, seemed to lift his spirits even higher.

About forty minutes later he passed directly over a churning snowmobile with two figures hunched inside, his tiny shadow swallowed by the noisy machine; he thought nothing of it, a common enough sight in the winter months.

Two miles ahead and slightly off course, he caught sight of a towering structure. He didn't perceive it as a menace, just a curious object easily avoided. He glanced at the altimeter on his watch, pegged at three hundred feet; with the weather clearing, he climbed to four hundred-fifty feet and leveled off. Three minutes later, at a mile out, he became aware of a large home and a slender human, surely a woman in shape and grace, walking slowly across the landscape. On the home's front steps stood another, much larger figure, hands on hips, a pose of anger, or perhaps, disrespect.

Owen saw them before he heard their motors. An enormous drone, maxed out at sixty miles per hour, came at him from slightly above. Another drone sped from the right at the same altitude and speed. Though Owen had not been trained in drone warfare, their aggressive action toward him set off an ancient self-preservation alarm in his brain. His ancestors, from the beginning of time, built the foundation of their (and now his) DNA on two crucial principles: anticipate danger before it sees you, and react to it before it reacts to you. Two attacking eagles or a pair of owls would have triggered the same instantaneous reaction. With a simple flick of his wingtips he rolled into a standard corkscrew dive and easily avoided what might have been a catastrophic collision. The drones sailed harmlessly by, missing each other by the narrowest of margins.

In passing, Owen observed the drones carried weapons of some sort. He thought he heard projectiles whizzing by.

Untouched, he corkscrewed down, leveling out at one hundred feet, the altitude alarm on his watch beeping furiously. From his meager lunchtime reading in the school library's collection of advanced technology manuals, he knew these machines were human directed, and therein lay their weaknesses—human courage and fear cancelled each other out—attacking without restraint or joy, nor heart or soul—driven by mere electrical impulses from afar.

Twenty seconds later they were on him from the rear, and a third drone dove from high above. Owen was impressed by the drones' acceleration and speed capabilities, but sensed their maneuverability and reaction time was far less than his own.

A heartbeat before the three drones converged at the killing point, Owen stiffened his tail feathers into a Samurai's Fist, flared his wings hard against his forward progress, stalled, and dropped three feet in an eye-blink. There was a sharp ting of metal striking metal as one of the drone's landing apparatus clipped another drone, shearing off one of its four rotors and sending both into unbalanced, unrecoverable spins.

Another one bites the dust, Owen thought, smiling inwardly. Following his training, Owen dropped his head to regain speed, and after a precipitous Elevator Cable Snap of one hundred feet, he pulled out of the stall and immediately went into a vertical climb. He saw momentary puffs of powdery snow where his foes crashed. He allowed himself a moment of satisfaction and his eyes behind his goggles lit up and his beak opened wide into a wry hawk's grin.

A fleeting memory came to him then—a philosophical question Ms. Ride had once presented to the class as the topic of an essay: Why do humans sometimes kill what they do not eat? Owen sensed the man directing the drones from his lookout post on the steps would not have eaten him had his drones been successful in the kill. Then why bother? His presence did not harm the man in any way. The man did not own the sky above his home. The sky, to Owen, was a limitless gift for all to use as a pathway to life.

Owen felt a twinge of guilt when he realized he had killed many crows recently, crows he had no intention of eating. He remonstrated against himself for breaking one of the sacred pillars binding and directing the red-tail hawk community—*take no life unless thy stomach demands it*. This violation stung him now, leaving him with an uncomfortable feeling of uncertainty. This was, to Owen, a terrible mis-step down a dark path he did not care to follow.

Owen noticed the man standing on the steps, almost directly beneath him, head tilted far back, dark eyes staring. The man raised his rifle, wasted a single harmless bullet. He might as well have thrown a stone at the moon. He leaned his weapon against the porch railing and punched his cell phone, calling off his guard dogs lest he lose them all to a lion of the sky. Popeye and Scout's mid-air collision had cost Chuck Bakken just over twenty-four thousand dollars.

Owen flew on.

. . . and stored deep within human nature is the need to spin stories, to explain the day at the dinner table or around the campfire. If exaggeration or embellishment twists the tale, no harm has been done. What, pray tell, is the lowly hotdog without mustard and onions?

OWEN HAD JUST CROSSED LAKE OAHE, PASSING directly over a popular fishing and hunting resort called Pike Haven when he recognized the shape of an oncoming red-tail hawk at one mile out. At a thousand yards his heart leaped with joy at the sight of a goggled face. In all of South Dakota only two red-tails—he and his father—wore goggles.

A shrill cry of greeting, *Kyreee,* flew across the remaining space as father and son quickly closed the distance. At approach, Orville slowed almost to a stall and opened his wings wide to embrace Owen in a gentle chest-to-chest collision. In an instant they were falling, unable to sustain flight, delirious with family love, a cherished son returned from the dead. They began a wobbly spiral, half a second ticked by, and a quarter of another, their speed accelerating—almost unmanageable.

Orville opened his wings, pushed Owen away and dropped his head; he gained even more speed as he hurtled downward; fifty feet off the ground he forced his wings open, caught air, pulled out of the fall. Owen mimicked his father's acrobatic move, escaped Splatsville, an English slangy term most young red-tails use to describe catastrophic collisions with the ground; the two climbed side by side before leveling out at four hundred fifty feet.

They banked in unison, moving into a slow and wide circle. Orville moved his goggles to his neck—a gush of tears had fogged them, rendering them useless.

"Where are the others?" he asked, his wingtip brushing Owen's as if to reassure himself his son was actually alive. "We must go there to secure the graveyard."

"What do you mean, graveyard?" Owen's voice reflected genuine surprise. "Aren't they home yet?"

Orville's eyes widened. "Of course not. Higgins and I came upon Quinn yesterday. He told us all are dead and only he survived. Why would he say such a thing if not true?"

For a moment Owen could not speak. He turned his head toward his father. "Dead? They're all dead?" He shook his head in disbelief. "No. I don't believe it."

"Were you not there to see it with your own eyes?" his father asked, his voice incredulous. "Were you not flying in formation?"

The questions stunned Owen. For a long moment he could not speak, then in a halting voice he began to explain. "Ms. Ride was injured and she could not keep up. She assigned Rowdy to point, while she trailed behind as best she could. The snow was so thick . . . and the wind, at first in our faces out of the west; then it badgered us from the north, and drove us sideways, pushing us, swirling left, then right, always a headwind. Dark clouds forced Rowdy to fly low . . ."

Owen faltered, and was suddenly bludgeoned with grief; the stark realization his classmates had perished began to seep in. "Papa. Rowdy was my best friend," he said, his voice a whisper.

"How did you escape the turbine's blades?" Orville asked. "Quinn told us he alone survived."

"Emma." A fresh wail of anguish escaped Owen's beak. "She and I started the flight in row two, and then, after the first rotation, Oliver and Gabe replaced us. Emma and I dropped back and flew the left and right flank at rear guard. While making the rotation Emma realized Ms. Ride was no longer in sight. Emma flew up to point, conferred with Rowdy, and he gave Emma and me permission to fly back to locate and help Ms. Ride. He told us to search, and if we could not find her we should rejoin the formation immediately, at our own peril."

Father and son flew in silence then, stitching the air with lazy wings. "And you never made it back to the group?"

"We flew nearly eight miles retracing the exact way we had just come. We didn't see her."

"Then your teacher must be dead too," Orville said. "She could not survive the cold and predators alone for two days. I'm sorry you could not save her."

Owen swiveled in the air so he could see his father's face. "Papa, the outcome has not yet been decided. Emma had promised Rowdy we would turn back after fifteen minutes and rejoin the formation. We know our ultimate responsibility is always to the group, and yet we could not bear to leave Ms. Ride to die alone. Because of the gloom caused by low cloud cover, the swirling wind, and thick snow, we felt we must have overlooked her. So we decided to return to the formation by scraping the earth at twenty feet above ground. We were certain Ms. Ride was down."

"You were brave to fly so low. Many expert flyers have died attempting such flights."

"We were lucky, Papa." Quickly Owen explained how they had discovered their teacher and what must have happened to her.

"Did the crows attack you too? Your feathers seem ragged and torn, especially those about your face and neck."

"The three of us spent the night out of the storm, hidden in a nearby barn. In the morning, I went back to search for Ms. Ride's cell phone; her holster was missing when we found her. I knew everyone would be worried when we did not return with the others. If we found the phone we could call you for help to transport Ms. Ride to Doc Higgins' clinic. When I returned to the spot where we found Ms. Ride I was immediately set upon by a cowardly pack of crows. *'Take his eyes'* they screamed. *'Rip out his eyes.'* I fought as you and grandfather taught me, but still they pinned me down. Emma heard their bloody shrieks and joined the battle; she fought with great skill and fury, saving me at the last moment."

Owen's eyes filled while revisiting the memory. "Ms. Ride taught us revenge is never allowed in a red-tail's heart, but I was so furious I killed their leader as she tried to escape. Forgive me, Papa. I have dishonored myself and our family." Owen, unable to meet his father's eyes, hung his head in shame.

"If our adversary has no honor, why should we?" Orville said. "It's true we pledge to kill only for food or self-defense, but you are not the first of our tribe, nor will you be the last, to eliminate a ruthless leader. Well done. Your bravery makes me proud."

"Emma was a tigress, Papa. She saved me from certain blindness or death."

The story out, silence prevailed; Orville's mind reeled under the full realization of the tragedy as it had unfolded, and what must be done about it. At last he said, "We must first locate the sacred ground where your classmates have fallen. It is our duty to protect their remains. Once we land there I'll call for help. Then we must go to Ms. Ride. I'll call Doc Walters in Dupree and he will advise me of her care."

"Blood has caused pressure in her brain, Papa. I have read of it online."

"Doc Walters will know the remedy. Perhaps her life can still be saved."

"I flew near the turbine just twenty minutes ago," Owen said. "It sits about four hundred yards south of our flight path. No matter how hard he tried, Rowdy could not keep true in such powerful winds."

"No one will blame Rowdy," Orville said. "He will always be a red-tail hero, one who led and navigated in impossible conditions. In our community his name will live forever."

"He was so strong, Papa. It is certain he was unmatched in our class. No one could keep up with Rowdy Gowdy. I will miss him forever."

"Not just Rowdy. We've lost so many precious young flyers," Orville said. "Each was unique and we mourn them all."

"Danger is thick at the killing site," Owen said. "We must be vigilant. Drones patrol the property. They attacked me as I passed by, but are mindless machines, and easily avoided. Two of them crashed trying to kill me. Their owner fired his gun at me even though I did nothing to provoke him."

Orville lowered his goggles, came out of the circle, and headed southeast, Owen tight beside him. They checked the coordinates and accelerated to thirty-two, then forty, a speed comfortable to both. Orville turned his head, spoke loudly to his son. "Humans are the most unpredictable and dangerous of all creatures. They are worse even than badgers. We red-tails cannot fathom nor underestimate such a man's actions."

Profound grief causes heavy hearts, weary wings, and muddy minds—opposites of what is necessary for successful flight. Their spirits, though, were buoyed by a desperate need to save a treasured teacher. Father and son raced hard over dark water.

*. . . and money will destroy a man's mind
faster than rat poison. Greed's bounty
comes cheap.*

CLAIRE HEARD THE RIFLE SHOT A MILE BEHIND
her. She glanced back toward the house, her quickened breath, a cumulus cloud before her face. But she
was low on the hill now, her view obstructed. Past the
lazy blades of the turbine her eye caught movement: a
large bird flying past. *Why is Bakken even outside? He
detests the cold.*

Daisy hovered not fifteen feet away, red power-
light blinking, its camera staring, and tiny microphone
recording every sound. Frightened, Claire quickened
her pace, slipped on the glazed tire track, lost her balance and fell hard on her bottom. She glanced over her
shoulder at Daisy, and wondered if Bakken was monitoring her by cellphone; or had he returned to his den, and
stationed himself in front of his monitors?

She scrambled to her feet, her breathing erratic, a
cold sweat glazing her neck. She forced herself into a
slow jog; fearful of slipping again, the jog became more
of a shuffling trot. It was still a quarter mile to the road.
She surveyed the landscape for a hiding place, her mind
reeling, but she knew as long as Daisy followed there
could be no hidden shelter.

Predators focus their senses to notice minimal changes in the environment—the slightest muscle twitch or sound amid dead stillness signals prey. Daisy transmitted Claire's anxious eye blinks, the jiggling tassel on her wool cap, and the raspy sound of her labored breathing back to the watcher.

Just a week earlier, she and Bakken had had a heated argument about Claire's supposed frivolous spending. A brown UPS truck had appeared in their driveway with an Amazon order of ten books. The driver, a young man sporting a friendly grin, had popped out of the truck as if his legs were spring loaded. Dressed in the familiar dark brown shorts, matching company shirt, wool socks and high-topped black boots, he looked more the Swiss hiker than an industrious deliveryman. Bakken stopped him at the bottom step of the entry deck with a cold stare and upraised hand. "Are you blind?" he asked, his voice bathed in a stinking broth of insult.

The youthful alpinist stopped in his tracks, cheerful smile fading to a look of faint surprise. "What do you mean?" he asked.

"You just drove a mile and a half on private property up a road clearly marked with no trespassing signs. Can't you read English?"

"Just doing my job, sir. I was told to deliver this box to the front door of this address." He placed the box gently on the bottom step. Didn't mean to trespass."

"Next time I'll shoot your dumb ass. Get the hell off my property."

Inside the house Bakken had ripped open the box and inspected the bill. "You charged two hundred and seventeen dollars for ten lousy books?" he yelled at Claire.

"Are you crazy? Did the library in Blunt burn down? Am I so rich you can throw money away on books that can be had for free?" He glared at Claire as if she had just given away one of their cars.

Claire forced herself to stay calm. "I intend to pay for them myself." She challenged him with an enigmatic smile. "Books are my refuge. They are my only pleasure."

She lifted her chin—for the first time openly defiant—locked eyes. "The library in Blunt is tiny and the books are few. And," she paused for emphasis, "I definitely don't need your money, Mr. Cheapskate. I've plenty of my own."

Her words bit, a scorpion's sting to his ego. "I'll give you your refuge and pleasure," he roared, his face purple with rage. He grabbed the stack of books and threw them underhanded into the fireplace, one by one, as if he were pitching horseshoes at a family picnic. Glowing embers from the morning fire quickly crinkled the covers, turned them brown, then black, before igniting in orange flame and slowly consuming them.

She had turned and ran out the front door without pausing to grab even a jacket. When she reached the driveway she gasped for breath, blinded by angry tears. *How could I have married such a man? I've made the worst mistake of my life. How, oh how, could I have been so stupid?*

She had jogged on, tears flowing, a quarter mile downhill toward the turbine before slowing to a walk, her breathing ragged. Daisy, as always, had stalked her from above, a black and gray oversized mantis. Without thinking, Claire stooped, picked up an egg-sized rock and hurled a fastball at the buzzing pest.

"Go away!" she screamed. The rock missed its mark, sailing harmlessly by. Overwhelmed, she covered her face with her hands and sobbed, sank to her knees. Daisy—ever vigilant, unfeeling—did not retreat.

Twenty minutes later Claire had reached the county road leading to Blunt. On a whim she decided to walk to the nearest neighbors' home, people she had never met. To her surprise, Daisy flew to the point where the driveway joined the road, abruptly stopped and had not followed. She guessed Bakken had programmed the drone to fly only as far as the property line. For the first time in several months Claire felt free and safe.

Forty-five minutes later, she was standing in the kitchen of Karl and Elsa Soderberg's home.

They had greeted her warmly, as one of their own. Elsa, in her late seventies, softly round-faced and bodied, had hugged Claire and sat her down at the kitchen table; pleased at having company, she offered coffee and fresh made zucchini bread, still warm from the oven.

Karl, at eighty-one, a tall raw-boned farmer of ancient Swedish stock, sat quietly across from Claire. Not one to intrude, he sipped coffee from a big mug and nibbled at his wife's zucchini bread, listening. Finally, he asked, "Did you walk all the way from your place? Must be a good three miles from here."

"I did," Claire replied. "We've driven past your place many times and . . ." She paused, searched for the right words. "Well, I just wanted to stop in and meet you. I get so lonely sometimes." She smiled, trying to disguise the despair in her eyes.

"I knew your husband's father, Bud Bakken," Karl said. "He and I went to school together. Then he went off to college in Chicago, and never came back."

He glanced at Elsa. "Bud reeked of arrogance. Thought he was too smart to farm like us bumpkins. Bud's mother, your husband's grandmother, lived into her nineties. Real nice lady. She died quite some time ago and the place has been empty ever since. Happens a lot around here. Kids and grandkids don't want to farm no more. Rather work at Starbucks or run a computer in Pierre."

"Are you from Chicago?" Elsa asked. She wondered about the hurt stored in her neighbor's face. Didn't seem proper to ask.

"No," Claire said. "I was raised just outside Seattle in a small village on the banks of a slow moving, do nothing slough of a river. Grew up there, went to college, and worked at Boeing as an engineer for a little over twenty years. Now I'm here." She paused, unsure if she should say more.

Karl stood up. He carried his plate and cup to the sink. "You girls have a nice gab. I've got some animals to look after. Let me know when you're ready to go home. Elsa and I'll run you down in my truck. Too far to walk." He patted her shoulder, neighborly. "Real nice meeting you, Claire. Never met a Seattle girl before."

An hour later Claire was let out at the mailbox. Karl had wanted to drive her up the driveway to the house, but she'd insisted she wanted to walk from there. *Need the exercise,* she'd said. Karl turned his pick-up around in the driveway. Claire stood in the road, lingered, and waved goodbye.

A moment later Daisy appeared and escorted her up the long driveway.

Claire followed Bakken's tire tracks in the deep snow; the rifle shot behind her had renewed her fear and she forced herself to jog as fast as possible. She could see the county road now, less than one hundred yards away. In the distance behind her she caught the faint, deep-throated growl of Bakken's Range Rover starting up. Fear caught in her throat, restricted her normal breathing. *If only I could get to the main road and out of Daisy's sight, I might find a hiding place.*

The day she had walked to the Soderberg's she had noticed a small culvert passing under the road, allowing a tiny creek to flow uninterrupted down the slope.

At the road, heart pounding, thighs on fire, she glanced over her shoulder. Bakken's Rover was still out of sight. She knew he often stopped while driving to toy with his cell. A cry of helpless terror escaped her lips, cutting through the still air. An evenly spaced line of trees, planted a hundred years earlier as a windbreak by Bakken's grandfather helped obscure her from the drive-way. Another glance over her shoulder told her Daisy was stalled at the property line. The culvert loomed, a small dark opening to a tunnel in the white landscape.

She ran another twenty yards before veering off the road through shin deep snow; she lost her balance and tumbled, rolling down the embankment. On hands and knees she crawled through the accumulated snow toward the sound of small water gathering, snow falling in on itself, drips joining, a million tiny rivulets joining hands to become one.

The culvert was so small she was forced to crouch low; she straddled the main flow, her legs quivering; the gurgle of water sounds multiplied and mingled with her gasps for air. Dim light added to the desperate cacophony.

. . . and adrenalin, that magical "fight or flight" elixir concocted by the body's endocrine system, stimulates action—to face the danger and fight for life—or get turned around and scoot the other direction.

JUST LEAVING BLUNT. HP TO FND HAWKS SOON. Am safe. Kate squinted at the cell's screen in the brilliant sunshine; she hit the send button, and slid the phone into the back pocket of her jeans. Optimistic their journey was nearing the end, and strengthened by the meal, she pulled the helmet over her head, and snugged it down. The Yamaha's roar reverberated down Blunt's narrow street, glancing off brick storefronts and surging around parked cars. The minister smiled and raised a slender fare-thee-well hand from the sidewalk as Liam maneuvered away from the curb.

For the first time in three days the skies had cleared and the temperature was climbing. The clouds had divided and fled, leaving crystal clear blue sky and blinding light. Everywhere, snow lost its grip and dripped incessantly. The street's gutters sang a cheerless melody with the flow of gritty water following its master—gravity.

A moment later they were outside the town limits cruising northwest toward Lake Oahe. Fifteen minutes later, they paused at the crest of a small hill overlooking what seemed an endless valley; they stood beside the purring machine, basking in the warmth; the vantage allowed them an uninterrupted view of a landscape dotted here and there with the works of mankind—bulky structures needed as protection from the world. The land also had been carved and lined with narrow passages allowing ease of movement. At the far extremity of their vision, ten miles or more, stood a thin dark smear marking the eastern shoreline of Lake Oahe.

Liam removed his coat and hat, and stood tall beside his parked machine in t-shirt and jeans. He pointed across the valley. "There's the wind turbine and the lake he told us about. The turbine is very close to the hawks' line of flight. Maybe they sheltered there."

"The weather is perfect for flying," Kate said. "I'm sure they've left by now. We've come all this way for nothing."

"No, we've tried to help." He draped one arm around her shoulders, gave a gentle squeeze. "Only one way to find out for sure. A road runs right by there." He gestured toward a snow-covered narrow lane flanked on both sides by towering trees. "Let's go."

He turned the snowmobile down the slope in the general direction of the road. They followed it past two or three neatly kept steep-roofed homes set back from the road.

Faded names on dripping mailboxes slid by announcing the Swedish and Norwegian heritage established there by early immigrants—bold, courageous, ambitious people who dug and built and planted.

They came around a slight bend in the road and Liam was forced to slow. A car, the driver's door flung open, motor still running was parked in the center of the road. A man carrying a rifle stood behind the car. Liam idled his machine and stood up beside it.

"This road is closed," the man called. "You'll have to turn back."

"What's going on?" Liam asked. He took a few steps toward the man.

"I've lost something in the snow. Go back the way you've come."

"Maybe we can help you find it," Liam replied. "We're both young eyes."

"No. I don't need any help." He lifted the rifle, pointed it over Liam's head. "I'm not going to tell you again. Turn around and get the hell out of here before you get hurt."

Liam didn't reply. He jumped in and swung the snow-mobile around in a quick, tight maneuver. Kate had to hug him from behind to keep from being thrown out. Three miles down the road, at the first driveway, Liam turned in, sped up the narrow lane and parked in front of the porch. He shut the machine off. "We need to report him. He's nuts."

Karl Soderberg opened the door just as Liam knocked. He looked over Liam's shoulder and saw Kate. "Come in," he said, swinging the door wide. He turned, and called to his wife. "Elsa, there's company."

They followed the man down a short entryway into the kitchen. Elsa turned from the sink, wiping her hands on her apron. "Hello," she said, smiling at the new-comers. "I'm Elsa."

"A man with a rifle is blocking the road," Liam said. "Down the hill toward the lake."

"Did you talk to him?" Karl asked. "I know most every-body round here."

"Not really. His car was in the middle of the road. I asked if we could help. He told me to turn around, go back the way we'd come. He said he was looking for something in the snow. I told him again we could help, but then he sort of pointed the gun at me, so we took off, came back this way as fast as we could." Liam glanced at Kate. "How'd he look to you?" he asked.

"He was big, quite tall," Kate said. "We didn't get real close to him because he was standing behind the car. Looked scary holding a rifle."

"The car was a white Land Rover," Liam added. "Looks almost brand new."

Karl looked at his wife. "Could be Chuck Bakken," he said. "A neighbor of ours. He drives a white Rover." He scratched his forehead with a thick finger. "Please sit down," he gestured toward the kitchen table. "I'll call the sheriff. Doesn't sound right. Sure shouldn't be pointing a gun at people."

When they had settled around the table, Elsa said, "What can I get you kids? I made fika this morning and I have fresh coffee."

"What's fika?" Liam asked.

"From the old country, my mother's recipes. Fika is a Swedish pastry. It's Karl's favorite. We call it *vaniljhärta*. In English it's *vanilla hearts*. I'll get coffee too." She looked at Kate and smiled. "Please take your coat off, hon, and make yourself at home."

Karl held the landline up to his ear, leaned against the kitchen wall. "This is Karl Söderberg out on Halvorsen Road near Bent. One of our neighbors has a rifle and has blocked the road." There was a short pause. "We're seven and a half miles due west out of Blunt. He's a bit farther, another three miles or so toward the lake." Karl watched his wife place a large plate of delicate vanilla hearts on the table. "I don't know what he's doing. He threatened some young people. Yes. He pointed it at them." He looked at Liam for verification, got a head nod back.

Elsa poured coffee. She beamed at Kate and Liam, pleased to have visitors under any circumstances. Judging from her face she'd probably be happy serving breakfast to a burglar during a spring twister.

"Could be a man named Charles Bakken, but I'm not sure. No, we don't have his license plate number. Sorry. It's a white Land Rover. Okay. We'll stay put. Thank you. Goodby." He put the receiver down, nodded at the group. "They're sending a deputy out. Should be along pretty quick."

Elsa hovered over her guests. "I should have offered tea," she said. "Karl and I don't drink much tea, but I can fix some easy enough."

"Coffee is fine," Kate said. She gazed about the old-fashioned kitchen, the tall ceiling and linoleum floor, and felt the intense memories of her own home near Dupree where she'd grown up, so similar to this one. New cabinets and stainless-steel appliances had modernized it without detracting from the warmth.

"These fika are wonderful," Kate said. "My grandmother bakes something similar."

Carl interrupted. "If it's who I think it is, his wife could be in big trouble. I've got a feeling they've been squabbling. Somebody needs to get down there real quick and see if she needs help."

"We didn't see a woman," Liam said. "Just the man."

Elsa turned to her husband. "You just called thirty seconds ago. The sheriff will be here soon. Let them take care of it. You know how dangerous Bakken is better than anybody."

Chapter Thirty-one

Danger, the constant and potent child of nature, and the endless manufactures of man, presents itself in a myriad of forms, bringing destruction to those unfortunates who encounter it.

OWEN SAW THE DARK SPECKS FIRST, STILL A MILE out. He drifted close to his father, touched a wingtip and motioned toward his ear. Orville quickly responded, pulled his earflaps up and moved even closer.

"Bogeys at twelve o'clock, Papa," Owen shouted across the rushing airstream.

Orville snugged up his helmet, scanned the sector dead ahead and spotted the smudges of black, closing fast. He recognized the silhouette as a simple flying machine, and dismissed the threat immediately, concentrating his vision slightly off course toward the looming turbine tower. *There's the real danger.*

Bakken's two remaining advanced capability drones, (ACDs), Rodeo Joe and Batman, also programmed to intercept all air-space intruders at the margins of the property, functioned primarily as flying cameras. Like the others they were armed with two cannons each.

When fifty yards separated them from the onrushing drones, Orville feinted left using the classic Scrambled Eggs maneuver, held it for one heartbeat, and then dove hard to the right. Owen mirrored the move, tucking in inches behind his father's bright red tail feathers; both were beyond the drones in an instant; they quickly descended to the base of the tower.

The air temperature, rising fast, had rendered the snow covering scabby, and at landing their talons dug sharply into it making a crunchy sound. The tower's murderous blades spinning high overhead created long shadows moving across the terrain. Batman and Rodeo Joe hovered directly above, rotors humming, and their cameras recording.

Orville slipped his goggles to his neck and loosened the chinstrap of his helmet. "Smile, Owen," he called, "someone is watching." He gestured toward the drones. His own face remained grim, frozen with the realization he was standing in an unmarked graveyard; he dismissed the drones from his mind as a mere nuisance and began the search.

The landscape surrounding the tower, dazzling in the afternoon sun, was dimpled here and there with small mounds reminiscent of ancient burial sites scattered about the world. One nearest the road seemed larger than the others and drew Orville's attention as a starting place. The skimpy snow blanket had shrunk and crystallized in the warmth; feathers just below the lattice of melting ice could be clearly seen. Orville scraped lightly with his talons and the side of his beak.

Lily had died with her wings surrounding Oliver, encapsulating and protecting him from the cold—a futile attempt to save his life—perhaps at the expense of her own. Orville put his ear to her chest, but the heartbeat had ceased to drum, a stilled life's cadence. He turned and looked at his son. "She's still warm. We've just missed her." His honey gold eyes widened with regret. "She's just passed us by."

Owen stood weakly to one side, unable to help his father in the grisly task. "Lily and Oliver," he whispered, his beak barely opening to pronounce the names. "Oh, Papa, not Lily."

He felt faint, dizzy, his brain collapsing with the enormity of his friends' deaths.

Just two weeks ago Lily had shyly approached Owen in the school cafeteria. Two of her best friends, Olivia and Isabella, flanked her, offering moral support and giggles.

"Owen," she began. The feathers on her cheeks had flamed red with embarrassment. "We've been wondering," she glanced at her two pillars of support, "I mean, *I've* been wondering if, well, if you'd go to the Hawk Hop Tolo dance with me when we come back from the Sioux Falls competition?" Her eyes glittered with youthful verve.

"I'd love to, Lily," he'd replied, flashing a shy grin. "I've been hoping you'd invite me. And, I promise I won't wear my goggles or helmet."

Owen stumbled and Orville reached out and steadied his son with a strong wing, and then pulled him into a tight embrace. "Oh, Papa, life hurts too much sometimes."

"They're all here," Orville said, his voice quaking with an unbearable, numbing grief. He pulled Owen to the ground and they sobbed together, emptying their sorrow upon the snow. They sat for several minutes before Orville regained his composure enough to stand. He stroked his grieving son's head with his wing; he gazed about, steeling his resolve for the grisly task before him. "There's work to be done," he said.

Rodeo Joe flew lower, hovered just above the bodies; its ghoulish lens whirred, snapping close-ups of the two departed angels.

There was a sudden explosion of feathers, and Owen, in an unstoppable rage, flew viciously at Rodeo Joe. The drone, filming without a brain or heart or soul, could not react fast enough. Owen snagged it by its tether ring with his fore-talon; he carried it to the nearest leg of the tower, and bashed it again and again against the iron. Metal clanged on metal. The plastic components were shattered, the electrical impulses snuffed, and the drone's incessant buzzing was silenced. Owen flung it into the air and watched it plummet to earth.

Batman had turned tail toward the house. Owen, still in a rage, caught air and followed in hot pursuit. Initially the drone was faster, but it had to slow while the garage door slowly rose. Owen, not wanting to be trapped inside the garage, sailed by an instant too late as Scout ducked under the closing door to safety.

Owen gleaned no satisfaction from his act; he knew the drones were mere mechanical puppets directed by distant human hands. They suffered no pain, dripped no blood—left behind no cherished parents, brothers, sisters or best friends. A drone was replaceable. Lily and his friends were not. Lily would never cut loose at the school dance—not now or ever.

Hoping to locate the man outside his residence, Owen floated above and safely off to one side of the house and watched while his father excavated body after body—all those Owen had schooled with, teased, and loved.

But the door remained shut and Owen's heartbeat slowed, resuming its normal pattern. Unable to continue the fight, he turned back, landing softly beside his father and the lifeless bodies of his friends.

A moment later both hawks were startled by the sharp crack of a rifle shot. They turned their attention toward the county road, where the sound had ricocheted almost a mile below them; but a far-off stand of windbreak trees blocked their vision.

"Something is terribly amiss in this foul place," Orville said. "Death is born here, much too common, delivered by a careless midwife. Go investigate, but be cautious," Orville ordered. "I will stay here and finish my work."

Chapter Thirty-two

*...and the terror of being hunted. It freezes
the mind and limbs, allows the hunter to
gain the upper hand.*

CLAIRE COWERED. ALMOST PARALYZED WITH
fear she realized too late she had trapped herself;
Bakken would find her soon enough simply by following
her tracks in the deep snow and peering in the end of the
culvert pipe. In the two years of their marriage he had
never actually threatened to kill her, but on more than
one occasion she had watched in horror as his face con-
torted into a mask of outrage, cheek muscles twitching
over the most trivial of matters. During these brief flare-
ups of uncontrollable anger his eyes would transform
themselves into grayish slits—vials of viscous poison.
She feared those eyes most of all.

Her mind raced, tried to imagine another, safer hiding
spot where she might be camouflaged before it was too
late. Did she have time to jog up the road to the Soderberg's home? Could he reprogram Daisy or one of the
other drones to seek her out beyond the property line?
Even if Bakken followed her up to their neighbor's home
she felt certain Karl Soderberg would protect her.

Logic drove her into action. Better to leave this tempo-
rary concealment and certain discovery. She skittered back
out into the muted sunlight beside the road, and using an

old convict's escape trick, waded into the shallow water of the creek leaving no footprints in the snow; soaked almost to her knees, her feet numb in the icy flow, she splashed downstream away from the road for fifty yards.

There once had been a barbed wire fence, now fallen and decayed, sprawling in the snow; beyond the fence line sat an ancient apple orchard. It had been neglected for twenty years or more, the trunks and limbs now gray and gnarled. She left the stream and scrambled up the bank bordering the orchard, picking her way over the decayed fence; she ran between the apple trees dodging the hateful, clutching, snagging branches.

Finally she reached the creek again where it turned to follow the natural contour of the land and marked the orchard's extremity.

Abandoning the orchard, she scurried through the creek again, and clambered up the steep bank to the road on hands and knees; she glanced behind her, but all was motionless and silent; At the place where she had emerged, the road remained pristine except for a blurred set of what seemed to be ski tracks; there were no snow packed tire tracks for her to follow, to ease her way. She forced herself into a slow but determined jog.

Thirty years earlier, on a warm spring day at a high school track meet in Seattle, she had run a swift mile in five and a half minutes. The race was ancient history, and the years gone by had added baggage, clinging to her slender frame and weighing her down. Claire jogged in shin deep snow, her breathing raspy, lungs laboring to fuel her muscles, but she plowed on with determined resolve; she turned a slight bend in the road, drew a measure of concealment and safety from it.

At last she came to the driveway, the house sitting just a hundred yards up a slight rise on a picturesque hill, outbuildings some distance behind; exhausted now, and unable to catch her breath, she bent over, hands on hips, waiting for her heart and lungs to catch up, restore themselves. She was startled by the noise of chained tires clattering on crushed snow; she turned in time to see a sheriff's car, a white sedan with a green and gold logo on the side. It passed by before she could think to raise her hand and wave, signal for help. A surge of relief came to her then—she was safe. Karl Soderberg and the sheriff would protect her from Bakken; the snow was melting, the roads would be safe, and soon she would be on a plane to Seattle—this worst of all nightmare marriages put behind her.

Refreshed, she began walking up the sloped driveway toward the house; she could see a sleek snowmobile parked near the front porch. She slowed—no need to hurry now. Looking neither right nor left, her legs on fire, she trudged up the narrow lane, dodged the snowmobile and climbed the porch steps. Suddenly too warm, she removed her gloves. At the top of the stairs she stopped and turned, looking back the way she had come. Almost giddy now, she reached for the doorbell.

Just as she extended her arm, far off in the distance, a gunshot reverberated through the valley.

. . . and in John Wayne's day, at the Saturday afternoon matinee, cradling a box of popcorn in lap, eyes glued to the screen, the good guys in the white hats always caught and punished the evil, cigar smoking bank robbers, or the thieving, foul smelling Indians. But movies are not reality.

BAKKEN HEARD THE CAR'S CHAINS BITING THE snow. He had followed Claire's footsteps to the culvert, peered in. Her fear had left a slight pungent odor, but she'd waded into the stream, leaving no footprints for him to follow.

Bakken put a knee down, crouched out of sight from the road as the car stopped above him. It idled, a low, pleasant rumble. The car door opened and Bakken caught snippets of radio transmission, short bursts of conversation. *It's a cop.*

Duncan Taylor, a sheriff's deputy, had been following ski tracks in the snow, the only marks on the untraveled road. When he came out of a slight downhill turn he was surprised to see a large white vehicle stopped in the center of the road, headlights facing him. The driver's door was open, no one in sight. He sat for a moment, engaged with a female dispatcher. Announced his arrival and the presence of a white Land Rover blocking the road. Requested back up.

Finally, he emerged from the cruiser and stood by the driver's side; he unbuckled the strap of his holster while surveying the scene. Water trickled nearby on both sides of the road, a creek being fed by melting snow. The parked car appeared to be empty, no apparent movement or presence. He sang out, "Hello? Anybody here?" He waited a few seconds, then called out again. "Are you okay?"

Bakken heard footsteps above and slightly to his left. His heart was racing, but he remained completely motionless while controlling his breathing.

The deputy walked toward the driver's door of the blocking vehicle. Careful of his trooper's hat, he ducked his head to look inside the open door; seeing nothing of interest he stood and walked alongside the car toward the rear. He fished out a small notebook from his jacket pocket and jotted down the license plate identifier and the car's color, make, and model. Glanced at his watch and noted the time.

"Get away from my car." The voice was off to the officer's right.

Duncan Taylor was still writing, and the voice startled him. He turned his head to the side where Bakken stood slightly below the road, rifle in hand.

"Put your weapon down, sir," Taylor said. His voice was firm, definite, leaving no options.

"I have as much right to a gun as you do," Bakken said. "I'm protecting my property." He took a quick step up to regain the road. "You're snooping where you've no business."

"Stay where you are and put down your weapon," Taylor repeated. He laid his pen and notebook on the car's roof above the back window; he turned slowly and faced Bakken. His right hand brushed the handle of his Glock, the movement almost imperceptible. Almost.

"This is a public road," Bakken replied, his eyes tightening down. "It's as much my road as it is yours. I go where I please, do as I please." He chuckled. "This isn't kindergarten. You don't tell me where to sit or when I'm allowed to sharpen my pencil." The muscles in Bakken's face twitched, contorting his mouth.

"Looking for my wife," he said. "Bitch ran off."

Bakken lifted the barrel of the gun an inch, pointed it at the deputy's chest. The two men were twenty yards apart. "I don't like folks meddling in my business. Especially badge people."

"Sir, we can't have a conversation while you're threatening me. Put your gun down and we'll help locate your wife. I'm here to help you." He put his left hand out, palm facing Bakken, a magician's diversion and subconscious signal to stop. His voice remained calm though his heart hammered. "Don't turn a small matter into a big problem. We can work this out."

Deputy Taylor's face stayed composed, professional. Elbow bent, deft fingertips curled around his pistol. His hand ached to grip, lift, and point—trained, practiced—quick and efficient—but death came too fast, was upon him before he could execute and complete the movement. Just as three deuces always beats a pair of jacks in a poker game, so too a tiny squeeze on a hairspring trigger always beats a draw from a holster. On this particular day, on this particular lonely snow-covered county road in South Dakota, hotshot marksmen the likes of Wyatt Earp, Doc Holiday, or Billy the Kid could not have beaten Bakken's squeeze. Duncan Abraham Taylor's weapon never cleared his holster.

Bakken's right index finger, cuddling the trigger, fired one shot. He walked past the fallen deputy without so much as a downward glance. "Damn meddler," he muttered. He did not recognize the cruelty his squeeze had just created: a young man's life shortened by more than half; a ten year marriage erased as if the love affair between Duncan and Lola Taylor had never existed. The cruel act robbed two children of one of their parents; no one to teach a boy how to shave or cuss or cast a fishing line; no one there for a girl to demonstrate how to pitch a softball, dribble a basketball up court, to eat her first batch of brownies, or enforce her curfew.

Bakken leaned in the still open driver's door of his Land Cruiser and placed the butt of the rifle on the floor on the passenger's side, the wooden stock against the front seat cushion.

Turning back to the fallen deputy, he grabbed the dead man's hands, still warm from the reservoir of blood recently coursing there; Bakken dragged him to the side of the road and with his foot rolled the body into the ditch. He climbed into the still idling police vehicle and nosed it slowly to the edge of the road.

Leaving the gearshift in neutral, he got out and leaned against the driver's open door. He pushed hard, grunted with the effort, and despite the slippery snow under his feet, the car rolled forward a few feet and slowly the front end tilted, until the front wheels and engine weight pulled it over the edge. It slid down the embankment into the ditch. The car's rear end pointed skyward, the way home for Deputy Taylor.

Bakken walked up the road a hundred yards or more. He stood for a moment staring toward an old apple orchard, one his grandfather had planted sixty years earlier when the road he was standing on was still just a dirt lane. Abruptly Bakken spit a coarse stream at the snow; he turned and hurried back to his car.

. . . and when two cars speed through a busy intersection, drivers hurrying home after a long day at work—distracted perhaps by thoughts or gadgets—collide and damage is done, and lives are lost, someone must be blamed. Accidents don't cause themselves the police will say. Insurance companies, eager to avoid payment, point the finger away.

OWEN, WINGS SPREAD WIDE, FLOATED HIGH above the results of the deadly confrontation between officer and citizen. He could see a man on his back being dragged over the snow by the other man. Owen watched as the body slid over the embankment and came to a stop just off the road. A large red stain pooled on the man's chest. The other man walked briskly away toward a large white car. Even at this height Owen was certain it was the same man who'd shot at him as he flew by after he'd eluded the drones.

Three miles off in the distance, in the direction the man drove, stood a small white farmhouse. From his lofty vantage point, Owen could see a narrow, snow-covered drive leading up to the structure. A cluster of mature shade trees, their branches almost bare, surrounded the house. Gray smoke curled from one of two brick chimneys. Owen spotted a slender figure standing on the porch, appearing to rap on the door. A moment later the door opened and the figure disappeared inside.

Owen curled his wing tips upward, snapped his tail feathers into a closed position, lost lift, and dropped precipitously toward the shooting scene. He landed softly, hopped once and stood respectfully beside the lifeless man. Even young hawks are mindful of death; indeed, wedded to it, they live each day only because of it, but pointless death—death without reason—is so foreign to a red-tail's manner of thinking it caused a dark revulsion in Owen's mind.

The man's eyes stared, sightless, into the abyss. Owen leaned in and put his forehead against the man's neck as he had been taught in a first aid class. The pulse and warmth normally found there were silent and cold. Owen shuddered from head to talons, mourned for the man just as he grieved for his classmates so recently torn apart by the wind turbine's whirling blades. Nothing to be done about it, he lifted off and raced back to his father.

Orville had laid out twenty-five feathery bodies, arranged them gently, face down as they flew, wings extended, in arrowhead formation with Rowdy at point, an artifact so far removed from existence it could no longer cut through the air; so too, in the red-tail burial tradition, they would rest together—in an eternal pattern of arrowhead flight. There were but three gaps in the burial pattern—where Emma, Quinn, and Owen had flown.

As soon as Owen landed he approached his father. "A man has been shot and killed, Papa. A police officer."

"Policeman?" Orville asked. "Are you sure?"

"I saw the badge on his uniform. It's a shiny gold color similar to the one the county sheriff wears when he visits our school."

"Did you see the shooter?"

"No. He drove off as I approached."

"You didn't see his face then."

"No, but I believe it is the same man who lives on this land, the one who set his drones on me when I flew over his house. After his drones crashed he shot at me. There's a farm two or three miles east of here. He drives that direction. I fear for those who live there. It seems he chases after a woman. I could see someone, a female, entering a house."

"Police officers never work alone," Orville said. "They're always connected in support teams as loyal brothers and sisters. Another will be along shortly. The killer will be apprehended before he can harm anyone else. Humans have their punishments—jails, prisons, and executions. Their laws are complicated and many." He sighed, shook his head as if it were all a burden. "The man will be judged by his peers, and in the end, punished."

"Have you called Mother?"

"Yes. She knows you are alive. She rejoices for you, but is heartbroken for your classmates. Quinn and Higgins made it home safely and have informed our community of the terrible loss. Relatives—the strongest flyer in each family—will soon be on their way here to carry home the fledglings. All will be transported back to Dupree for proper burial and memorial ceremony."

"We must hurry to Emma where she tends Ms. Ride," Owen said. "I promised her I would return as soon as possible. Ms. Ride is very near death."

"When the family members arrive our work here will

be done. Then you and I will go to Emma. Until then we must be patient. Perhaps Higgins will help us too. If Ms. Ride is still alive we will carry her home to Doc Walters. If anyone can save her it will be him."

Orville fished in his wing holster. "I found this," he said. He held up a silver medal and chain. "It was near Rowdy's body."

Owen, unable to help himself, began to sob, the tears rolling down his feathery cheeks.

Orville gathered his son in his wings, offering comfort in a terrible moment.

Finally, Owen could speak. "It is the medal we earned for second place in the competition. We were so proud, Papa. The chain has twenty-nine links, one for each student, and one for Ms. Ride. Now we are linked in death."

Orville was quiet for a moment. "Your class celebrates still," he said. "This story will be told over and over again to the future flyers of our community. The legend of your class's exploits will never end. We will bury the medal with these." He swept his wing over the silent formation on the snow.

"Papa? I need to know something, but I'm not sure how to ask."

"What is it?"

"Why do wind turbines exist? They pose great danger to all flyers."

Orville turned toward his son. "Because the man wanted to generate electricity."

"But all houses require power. Couldn't he use the same power as others?"

"I suppose. But, for some reason he preferred to create his own." Orville shrugged his shoulders. "Perhaps to save money."

"Papa?"

"Yes?"

"Can you explain who is to blame?"

"What do you mean?"

"Was it Ms. Ride's fault?"

"On what basis would we blame her?" Orville asked. "She was injured protecting her class. Her duties as a teacher are to teach, inspire, and protect. Should we blame her for carrying out her duties? No one has control of the weather."

There was a long silence. "Was it Rowdy's fault, Papa?"

"Why are you so eager to blame?" A trace of exasperation tinged Orville's voice. "When the wind blows and a nest falls, should we blame the wind or the coyote for coming along? If the river floods and fish are stranded in the mud, should we blame the storm? When the lightning strikes and the forest burns, who's to blame?"

Orville's eyes glowed. He took his son by the shoulders. "Live *your* life, Owen. Do not lay blame on others. Understand this—all living things in this world do the best they can."

"Papa?"

"Yes?"

"Why was I disappointed when Ms. Ride picked Rowdy over me to fly point? I know he's a stronger flyer, but still I was disappointed. I thought I was the better navigator and almost his equal in the air. I felt resentment during the flight—her choice of Rowdy over me; he was my friend and a fantastic flyer. I've shamed myself, Papa."

"Owen." Orville paused, made powerful eye contact with his son. "Every student in the class should have been disappointed she placed Rowdy above them. My own flight instructor, RT Boyd Higgins, taught us envy and arrogance are fundamental weaknesses in the nature of our red-tail character. Each one of us thinks we are the superior navigator, the top flyer, the bravest, even the best looking. When others win awards, we envy them instead of celebrating their success. You have not shamed yourself. You have proved yourself to be a red-tail, and I love you the more for admitting it."

He reached out a comforting wing and pulled his son tight.

. . . and is there anything more comforting in the whole wide world than a compassionate friend or neighbor when troubles pile up?

To Karl's surprise, the instant he opened the door Claire burst in like an uninvited dwarf at the hobbit's door; seeking only safety, she rushed past the startled man toward the kitchen.

"He's shooting," she said. Her face, flushed from the cold and effort of her escape, stood an open book; her eyes, frightened pellets as she entered the room, thawed, and turned luminous in the kitchen's sudden warmth and safety.

"Bakken?" asked Karl. He stood with his back to the door, his mouth gaping wide.

"I don't know for sure, but it must be him. Or the police."

"The police? Where are they?"

"Down the road somewhere. I'm sure Bakken's after me. I tried to hide near an old orchard by the creek. By now he's found my tracks in the snow." Her words, propelled by fear and relief, tumbled out, filled the room. "It's so hard to hide in the snow."

She looked at Elsa, standing with hands on hips next to her stove. "He hates me. Don't ask me why, because I don't know why; I think he hates the world."

Her voice shook with emotion. "We argued again this morning. Every day it gets worse. This morning he told me I'd never see Seattle or my children again. He said he was going to bury me face down so I'll never see heaven." She covered her face with her hands, and sobbed, her chest heaving.

In her distress, Claire seemed unaware Kate and Liam, complete strangers, were sitting there, attending her personal revelations. She uncovered her face. "I can't live with him anymore. I went for a walk so I could decide how best to escape him. He watches me wherever I go and I can't think properly." She reached for a napkin on the table and blew her nose.

"Last weekend I was ready to fly home to Seattle, but then the snow started and the roads became too treacherous; I wanted to leave, but I couldn't drive to the airport. I packed a bag and put it in the trunk of my car so I could leave as soon as the roads opened. About an hour ago, while I was on my walk, I heard him shoot at something; I knew he was coming after me and I needed to hide. I tried to conceal myself under the road, but it was like a trap, so I ran through an old orchard."

"You said the police . . ." Karl spoke softly in the hushed room.

"I got terrified when I heard the gunshot. He has a large collection of shotguns and rifles, but this is the first time he's shot one of them since we've been married. At first I thought I could hide, hoping he would just drive by, but the snow made it impossible. After the orchard, I came to a creek. I waded through it and then I came back up to the road; I jogged the rest of the way here. I was terrified he'd shoot me or run over me with his car. When he gets angry he loses all control of himself."

"Your feet must me frozen," Elsa said. "Slip your boots off and I'll get you warm slippers." She hurried off down the hall.

"If you didn't see Bakken, what makes you think he and the police are involved?" Karl asked.

"Just as I started up your driveway I saw a sheriff's car going down the hill toward our place. I don't think the officer saw me because he didn't stop. I could have warned him. Bakken is a very dangerous man. I'm sure he's going crazy. No, he is crazy. Just now, on your porch, I heard another gunshot."

"I called the sheriff's office about a half hour ago," Karl said. "The deputies are well trained and very careful. They have to deal with people like Bakken every day."

Elsa interrupted, handing a fluffy pair of knit slippers to Claire. Elsa seemed unable or unwilling to comprehend such a hateful relationship. "Please," she said, "take your boots off and put these on. I'll pour you some coffee. You've had a terrible fright and chill."

"Thank you," Claire said. She sat down at the kitchen table next to two stunned college kids, covered her face with her hands, and began to cry.

Elsa knelt on her spotless kitchen floor, and began working Claire's frozen leather bootlaces with her gnarled fingers. "Let's get these wet things off, honey," Elsa said. "You'll catch cold."

Liam and Kate, silent ashen-faced witnesses, cast their eyes downward; they felt themselves intruders on too many ugly facets of adulthood still beyond their youthful understanding.

Karl crossed the kitchen, dangerous matters on his mind; in the living room a large picture window allowed him a view of his front yard and the long, narrow driveway sloping down with a few twists and turns toward the main road.

Behind him he heard Elsa making introductions, offering food, drink, and soft, kind words. The mantle clock began to chime the hour and he knew Elsa would be eager to serve their guests dinner.

He crossed his arms against his chest, a defensive posture he sometimes used unconsciously when troubles were about. Looking through the window he noticed nothing out of the ordinary, other than a tiny river of melting snow coursing down the edges of the driveway where countless tires had grooved the dirt.

Karl had lived on this property for over seventy-five years in the same home he'd been born in. He and Elsa had shared it for fifty-three years and raised three children in it. The home had always been a safe, welcoming place, but now an uneasy feeling gripped him. Oddly, he felt cold, and crossed the room to bump the thermostat up a degree. In the other room, he could hear the cheerful voices of his guests and Elsa chatting, sipping coffee, nibbling Elsa's cookies. He hurried back to the window. Still quiet, nothing unusual.

He wondered if he should call the sheriff's dispatch office again, inform them a gunshot had been heard. But Karl, a patient man, as all farmers must be, dismissed the thought. The sound of a faraway shot was not uncommon in the country. He turned away from the window and hurried to a small bedroom he'd converted into an office after his youngest daughter had gotten married and moved away for good. He went to his desk and kneeled down on the hardwood floor in front of the bottom drawer.

He reached in with both hands and grabbed a brick in each, set them on the floor. Dipped in again, two more bricks. He'd built a crude barrier to keep his children safe. He bent down, his head nearly touching the floor and snaked a long arm way in the back of the drawer. His hand closed on a leather holster. He rocked back on his knees, and removed the Colt single action from the holster. He popped the chamber open. It was loaded with five shells, just as he'd left it over twenty-five years ago.

Karl shut his eyes, unwilling to see the hateful instrument. Then he closed the hammer on the pistol's empty chamber. No safety catch. His hand seemed uncertain about the pistol it was holding. He stood and pulled his flannel shirttail out of his jeans, took his belt off and threaded it through the holster openings.

He put a hand on his desk for leverage and pulled himself to his feet with a deep groan, born of a lifetime of heavy lifting. His back, knees, and hips ached all the time now. He returned the belt to the loops in his jeans, fastened it tight around his waist.

The gun disappeared under his shirt. Except for Valentine's Day or a birthday card, he had never hidden anything from his wife. But this was different.

He returned to the warmth of the kitchen and smiled, trying to mask his feelings. "It's gettin' near time for supper," he said. "We're probably better off just waiting this thing out. Bakken and the sheriff will sort it all out soon enough. Once it's resolved I'm sure the sheriff will come up here and let us know what's what."

He looked at Claire, sensed the danger stalking her. "The roads should be fine in the morning. You can spend the night here with us and we'll drive you to the airport in Pierre first thing."

Elsa scooted her chair away from the table and stood up. She turned and smiled at her husband. "I'll heat up the stew left over from last night," she said. "There's plenty and I've baked a pan of honey cornbread to go with it." She turned toward the table and pointed down the hallway connecting the kitchen to the rest of the house. "If you'd like to freshen up, the bathroom is the first door on the right. I'll just be a minute fixin' dinner."

Liam had been sitting too long. He stood up and stretched his arms overhead. He faced Karl.

"Mind if I go out and look at your barn and equipment?" he asked. "Need to get some fresh air."

"Not at all," Karl said. "I'll show you around while Elsa gets supper." He touched Elsa's shoulder with a big, gentle hand. "Be right back, El. Gonna show this young man the place."

Kate, also weary of just sitting, stood up and stretched her arms over her head, twisting her pliant body to loosen the muscles. She crossed the room to the refrigerator where Elsa was removing glass containers of food and placing them on the counter. "Anything I can do to help?" she said.

"No need, honey," Elsa said with a smile. "Look about the house. It's nothing special, but it's been home to us for over fifty years. I'll call everybody as soon as supper is ready."

Kate wandered into the living room and admired the comfortable looking furniture, family photos displayed on the walls, and many shelves of collectibles. Her back pocket buzzed and she reached for her phone. **Where Kate be? Turban deaded all class. By Villige Blunt.**

Orville's message caused her to gasp out loud.

Elsa came to the doorway wiping her hands on her apron. "Are you okay?" she asked.

Claire moved beside Elsa, the two women filling the doorway. "What's wrong?" Claire said.

"Is there a wind turbine on your husband's property?"

Claire looked puzzled. "Yes. But why do you ask?"

Stunned, Kate only managed, "Something horrible has happened. I've got to tell my friend." She squeezed past the two women and ran down the hall to the front door.

Chief among life's priorities is education. Those without it are shackled to menial tasks, low pay, and the snooty pity of others.

RVILLE AND OWEN PERCHED SIDE BY SIDE ON the lowest of the tower's support crossbeams, about twenty feet above the ground, an elevation more suitable to their nature. Red-tails are always uneasy on the ground, more vulnerable to their land-based predators, and prefer spending as little time walking about as possible. Talons are not sneakers. The sky was crystal clear now, and the snow, melting rapidly everywhere, fell in upon itself, as if crushed by an invisible hand and then squeezed back to the fluidity of water. Directly above them the turbine's three blades revolved lazily, the constant hum creating a slow unthreatening tune.

The two hawks were perched high enough they could see the sheriff's car, a mile away, slanted all catawampus in the ditch beside the main road. Everything else in their vista fit the normal pattern of autumn life on the prairie.

Owen broke the comfortable silence between them. "Papa."

"Yes."

"Will the other Iron Lightning hawks be angry?"

"At whom or what would they be angry?" Orville asked.

Owen turned his head, pulled his goggles down so he could see his father's eyes more clearly. "At Quinn, Emma, and me."

"Why would they be angry at you three? You've done nothing wrong."

"I know," Owen replied, "but we survived. Perhaps some will resent their loss while we three live still."

"I doubt it," Orville said. "More likely they will be thankful you three yet live. In the years ahead, each of you will be important members or our community and make it a better, safer place."

"Papa?"

"Yes, Owen." There was a hint of irritation in Orville's voice. "There are only two of us perched on this bar. You do not need to keep repeating my name. I am your father and there is no confusion as to whom you are speaking."

"Sorry," Owen said. "What will happen to us?"

"You mean, us two, or you three survivors?"

"Emma, Quinn, and me."

"Nothing will happen to you. What do you mean?"

"I mean about school. Only three in our class remain, and if Ms. Ride dies we won't have a teacher."

"Your mother can homeschool you if need be, like she did until you were old enough to wear goggles. Or perhaps you can skip the rest of this year as juniors and be promoted to the senior class right away. Your mother and I will decide what's best for you. We'll talk to RT Higgins and Dr. Richfield about it. Your education is too important to be disrupted."

"Oh," Owen said. "I hadn't thought far enough."

Bouncy boogie-woogie piano music interrupted their discussion and startled them both. Orville reached for his wing-holster and grabbed his cellphone.

Orville read Kate's text silently, each word a hurdle for his beak to pronounce and mind to understand.

"Kate Flannery, Papa?"

"Yes. She's in some danger nearby and needs me right away. I must go. You will stay here and guard your classmates. Scavengers abound. Food has been scarce for three days and they will eat anything. Honor your classmates with vigilance."

"Be careful, Papa," Owen called, but Orville had lifted and was already maneuvering past the turbine's supports. There was not an instant of hesitation as Orville accelerated to two hundred feet in mere seconds, his wings angled perfectly to catch, pull, and throw the air behind him; his tail extended and fanned wide, like a stately empress's fan, for stability and direction.

Transfixed, Owen could but stare as his father climbed and gathered speed; the scene made his heart ache to be flying alongside. With a deep sigh of resignation Owen turned his attention to the ground where his classmates lay frozen in their final motionless flight formation—a snapshot of eternity.

It was at then his ears caught a faint buzzing sound approaching from behind. He turned his head a moment too late.

*. . . of course there's always been killing,
one way or another, clear back to the
caves and earlier.*

KATE LEAPED FROM THE TOP STEP OF THE PORCH, nearly landing on the snowmobile parked at the foot of the stairs. She skidded, lost her balance, and landed hard on her butt when her feet slid out from under her. She picked herself up, and started running. She shouted, "Liam!"

A large well-kept red barn of a similar design and age as the house, and a stern, more modern looking large rectangular building sat side by side about sixty yards behind the house.

"Liam!" No answer. She kept running toward the buildings. She stopped and turned at the loud roar of a boxy white SUV fishtailing up the driveway. There were several undulations in the narrow road and the car would appear for a second, and then momentarily disappear below the terrain. The car's roar stayed steady, an outraged bull charging.

Karl and Liam, hearing the ruckus, emerged from the storage shed and workshop. "It must be him," Kate called. "Claire's husband. He's coming to kill her!"

A loud crash stopped her in her tracks. Bakken had lost control of his speeding car and it plowed into the snowmobile and cart, catapulting them up onto the steps of the porch. A thick wooden support for a corner of the porch snapped and its roof partially collapsed. The car stopped amid the wreckage, its front end bashed in.

Kate watched in horror as Bakken climbed out, holding his rifle. She turned away and ran toward Karl and Liam.

Amazingly, Karl calmly stood his ground. "You two go in my shop. There's no lock, so barricade the door. I'll handle this."

Bakken leaned his rifle against the side of the Land Rover. He held his cell phone up to his face, punched keys. A moment later he smiled and shoved his phone into his back pocket. He grabbed his rifle and for the first time looked up.

Karl strolled through the snow toward Bakken. "You've made a fine mess of my porch and snowmobile," he called. "Hope you've got good insurance." He managed a thin smile, then turned and took a few steps toward the porch, made a cursory examination for damage.

He faced Bakken. "Don't know if you remember me, Mr. Bakken, but I grew up with your father. We were high school buddies. Last time I saw you was at your mother's funeral, about thirty years ago."

Bakken ignored the information. "My wife here?" Bakken asked. "Need to speak to her a moment. Clear something up."

"Claire's not here," Karl said. "Haven't seen her in a couple weeks." Never having a need for deception made him a poor liar.

"Not sure I believe you, mister. I guess I'll have to look around." He started toward the mangled porch.

"You can't go in there. I don't allow guns on my property."

Bakken's mouth and eyes opened wide with surprise. "You don't huh?" he said. He smiled grimly, shaded his eyes with his hand. "A man has a right to make the rules on his own land. Believe in it myself."

He glanced up toward the living room picture window. Inside two shadows stepped back. "But somebody's in there." He waved one hand toward the window, then put the rifle to his shoulder and aimed and fired. The window glass shattered directly above and behind Karl's head.

Bakken lowered the rifle to his waist, pointed it at Karl's chest. "I think you're lying. She's in there, ain't she, Farmer Brown? I'm gonna get her. She's a dead woman."

Seemingly unfazed, Karl took several steps toward Bakken. The smell of gunpowder and the endless explosions of the Korean War had been seared forever in his mind; now the memories of death rushed back to him—bolstered his courage.

"If you seen somebody looking out the window," he said, "most likely it was my wife and her sister. They're just curious about the noise. Not everyday somebody crashes into our porch or shoots out our picture window."

Karl's right hand rested at his waist, felt the handle of the Colt under his shirt. "I told you, Mr. Bakken, I don't allow guns on my property. You can get back in your big car and go on home. Your wife is not on the premises."

"Let me tell you what *I* don't allow," Bakken said, "and that is my wife hiding on your property and you lying to me about it. If you take one more step, you'll be as dead as that meddling sheriff's deputy up the road."

Bakken laughed, like it was all a hideous joke. He slid the rifle to his cheek, and sighted down the barrel. Another man's life held no value to him. With the slightest pressure of his finger he could rip a hole in Karl's heart just to see if Farmer Brown's sternum could stand up to the bite of a high velocity bullet.

Karl stopped in his tracks. The two men were no more than twenty feet apart. Karl had sidled behind the bashed in front end of the Rover, protected now from the waist down. "Sounds like you've done enough killing for today," Karl said.

His hand was under his shirt now, the leather strap of the holster unbuckled. "Like I said, my wife and her sister are in the house. Wife and I been married for fifty-three years and I promised her father on our wedding day, I'd protect her with my life. You're not a going in there, Mr. Bakken."

He paused. Read the intent stored in Bakken's eyes. "Don't like to talk about it, but I did some killing in Korea during the war. Place called Pork Chop Hill. Terrible killing happened there. Hated myself for it, but it had to be done. I'm familiar with the process." As Karl spoke he seemed to grow in stature, diminishing the big man with the rifle. "Any minute now this place will be swarming with the law. They don't like it much when one of their own gets killed. They get real riled up about it."

"That so?" Bakken said. "So you're one of those war heroes, huh? What I read in the history books is a lot of innocent women and children got killed over there. Not all of you were heroes."

He lowered the barrel of the rifle slightly. If he touched the trigger now the bullet would catch Karl somewhere above his belly button, pierce the vital organs buried inside, and blow a hole as big as a man's fist out his back. He wouldn't have enough life left to whisper *I love you, El.* In half an eye blink, a single bullet would ruin everything a man lives three quarters of a century to accomplish.

"Deputy back there tried to tell me what I should do. Don't know for sure, but he was probably one of those soldier boys over in Iraq or Afghanistan. I guess he thought I was a kindergartner. Told me to put the rifle down. Said we could work things out. Kinda fooled him though. The tin badge boy was talking when he shoulda been listening."

He relaxed his grip on the rifle, moving it away and down from his cheek. "Instead of him working things out for me I worked things out for him, and now his wife will have to work a few more things out. Come tomorrow she'll need to order a nice shiny casket. Hire some fancy restaurant to cater a lunch for his memorial service. Buy herself a pretty black dress. Women are lovely in black, don't you agree, Farmer Brown? Slims 'em down some."

He laughed out loud. "Course she'll need a nice pearl necklace to go with it. She'll want to look her best at her husband's funeral, won't she? Next week she'll need to cash in his insurance policy. Spend it all soon enough."

Not used to holding ten pounds of weaponry with just his arms, he allowed the butt of the rifle to drop and rest on his hip. "Women don't mind spending their husband's money, do they? Mine likes books—and the libraries are full of 'em! Spend and spend, that's what women live for, isn't it? Tell you one thing, my wife has bought her last book." He laughed again, an ugly throaty sound.

As soon as Kate and Liam got safely inside Karl's shop, they put their shoulders together and managed to slide a heavy table saw across the concrete floor and jam it up against the door. The top half of the door was a glass window, affording laughable protection from a man with a high-powered rifle.

"Call 911," Liam ordered, his voice almost frantic. "They need to get somebody out here quick before he shoots Karl. He'll kill Claire too. Maybe us."

Eyes wide, Kate dug in the hip pocket of her jeans.

A pleasant female voice said, "Nine, one, one. What is your emergency?"

"We need help fast. There's a man with a rifle. He might kill his wife."

"What is your address?"

"I don't know. We're about seven miles west of Blunt on a country road. You sent a deputy out here about an hour ago."

"Are you in a safe place?"

"Not really, but he can't see us right now."

"Is the deputy there now?"

"No. I don't know where he is. There was a gunshot a while ago."

"Please stay on the line. Someone is on the way."

"I can't stay on the line. I need to make another call." Kate hung up and tapped out a hurried text to Orville. **From turbine, first house east off main road. Crazy man with gun. Help!**

Liam peered out the window, keeping his body hidden behind the doorframe. "He's gonna kill Karl for sure. He's got his finger on the trigger."

Claire and Elsa had been standing at the living room window looking out when Bakken's SUV had smacked into the snowmobile and destroyed the porch. Both had jumped at the loud blast of noise and felt the whole house shudder. They watched as Bakken sat for a moment, then climbed out and studied his cell phone, and appeared to send a message. Their fearful curiosity changed to horror when he pointed his rifle at Karl. A moment later, when Bakken looked up and waved, Claire grabbed Elsa's arm and jerked her away from the window.

"We've got to hide," Claire said. "He'll be coming in here looking for me. Hurry." Just as they entered the kitchen the living room window behind them exploded, sending jagged shards of glass flying.

Without a word, Elsa led Claire down the hallway, past the toilet and two empty bedrooms to the oldest, original part of the house where Karl's grandparents had lived for two years while the main house was being built. At the end of the hall, adjacent to the back door, was a closet. When Elsa opened the closet door they faced a few winter coats hanging on hangers from a thick wooden dowel. On a broad shelf, a foot above the dowel, rested woolen hats and several pairs of gloves.

"Duck your head," Elsa said. Behind the coats was another, roughhewn door and when Elsa opened it a draft of cool air smacked them in the face. "This is the old cellar," Elsa whispered. We don't use it much anymore except for tornado warnings. Careful. These steps are rickety."

She fumbled with blind fingers on the inside wall and flipped on a light switch; a bare light bulb, all cobwebby, dangled overhead, illuminating a dusty set of wide wooden stairs in dull yellow light. Elsa pulled the outer closet door shut and straightened the array of coats before the two women descended down the steps. The room was small and windowless, but strangely not stuffy. The bare dirt floor gave off a rich earthy odor found only in cellars, abandoned wells, and fresh graves. Here and there light peeped through thin cracks at eye level where the outside wall sat on the rough foundation. The cellar's four walls were lined with shelves packed full of jars, mostly empty.

"I still can a little fruit each year," Elsa said, nodding toward the shelves. "Mostly peaches and pears. Some blackberry and strawberry jam, maybe a bushel of beans. If Karl didn't mind the store bought canned fruit or jam I wouldn't go to all the trouble, but he hates the stuff. Course it's not like it was when our kids were growing up. Used to can my heart out every fall. We store bottled water, a little bit of food down here too. Just in case."

There were two straight-backed wooden chairs for furniture. The two women sat down, side by side, each silent for a moment with their own thoughts.

Finally, Elsa said, "I guess Karl will have to rebuild our porch." She sighed, as if tired of the project before it even began. "He's getting too old to be climbing around on ladders, doing carpentry. He's been doing it all his life, but it still worries me some."

"Does Karl have a gun?" Claire asked. Her visions were much darker than ladder falls.

Elsa let out a small laugh. "He does. My father gave him one for a wedding gift the day we got married. Dad told Karl he'd kept me safe for twenty years and now it was his responsibility to protect me. You know what Karl said?"

"Can't imagine," Claire said. Her eyes kept darting to the top of the stairs. She knew if the door opened they were trapped and doomed.

"Well, Karl had just got back from fighting in the Korean War. He was twenty-four years old and looked like a movie star: big and strong, hair so thick I could barely get my fingers through it. Karl looked my dad in the eye and says, 'I'll protect her with my life, but I don't need a gun. I'm through with guns. These Swedish fists of mine will do me just fine.'

"Dad looked at him a minute and got this little grin on his face. Dad was a pretty serious man, Norwegian to the bone. He didn't smile much. He said, 'Son, there are some fights can't be decided by fists. Some men will always want the advantage, and I want my daughter's husband to have it, Swede or not.'"

Elsa laughed again. "Dad had fought in France and Germany. He survived it, but learned how cruel war can be. Never talked about it much though."

"Did Karl take the gun?" Claire asked. Her eyes strayed to the door at the top of the stairs.

"Oh yeah, he took it, but he put it somewhere, and I haven't seen it since. Doubt it still works. He told me once when I asked him about it, he'd hid it so our kids would never find it. He probably couldn't find it if he tried. His memory ain't so hot anymore." She giggled, nerves bubbling out.

"You know how kids are, real curious about guns and and all harmful things. Karl never even taught our two boys how to shoot. Said he was all through with guns. All these years later, and now I have to worry more about him falling off a roof."

Claire could not bring herself to say what she was thinking: *It should worry you a whole lot more that Bakken is pointing a rifle at your husband.* Instead she said, "I wonder where Kate and Liam went?"

"Most likely ran to the barn or Karl's shop," Elsa said. "Don't worry, Karl won't let Bakken hurt them."

"Can we lock the door at the top of the steps?" Claire asked.

"No," Elsa replied, "there's no lock to it. Karl's grandfather built it himself. "He figured there was no reason to lock a cellar full of canning. Nobody steals canned peaches. He and his wife lived down here one whole year while he finished building the rest of the house. Can you imagine living down here for a year?" She didn't wait for Claire to answer. "We're safe even without a lock. I don't believe my husband will allow Bakken in the house."

The conversation ended abruptly when the women heard a dull, muffled gunshot coming from the front of the house. "Something just happened," Elsa said. She stood up and wiped her hands on her apron.

"I think we better wait here," Claire said. "Hopefully a deputy came and ended it all."

Chapter Thirty-eight

Violence is not the proper answer to any reasonable question, but bullies, lunatics, and terrorists, their minds and values misshapen, must be prevented from doing harm. It often leaves a trail of blood.

DAISY TOOK OWEN JUST ABOVE HIS SHOULDERS. She slammed into him at fifty-five miles per hour, her top speed; to make matters worse she outweighed him by close to twenty pounds; worse yet, she was made of high tensile plastic and metal, he of soft feathers and hollow bone.

He was knocked from his perch and landed hard, a limp mass of rumpled feathers amid the bodies of his classmates. He seemed to bounce an inch off the snow crusted surface before settling unconscious upon it.

Daisy, reprogrammed by Bakken to be a flying weapon without restriction, swooped low, hovered a moment inches from Owen's inert body, then accelerated and climbed, electrical impulses driving her into the exact same flight pattern Orville had taken just minutes earlier.

Orville cleared the trees. Wings wide and motionless, he circled the farmhouse and outbuildings, his body tilting back and forth amid the currents, analyzing and planning. Though he couldn't see Kate, he was certain this was the location she had texted about. Five hundred feet below him stood a man pointing a rifle at another man. Orville reasoned the man with the gun must be the target. The other man, standing in such a nonchalant manner, seemed to pose no threat to anyone. Orville needed to be sure. Since he could not see Kate he felt she must be safe inside the house.

Focused on the scene below he did not see or hear Daisy until she plowed into him from behind. He took the blow on his right side where his wing intersected his body; the collision threw him into a steep spiral and he twirled through the air, gathering speed and momentum as he fell. He slowly reopened his wings, forcing his tail feathers wide; using brute force, he braked and reversed the spin, stabilizing his fall less than twenty feet off the ground. He had been soaring above the empty space between the house and Karl's shop building when Daisy had sucker punched him, and now as he swooped low he caught a glimpse of two young faces in the door's window. He wasn't positive it was Kate, but it was enough evidence for him to attack.

He abruptly climbed, pushing himself to the edge of his speed range. Violating one of the red-tail basic tenets of air combat he had lost sight of Daisy. Even though she had given him quite a blow, he didn't consider her a real threat. Ordinarily, in air combat with eagles and owls, he would climb steeply and then when he knew he was above his opponent, level off and make a visual on his foe before striking. He knew the drone was stalking him, but he considered it a secondary issue. He felt he'd already taken the drone's best shot and the man holding the rifle was his main objective; he decided he would deal with the mechanical bird later.

He needed air speed and he sacrificed altitude to acquire it. Without even glancing at the altimeter on his wing watch, he dove hard from behind the man pointing the rifle at the other man. Orville chose a favorite maneuver, Low Yo-Yo, to gather speed, diving to seven feet off the ground. At fifty-yards—closing at forty-five miles per hour—his silhouette flattened and his body streamlined into Fire on the Wire, a lethal tactic first used by the South Dakota red-tail military and adopted by red-tails all over the world.

The man raised the rifle to his cheek and moved his finger to the trigger when Orville struck him on the cheek just where he squinted down the sight. Orville extended his talons at the last instant and raked Bakken's face, making a shredded carrot of his right ear and cutting deep furrows across his cheek and nicking the corner of his eye.

When Orville struck, the gun went off, but the bullet flew high, whizzing over Karl's shoulder, and slamming into the side of the house. Bakken let out a horrific cry of pain and dropped to his knees. He put his hands to his face in a vain attempt to staunch the rich flow of blood. He staggered back to his feet, still clutching the rifle, a wounded, blinded madman.

Karl, almost as surprised as Bakken by Orville's sudden attack, was unsure of what had just happened; he ducked down behind the Land Rover and quickly pulled his pistol. He lowered himself to the snow, peeked under the car. He saw shaky legs moving toward the front end: Karl got back to his feet, moved cautiously toward the rear of the car. He inched up and peeked through the rear window. Bakken, sensing danger behind him, shot without aiming; the bullet shattered the windshield and the back window, spritzing Karl with a shower of glass.

Orville knew he'd hit and damaged his target, but as he elevated and turned he could see the man was not yet out of commission; he needed to make certain the man holding the rifle would be unable to attack anyone else. He climbed rapidly to Cherubs One and, leveling off, dove hard; his goggles were pinned to his face, and his white scarf flapped wildly in the rush of violent flight. This time he chose a rarely used, almost antiquated maneuver called Oliver Twist, an advanced variation of the less lethal Here I Come, Ready or Not.

Bakken was looking around to see how he'd been wounded, his face bloody and eyes wide with fear. The hair on the back of Bakken's neck bristled just as Orville's talons dug into his head and ripped upward—taking a round bit of scalp, about the size of a coffee table coaster; a sizable chunk of Bakken's hair also came along for the ride.

It was somewhat reminiscent of the famous Crow Creek Massacre fifty miles south on the Missouri River some seven hundred years earlier where almost five hundred of the ancients, called Plains Farmers in the history books, were killed in a single attack; ninety percent of them were scalped by an unknown enemy. To this day the massacre remains the worst killing South Dakota ever suffered.

The red-tail constitution forbids scalping as an attack strategy, and Orville was flying a very sketchy line between right and wrong. He, like the rest of the Iron Mountain hawk community abhorred scalping and considered it a distasteful, extreme, and cruel method to disarm or disfigure a man; but, in this instance Orville felt he had no other option but to eliminate the man's ability to harm others.

The force of Orville's second strike caused Bakken to drop his rifle and pitch forward, face down into the snow. A few seconds later, hearing nothing but blood curdling groans, Karl came out from behind the car, and hurried to where Bakken lay writhing in blood drenched snow.

Karl picked up the rifle and said, "Mr. Bakken, that's a pretty nasty wound you've got there. I'll call 911 and we'll get you some medical attention real quick like." He smiled. "Just so you know, you're probably gonna need the services of a wigmaker."

It was then two county sheriff cars roared up the driveway and slid to a stop behind Bakken's ruined vehicle. So there would me no misunderstanding, Karl laid the rifle and his pistol on top of the Rover. He faced the officers, hands in the air, clearly unarmed.

The officer in the first car popped out, his weapon pointed at Karl. "What's happened here?" he shouted. A brown patch above the man's khaki shirt pocket announced **BUTTER** in bold black letters. Across his back in six-inch block letters the word **SHERIFF** further informed.

Karl bent his elbows, letting his arms droop. "This man is my neighbor. Name's Charles Bakken. Claims he shot one of your deputies this morning. Not exactly sure where it happened, but most likely down the road near his house. Told me a bit ago he came over here lookin' to kill his wife. She's safe inside with my Elsa."

Two sheriff's deputies from the second car hurried up; One bent over Bakken, still face down in the snow. He stood up, pointed a finger at Karl. "My God, man, it looks like you dang near scalped him. Come take a look, Drew." The man turned away in disgust, retched.

Sheriff Drew Butter bent over, filled his eyes with the carnage. He stood up, faced Karl. "You got some explaining to do, mister."

Karl said, "I never touched the man. He tried his best to kill me. Shot at me just as a big red-tailed hawk smacked him real good, talons wide open. Raked him twice matter of fact." He turned toward Sheriff Butter. "Mind if I put my hands down? Arms are gettin' tired."

"Chet, check this man for a weapon."

The deputy patted Karl down. "He's clean," Chet said.

"You can put your arms down," the sheriff said, "but stay right where you're at. Don't you move."

He pointed at the Rover. "Chet, secure that rifle and pistol for evidence."

"The pistol is mine," Karl said. "Today is the first time I've touched it in fifty-some years. Never fired it though. Didn't have to. Like I said, the hawk took care of the problem."

Sheriff Butter walked over to Bakken, pulled his arms behind his back and handcuffed him. Then he pulled him up to a sitting position. Bakken's face, neck, and head were a smear of blood, but his moaning had stopped.

A siren could be heard in the distance, a wail of despair approaching fast.

"Phil," Sheriff Butter said to the other deputy. "Need you to go check on Duncan. Should be west of here a mile or two. Dispatcher sent him out over an hour ago, and he's never checked back in. Nobody's heard from him. Could be this man done him some harm. Chet, you stay here with me."

It was then Bakken laughed out loud. "Didn't harm him so much," Bakken said. "Just put a little bullet hole in him is all. Went clear through him. Made a pretty big hole on the backside. Man tried to tell me what I should do. I don't take orders from the law."

"Well mister," the sheriff said, "from now on you're gonna be taking orders from just about everybody, starting with me." He grabbed Bakken by the front of his shirt with a gloved hand. "Stand up, you coward piece of shit." He jerked Bakken to his feet and shoved him hard face first against the side of the Rover. He kicked Bakken's legs wide, and patted his pockets. Butter looked over his shoulder at his deputy. "Dammit, Phil! Whatcha waiting for? Go check Duncan."

Deputy Phil hurried toward his car without a word; the engine revved and he backed hard down the narrow driveway. As soon as he made the main road and turned west, a red and white Medical Emergency vehicle slid to a stop, turned in and roared up the driveway.

Sheriff Drew held Bakken by the upper arm, nose to nose with the man. "These guys will patch you up. If my deputy is dead, then you're under arrest for murder." He handed Bakken off to Chet.

He turned back to Karl. "Who're those people?" He nodded toward the barn and Karl's shop.

Karl turned and looked, shading his eyes from the late afternoon sun's glare, sliding down fast toward a peaceful sea to the west. "Friends. Kate and Liam. They seen it all."

Chapter Thirty-nine

In times of pain and grief, a simple smile,
a light touch on the shoulder, or a happy
word full of surprise and joy, is often a
welcome palliative to ease the suffering.

DAISY WAITED, NO SENSE OF TIME PASSING, HER inanimate soul no darker than the grim shadow cast by a gallows; her blood red eye blinked monotonously, winking at the death she was programmed to cause. She flew in a perfect circle around the house ten feet off the ground, pausing for three seconds at each window and door. In her arsenal she carried twenty ball bearings the size and shape of blueberries. Her mechanical cannons, triggered only by face recognition, could fire a lethal steel ball up to fifty yards with laser-guided precision.

Her attack instructions allowed her to fire only at one person—Claire Bakken. Daisy's computer would identify the target by focusing on Claire's eyes and when target recognition was achieved and verified, firing would commence at her face, one inch below her eyebrows. Bakken not only wanted death, he also sought disfigurement—to pull the petals off the rose until only the naked stem remained.

Daisy was unaware she had less than an hour of flight time remaining on her fuel cell. When ten minutes remained, an electrical impulse would direct her to return to her recharge station in the garage at Bakken's house. Nor did she know Orville had carved up Bakken's head, or that Bakken had been arrested, handcuffed, and would soon be on his way to Avera St. Mary's Hospital in Pierre and then to the lockup at Solem Public Safety Center. To a lifeless drone, commanded to perform mindless tasks, nothing beyond electricity matters.

Orville, satisfied he had disabled the man with the rifle, was also waiting and watching. He wanted to return to Owen as soon as possible, but if Kate were nearby he wanted to contact her and explain what had happened to the students. He soared in a lazy circle high above the house and the chaotic tangle of vehicles and people milling about. He noticed Daisy slowly orbiting the house, but her presence did not really concern him. If the drone became aggressive toward him again he would deal with it.

The moment Kate and Liam started running from Karl's shop toward the front of the house Orville recognized her. He dropped to five feet off the ground and flew toward her at eye level to make certain she would see him and not be startled.

"Orvie," she shouted. "I knew you'd be here if I needed you. It's so good to see you again."

Orville skidded into a precarious landing on the hood of the wrecked Rover. Kate picked him up, held him close, felt his quivering strength. "Liam," she said. "I want you to meet my friend, RT Orville Hampstead. Five years ago he helped save my life."

"Hi," Liam said. "I'm one of Kate's college friends."

"What does you study?" Orville asked. "Vet like Kate?"

"Not sure yet. But I hope to work in wildlife management someday."

Orville's eyes glittered pure gold. "Cool," he said. "I be wildlife. For sure wild. Study me."

Kate and Liam laughed out loud. "I'll keep you in mind," Liam said.

Karl and Sheriff Butter walked up. Orville, nestled in Kate's arms, smiled up at the two men. But a red-tail's smile is difficult to interpret and easily mistaken for a grimace. "You better be careful if that's the hawk tore into Bakken," Karl said.

"Not mean kill," Orville said. Uncertain of the men's intent, he struggled against Kate's grasp to open his wings.

"They're friends, Orvie," Kate said. "It's okay now."

"Man no nice," Orville said. "Kill police officer."

The two men looked at Kate. "He can talk?" Karl asked.

"Yes," Kate replied. "His grammar needs work, but I understand him just fine." She caressed Orville's head. "He's really brave."

"Well," Karl said, "he pretty much saved my life today. Bakken was fixin' to shoot me when . . . what's his name again?"

"Orville," Kate said. "I call him Orvie."

"Bakken was ready to pull the trigger when Orville came along and 'bout ripped Bakken's ear off. I'm positive if he'd shot me, Bakken would have gone in the house after Claire and Elsa. No telling what all he had on his mind. He's a real sicko."

"Not mean hurt bad," Orville said. "Just him make stop. I not like shoot people. Red-tails no scalp. Scalp no permission. But, Kate tell me sometime, 'Shit happen, Orvie.'"

The three men laughed at Orville's expression, and Kate blushed.

Sheriff Butter's cell rang and he moved a few steps away. "Butter." There was a long silence. The sheriff rubbed a big hand through his hair and gazed off into the distance. "Yeah," he said. "I'll call it in. Get a convoy out here right now. Yeah, me too. Okay. I'm not going to call her. We need to go out to the house. Yeah. Soon as we're done here."

He turned back, faced the others, his eyes filled. "My deputy is dead. Bakken shot him."

Chapter Forty

. . . and when help is needed in the worst way, it often materializes out of the thinnest of air—as if directed by an unseen hand.

IGGINS SPOTTED THE TURBINE FROM THREE miles out and adjusted his flight line. Five minutes later with a soft whoosh of feathers he settled beside a dazed Owen who was still pondering how he'd ended up face down in the snow.

"Something knock you cuckoo, lad?" Higgins asked. He pulled the young hawk to his feet, studied Owen's eyes. He fluttered a gentle wing tip over the fledgling's head. "Got a nice bump there. Something whacked you good."

"Drone. Better watch your back."

"Where's your father?" Higgins asked.

"Kate Flannery called him. The owner of this property killed a police officer down by the road. Kate asked Papa for help."

"On my landing approach just now, I saw several police cars and an ambulance over yonder. Lots of blinking lights." He gestured with a wingtip toward the county road. "How long ago did Kate call?"

"Not sure. Papa told me to stay here to protect my classmates from scavengers, but then the drone came out of nowhere, bushwhacked me, and that's all I remember."

"Do you know where Orville was headed? If you're okay for flight, he might need you. I'll stay here to guard the students. I need some rest. Wing weary. The others will be along soon. They're only a few miles out."

"I feel a little woozy," Owen said. "But I'll be better in a minute. Kate said it was first farmhouse east of here on the side of road. I saw it earlier."

"One more thing," Higgins said. "I need to ask you something." Unbidden a lump clogged his throat, and he had trouble voicing the question. He looked away, brushed his eyes with a wing tip. Finally, he asked, "Did Ms. Ride die here too?"

"No. As far as I know Ms. Ride is still alive. She was injured protecting the class in Sioux Falls, and then on the way home she was attacked by a mob of crows. They ganged up on her and managed to pull her out of the sky. She fell from a great height. When last I saw her she was unconscious and wouldn't wake up. Emma tends her now. We must go there as soon as we can."

A weak ray of sunshine and a faint ember of joy sparked in Higgins' golden eyes. "Alright then, lad. Fly hard to your father. The others will bear your classmates home. We three will tend Ms. Ride."

Owen staggered a few steps, and slipping in the melting snow, went down beak first. Higgins reached out a wing to help, but Owen popped back up. He pulled his goggles up over his eyes, secured his helmet strap, and opened his wings to test them against the currents.

He turned to Higgins. "Off I go, sir. Do be careful. Drones and scavengers lurk nearby." Then Owen caught air, wavered for a few weak beats, and began to climb, not exactly sure of his mission, but more than willing to help if need be.

Chapter Forty-one

The human eye, a masterpiece of design, pulls light from the stars, drains color from the sea, and sculpts its shape from the most delicate olive.

KARL CLIMBED SPIDERLIKE OVER THE WRECKAGE of the Rover and the snowmobile on his way to the front door. Kate and Liam followed silently. Karl had invited Orville to come in and meet Elsa and Claire.

Orville looked up at Kate. "No time visit. Teacher, Chawla, need help. Must go now."

Kate kneeled on the splintered boards. "Where is she? Can we help?"

"East here place," Orville answered. "Owen know. We carry her Doc Walters. He best fix vet. Higgins here soon. We fly fast."

"Can you wait just a minute?" Karl said. "I want you to meet my wife. Tell her how you saved my life."

"Okay," Orville said. "Meet wife. Then must leave."

"Darn porch is ruined," Karl said. "I'm gonna have to tear it all the way down and rebuild it. Maybe Bakken's car insurance will cover the cost. Never can tell about these insurance companies. They'll always wriggle out of it if there's a way." He grinned at Kate. "You better hope his insurance will cover the snowmobile too. It's probably totaled."

Inside, the house was silent. "Elsa," Karl shouted. "It's all over. Where you be?" There was no answer. He looked at Liam. "Wait here. I'll go fetch 'em. They're likely down in the cellar." With a weary sigh he walked down the hallway toward the back of the house.

"Did you notice a drone buzzing around out there?" Kate asked.

"Owen fight drone at house," Orville said. "Owen break one drone and two drone break self. Not so hotshot fliers."

"Maybe a drone followed Bakken over here and it's looking for him, Liam said."

"It's almost like a sentry dog or something," Kate said. "Sorta creepy. Just keeps going round and round the house."

Elsa, Karl, and Claire walked into the kitchen and Elsa went straight to the sink, started washing her hands. "I don't know about everybody else," she said, "but I'm starved. Now the excitement is over, I'll get supper on the table."

"El, before you start cooking I want you and Claire to meet Orville. He needs to leave right away. He just now saved my life, and maybe all our lives." Karl bent over and picked Orville up and cradled him in his arms. "He took on Bakken, and Mister Bakken lost the battle."

The two women stared at Orville. "Thank you, Orville," Claire said. "If Bakken had gotten in the house it's certain you saved my life too." She reached out her hands and Karl handed him over, like a precious newborn making the rounds at a family gathering.

"Hi, Orville," Elsa said. "I'm pretty busy right now, but thank you for seeing to my husband. He sometimes needs a little extra help these days."

Karl turned to Kate. "I need to wash up and set the table for supper. Why don't you take Claire outside and show her the mess our porch is in." He patted Orville's head. "Thanks again, young feller. Next time you're over this way, be sure and stop in to visit."

Grins do not come easily to hawks, but Orville tried his best. "You welcome. Visit my home too. Small place high in tree with nice view."

Kate opened the door and they all stepped out onto the ruined porch. "I wonder if we'll be able to move the snowmobile," Kate said. "Liam and I need to get back to the college by tomorrow morning for our classes."

Karl laughed. "That snowmobile isn't going anywhere by itself. I'll drive you back to the place you rented it right after supper, and they can arrange for a tow truck. Snow's melting so fast the roads'll clear up real quick like."

Liam spoke up. "Sheriff Butter called for a tow truck to haul Bakken's Rover to Pierre for impoundment. When he gets here we can ask him to pull the snow-mobile off the porch. Even if it won't run we should try to clear your porch off. Maybe I can come back during Christmas break and help you rebuild it. My dad taught me some carpentry."

"Appreciate your offer, young man. Be nice to have some help, but things always work out, one way or another."

"Karl, do you keep a drone?" Kate asked.

"Course not. What in the world for? No need for anything like that around here."

Kate looked surprised. "Well there's one flying around your house. Somebody has you under surveillance."

"Can't be," Karl said. "Why would anyone be interested in me and Elsa?"

Claire's face blanched. "Charles Bakken might be. He owns and operates five drones on his property. One of them is called Daisy. She follows me wherever I go, but normally she stops at the property line. Maybe he repro-grammed her."

"Bakken is a real sick man," Karl said. "Such a person doesn't deserve to be free. I'm glad they've got him locked up."

Claire shrugged her shoulders. "Daisy is harmless really. She's just an irritation, like a mosquito at your ear."

Orville twisted in Claire's arms, looked her in the eye. "Drone not harmless," he said.

"Can do bad shit."

The porch reverberated with laughter. For the first time in weeks, Claire graced the world with her beauti-ful smile. "Well said."

Kate's face blazed. "Please don't use that word, Orvie. It's not pleasant."

"Kate use sometime," Orville said. "Not okay?" He looked bewildered.

Liam interrupted. "It's a common word millions of people use every day. But, like any other word, it shouldn't be used all the time. I think Kate means you should save it for special occasions."

"Exactly," Kate said.

"Today pretty special," Orville said. "Orvie got clob-bered by drone." The whole porch rocked with laughter. He flashed a charming hawk smile at Kate. "Me try better grammar."

"Let's go outside and see Daisy," Claire said. "I want to make sure it's her, and not one of his other toys. I think the others are lots more dangerous." She bent over and placed Orville on the porch floor. There was a faint buzz-ing sound, but the porch's ceiling blocked the view of the sky immediately in front of the house.

"Sounds like Daisy is around the other side," Liam said. "We'll have to climb over all this stuff to get down. Be careful."

Orville hopped from the porch to the front of the snowmobile, and opened his wings. "Me check drone first. Wait here please."

Once Orville cleared the wrecked Rover he climbed to rooftop level, and searched out the drone. It was monitoring windows on the far side, gradually working toward the front entrance. Orville caught sight of the heartless, buzzing machine. He remembered Claire's comparison to a mosquito. But he knew mosquitoes could be much more trouble than an annoying noise in the ear. He had a nagging distrust of this mechanical version.

He elevated above and behind Daisy, just as he would any common foe. If Daisy were aware of his presence, it ignored him. Orville watched as it paused and hovered for a moment at each window, training the video camera on it briefly before moving on.

And then he understood. Bakken had searched out Claire with the intent to kill her, and just to make certain, in case he fell short, he had reprogrammed Daisy to be Claire's assassin. But how could a thirty-pound whirling dervish of a brainless machine know enough to select and kill a particular human among many?

Below him he could hear laughter. Claire, Liam and Kate had tired of waiting and decided to climb over the jumble. They were standing together beside the Rover looking up into the sky. Daisy's audio equipment picked up their chatter as well, and she came sailing around the corner of the house.

Daisy hovered for a moment at roof level, trained the video recorder on them. Liam noticed the drone first and pointed. "There it is," he said.

The camera locked on his eyes, scanned his right eye, snapped the image; the drone's computer considered first the pupil, the small circle in the center of the eye. Liam's pupil was too large by a thousandth of a millimeter. No match. Target rejected.

"I see it," Kate said, her eyes following Liam's pointing arm. The camera locked in on her eye, scanned and clicked. Pupil. Size, shape, and color. Match. Iris. Amazingly, Kate's blues sang almost the same as Claire's did. But, almost is never good enough for a computer. It did not take the next step in the sequence to examine the sclera—the white part of the eye surrounding the iris. Target rejected in less than a second.

"Is it Daisy?" Kate asked, turning toward Claire.

Claire held her right hand above her eyes, shading them from the dying sun. "Yes," she said, dropping her hand away. "That's her. My little watchdog."

The computer began to process Claire's pupil. A perfect match in size, shape and color. Sclera. Again, a perfect match. Only one part of the eye's anatomy remained to consider.

Claire's iris had been painted a rich blue by an uncountable number of her life's ancestors. Along the way, as a thousand generations lived and died, the blue in her iris family changed from the deep fjord blue green of the far north to a startling light blue, capable of awe and wonder and laughter and grief and fright all in one passing moment. Perhaps another thousand generations passed and minute chunks of pepper appeared in the iris, floating like black satellites.

In a fragment of a second the computer made the match for color. Large eyes to the female face were attractive to young men, giving them ample reason to seek, marry, protect, and reproduce with.

More generations marched by. The size of Claire's eyes, large and luminous, was a perfect match. Next came shape, the computer's last matching point. First it considered the eyebrow, eyelash, and eyelid, all three designed by nature to protect the eye from bright light and all foreign objects—dust, sweat, and gentle rain. They were perfect in size, color, and shape. The shape of the iris, nestled so lovely between the lower and upper lashes, had passed the final test.

In a microsecond, the computer sent an electrical charge to notify Daisy to activate the two cannons and commence firing. A green laser beam instantly appeared on Claire's forehead, moved slightly lower, and aimed at those beautiful eyes.

Liam's eye, seeing the sudden brilliant flash of bright green, reacted as he would have a million years earlier coming face to face with a saber tooth tiger. His lips parted and he sang out a yelp of warning as he hit Claire hard in the chest with the flat of his hand. She fell backward into the snow. Two steel balls whizzed past her face.

Orville, merely a puzzled observer while the computer's calculations were being made, reacted almost exactly as Liam had. He dove hard toward Daisy, but her whirling propellers would slice him to pieces if he attacked from above. She had weapons to the front so the drone's only real vulnerability was from below, in her plastic underbelly.

Daisy, robbed of its kill by Liam's life-saving reaction to the laser beam, could not fire again until it was locked on Claire's eyes. The drone maneuvered toward her face, but Liam was crouched over Claire. "Don't look at the drone!" he shouted. He grabbed her hands and pulled her to her feet. "Run for the porch. Keep your face pointed away from Daisy."

Kate was stunned, unable to process what had just happened. Liam grabbed her hand. "C'mon," he yelled. "The drone is a killer."

Daisy dropped straight down, and leveled off, Orville no more than a foot behind the slashing propellers. He tried to maneuver so he could attack from below, but the drone was a sprite, zipping about like a nimble hummingbird.

Claire scrambled past the first few broken steps, stumbled over a corrupt board, slipped down on one knee. From behind, Liam grabbed her, pulled her back to her feet. "Go," he shouted, and gave her a push from behind. Claire jumped toward the tilted seat of the snowmobile.

But Daisy zoomed to the door above them, and whirling about, faced them. First the red eye of the video camera clicked on, and the lens locked again onto Claire's eyes. Less than a half second elapsed. The kill impulse was resent, and the green laser clicked on, illuminating Claire's forehead in a ghastly green; at that instant, two-and-a-half-pounds of juvenile red-tailed hawk named RT Owen Hampstead ploughed into Daisy's underbelly at thirty-five miles per hour.

Daisy, her gyroscope knocked catawampus, began to spin, cannons firing steel death while spinning wildly out of control. Kate, her arms spread, dove on top of Liam and Claire, pinning them flat inside the snowmobile. There was a loud bang, and then silence.

In her crazy spinning flight, Daisy impacted the side of Bakken's Land Rover and lay in scattered smithereens beside it. No blood. No moans. No last gasps of breath. Just a useless heap of broken metal and plastic, corrupt technology.

Orville whooshed onto the porch beside Owen. He opened his wings wide, and pulled him tight.

Kate climbed off Liam and Claire. "Sorry," she said, "didn't mean to land so hard." She gave Liam a sheepish grin.

"Rather enjoyed it," Liam said. He grinned. "No problem."

He helped Claire to her feet. "You were safe as long as you were facing away from the drone."

Kate stood up on the seat of the snowmobile. "Orvie, did you put Daisy out of action?"

Orville laughed, "No. I not fast enough. Daisy fly too jerky. Owen young, quicker be. He knock shit out Daisy."

"Orvie!" Kate said, her eyes flashing. "Enough." They all laughed.

The door opened and Karl stood in the doorway. "I heard a big bang," he said. "What's going on out here?"

"Oh, nothing," Claire said. "Just a little skirmish between a hawk and a drone. The hawk came out on top."

"Well, dinner's on the table. You all need to sit down before Elsa gets her feelings hurt. She prides herself on good food, served hot."

"What about the hawks?" Kate said.

"We go now," Orville said. "We have hurry wings. Eat later. Thank you hospital."

"You mean, hospitality," Kate said.

"Beak not good English talk. Eyes good English read though. Cut Orvie some slack, Kate. You no fly so hot."

"I think you're amazing," Liam said. "Thank you for all you did today."

"Welcome," Orville said. "Bye, Kate. Study vet lesson hard. Someday Dupree need more good vet. Maybe Doc Walter old then. Bye Liam. I be ready you study. Me pure wild."

Owen hopped onto the crunched snowmobile and launched upward. Orville caught air, and they were gone.

The three humans, chins tilted, watched the flyers vanish into the sky's vastness. A moment later they turned toward the door. Claire pushed it open and entered. Liam stopped and, filled the doorway; he turned and faced Kate. His eyes locked on hers; his voice softened. "Thanks for saving my life. Claire and I would have been dead if you hadn't covered us." He reached out, and pulled her close; closing his eyes, he found her lips, thanking her most properly and tenderly.

Kate's heart roared, a sudden furnace. Her lips, starved, sought his; on tiptoe, her hand moved to his cheek, urging him to linger. Her hand slid behind his neck, pulling him closer still.

From the entry, Claire observed, but said nothing. She smiled.

Chapter Forty-two

. . . and friends, no matter how improbable the tale may be, even the very best of them must end when the silvery thread reaches the bald wooden spool—no doubt leaving smiles of bewilderment or tears of happiness on the doorstep—perhaps to come calling another time . . .

WEN FLEW POINT, HIGGINS AND ORVILLE, flanking him on either side.

Miles and miles behind, the cherished fledglings had been loaded into the air-travois by their loved ones. These were simple net structures designed and manufactured by the red-tails to allow flyers of all sizes to transport packages, or in this case, loved ones from place to place. The device had two adjustable padded leather shoulder straps for the flyer to slip both wings through; once aloft the package being transported dangled six to ten inches below the hawk. Some of the stronger hawks could carry up to five times their weight, approximately fourteen pounds.

The activity below the turbine had been a chaotic scene, with much loud wailing and angry cursing—quite unusual for red-tails who take great pride in maintaining their composure in almost all situations. But this was a tragedy of immense proportions, the worst ever recorded in the annals of the Iron Mountain red-tail community. Bakken's sullied name is etched forever in infamy for South Dakota red-tails.

Once the bodies had been safely secured into the air-travois apparatuses, the flyers caught air, laboriously lifting from the ground and climbing west toward the setting sun. Plans had already been made for a memorial service in the school cafeteria the next morning with burial in Air Haven Memorial Park Cemetery immediately following.

Orville and Higgins, acting as unofficial community leaders, had supervised the airlift; once everyone was airborne they left immediately, headed east toward where Emma and Ms. Chawla Ride waited. It had already been a long and tiring day for the three flyers, and Higgins especially was growing weary, but they were determined to transport Ms. Ride to proper medical attention as soon as possible.

When they came to the barn, the sun was just a brilliant crimson glow above the horizon. The snow in the pasture surrounding the house and barn had melted, leaving dirty white mounds here and there in the shaded areas. Owen landed first just inside the barn door, the two others soft beside him. "Over here," he said, heading for the nest they had built for Ms. Ride.

"Emma, I'm back. Papa and RT Higgins are here." He pulled his goggles down to his neck, the gloomy barn affording him almost perfect vision.

A wing stirred, emerged from under the blanket. Emma wriggled free, sat up. She smiled at Owen. "I was beginning to worry," she said. "I expected you hours ago."

"Sorry," he said. "Unexpected delays. We had a run-in with a mad man and a drone. Explain later. How is Ms. Ride?"

"The same," she said. "But I think she grows weaker every passing hour. She has not eaten since Sunday morning. She's melting away. What day is it now?"

Higgins spoke up. "Tuesday leaves us soon, lass. We must hurry Ms. Ride to Doctor Walters' clinic in Dupree. He is the only one who can save her now."

Orville moved a few steps away, pulled his cell out of his wing holster, and punched the speed call button, for Doc Walters.

"Orville call," he said using crisp English. "Your help need. I know dinner time, but wait must not."

He paused and checked his Breitling for the time. "Teacher. Chawla Ride. She unconscious more than two day. Severe head hurt. No blood outside head. Maybe coma. Very bad."

He listened for a brief moment, then interrupted. "Please not say, 'Perhaps save.' Fledglings need best teacher." Orville glanced up at the barn's rafters. "Three hours. We fly hurry wings."

While Orville spoke to Doc Walters, Owen and Higgins laid out an air-travois on the barn floor. They gently hoisted Ms. Ride, still wrapped in the horse blanket, into the netting, and secured the Velcro snaps.

"The blanket weighs more than she does," Emma said. "Can we carry that much weight so far? Will they think us thieves?"

"We must take the blanket," Higgins said. "Let them think of us what they will. In a few days, I will return it to the barn. It's a very cold night and it's imperative we keep Ms. Ride warm. We must gird our wings and endure the extra weight. We are three plus a navigator. If we rotate every thirty minutes we'll be fine. I may not be able to go a full thirty minutes, but you young ones have strong wings. The years have become an enemy to my strength."

"Doc Walters will meet us at the clinic in three hours," Orville said. "I told him we'd be there no later than nine o'clock. He said he'll drill a hole in Ms. Ride's skull to alleviate the pressure from the trauma she has suffered. He believes her brain is bruised and swollen, perhaps causing permanent damage. He's never done such an operation on a hawk before, but he's confident it can be done. We can be certain he will do his best."

Orville passed out Raptor Flight Mix to everyone. "We need extra energy, for the task ahead," he said.

They munched in silence for a moment. Orville studied his companions. "Who knows the constellations best?" he asked.

Owen pointed a wingtip at Emma. She flashed a shy grin. "I scored the highest in our last navigation test. I even beat Rowdy and Owen."

The mention of Rowdy's name brought tears to Owen's eyes. "Emma," he said. "I've horrible news. Something terrible has happened." He paused, looked to the older hawks for guidance.

"Go ahead, lad," Higgins said. "Tell all. It can't be kept from her."

Owen reached out, touched wings with Emma. "Our entire class—except for Quinn, you, and me—were killed by a wind turbine near the lake. Their bodies are being carried home for burial this very moment."

Emma appeared stunned, unable to utter a sound or even comprehend such a disaster. Her eyes filled. She stood motionless, her feathered face pale in the fading light. She closed her eyes and her legs buckled under her. Higgins reached out, wrapped his silvery wings around her, supporting her quivering body.

After a moment Orville said, "Doc Walters is waiting for us Emma. The best we can do now is transport Ms. Ride safely to him. We must away."

Orville turned, wiggled his shoulders and wings into the air-travois straps. "I'll carry first," he said.

"Emma, our flight is very dangerous, but it must be done. You know the sky best so you will navigate. The stars are our faithful guides and never play us for fools."

He turned to his son. "Owen, you inherited your night vision from your grandmother and me; to us, darkness becomes light. You will fly point."

He paused, searching their youthful eyes for reluctance or hesitation, but found only rich courage. "Our burden is heavy and delicate; we will fly at twenty-five. Emma will guide us by stars, and Owen will keep us level and true at five hundred feet. We'll be above all obstacles."

"Yes," Emma said softly, finding her voice once more. "I will read the stars."

"Of course, Papa," Owen said.

Higgins, his voice solemn, recited the familiar red-tailed prayer. "Deikrrt-Dimerrt-Deisoort." *God grant speed. God grant courage. God grant vision.*

And with that simple request for regal assistance, they defied gravity, put aside their natural fear of falling, and ascended into the salted night sky. Many long hours into the night they flew, like William Tell's arrow, level and true. They alone could see.

Far ahead, a grieving community steeled itself for the dawn. At such momentous time, when the eastern sky first calls forth its ribbons and streams of crimson, they were tasked to place their offspring, one by one, into pure white shrouds. Then they would break the cold ground, soften and warm it with their unending tears, and lower the phalanx—the entire Prairie Winds School of Flight's junior class, save but three—into the earth.

Sitting on her haunches on a nearby, frosty porch next to a hideous October jack-o-lantern, a curious Airedale named Kali, cocked her ears, and stared upward as if to see a hurrying convoy of angels. Her black nose quivered, sifting each molecule of the atmosphere, sorting and recording.

The strongest odor, clinging to a ragged saddle blanket, related the story. The noble dog's yellow brown eyes glowed in the luscious darkness and a soft whimper escaped her heart. She smiled then, as Airedales often do, jaws wide, almost the gesture of a nervous yawn. She stood at perfect attention, as if carved of the strongest teak; she understood it all without explanation—she had been chosen as a solemn witness to the odyssey—four daring hawks soaring through the glittering night sky, coming for to carry her home.

Acknowledgements

I'VE YET TO SIT DOWN TO LUNCH WITH ANOTHER author and discuss the process of writing out a long story. All I can say about it is a scant idea comes to mind and I sit down and begin. I start with a sentence and continue each day until it's done.

I've never cooked lasagna, but I've eaten several, and I've come to understand lasagna consists of layers laid upon layers of ingredients.

An apple is not lasagna. Once beyond the skin, an apple is not layered at all. As a writer I'm far more lasagna than apple.

What I mean is, everything I know about storytelling is layered in my mind somewhere.

I must give credit then to all the authors I've ever read. It first began ever so long ago with comic books and a novel written by Edgar Rice Burroughs about a proper English boy raised in Africa by gorillas. They called the boy Tarzan.

Hundreds of books later I read the adventures of two young scoundrels, Tom Sawyer and Huckleberry Finn, the creation of Mark Twain.

Piles of other books came along and finally I encountered J. R. R. Tolkien's masterpiece, *The Hobbit*. These three were my foundation, but hordes of other authors have contributed too.

All these countless storytellers, men and women, are the architects of any skill I have with words. I confess they are the carpenters of my imagination.

Only with the help of others does scribbling take shape and become coherent. My skilled editors, Vrai Kaiser and Forrest Gowen, must have stumbled through my manuscript like bewildered parents wading through their teenage son's messy bedroom.

They gently woke me from my reverie and pointed out my sloppy punctuation habits, old-fashioned constructions, and penchant for similes. Their knowledge of our language is remarkable, and I've done my best to follow their directions to make the necessary changes. If any errors remain, they are mine alone.

I also thank good friends Sandra Trask for her first reading and encouragement, and her husband, Lance Trask, for creating the helpful maps found inside.

And thanks to the countless others, family and friends all, who've so enriched my writer's life.

www.ingramcontent.com/pod-product-compliance
Lightning Source LLC
Chambersburg PA
CBHW030655260626
47157CB00007B/2665